# ORC BOUND

AN ORC MONSTER ROMANCE

THE IMMORTAL SORTING
BOOK 2

EMMA ALISYN FAE

# ORC BOUND

THE IMMORTAL SORTING BOOK 2

EMMA ALISYN FAE

## ONE

## GETHEN

I stalk the twisty cobblestone streets of Seanna City under cover of a storm scented night. Gaslamps flicker and dim in my wake, casting an eerie yellow-orange glow.

A carved bone pendant dedicated to the goddess of war warms my neck, confirmation she is pleased by tonight's offerings. I abandoned my uncle's god, the Eyeless Priest, three years ago and dedicated myself to Uthsha and her mate, Tueven.

Uther's voice is in my mind. "A warrior's honor is in his charge—forsake it and forsake all."

"But, Uncle, what if—"

His gaze went steely, though his voice remained kind. "Asking but is the first step to dishonor. There is no but."

*But* honor and serenity can't help me now; I need the

favor of warriors. I'll deal with my uncle once I'm done with this cursed City, once my mate is safe in my arms. Demand he explain how a warrior is meant to cling to honor when his female is under threat by those who have none. If I'd abandoned my upbringing earlier, this situation wouldn't have come to pass.

My mate attacked, harmed in the vilest way a female can be harmed, then imprisoned only to face the flock of vultures gathering to peck at her bloody bones.

Two of the hunters threatening her have met their end by my ax, lifeblood coagulating into the crevices of the cobblestones. I've spent two years countering any threat to Tleia, after ten as her personal guard—I've learned to be like her.

Outwardly emotionless. Vicious. Laying in wait and then quick to strike.

Though she'll use tears and her lush body to weasel out of the consequences of dishonor, and I don't bother with those games.

Unflinching, I face what I've become. A monster. . .her monster. Uthsha would approve—she'd stormed the lands of the Dark Horde to rescue her imprisoned husband, killing a host of malformed giants and the handmaidens of the Lord to distract him with grief while she escaped with Tueven.

Chill mist clings to my face as I pursue the third bounty hunter down streets and up crumbling stairwells in the ruins of brick and steel buildings, his frantic wheezing like breadcrumbs.

A movement in an alley I pass snatches my attention. I

slide into the murk, spying a shadowy figure attempting to hide. At my soft footfalls, he spins around in a panic, eyes widening with alarm.

"Mercy, mercy!" he cries.

He's a short man with a thin rat face hiding under a battered bowler hat. Small eyes dart around like cockroaches caught in a sudden light.

It's almost dishonorable to kill him; he's fast, but now that he's cornered, he can't put up much of a fight. His death insults the quality of my ax.

I bare my teeth. "I'll show same mercy you would show my female had I been weak enough to let you capture her," I say in Gaithean.

The language is standard on this once Human ruled planet where my grandparent's dreadnought crashed over two hundred years ago. Born here, I'm more of this place than I am of my ancestral home world, so I speak the mortal tongue well enough when I choose; there will be no misunderstandings why he's about to die.

He scrabbles for a weapon with dirt-encrusted fingernails, hurling a rusted pipe at my head. I bat it aside contemptuously and lunge, talons extended to rend flesh. He rolls away, another pipe clanging on the stones.

"I can take you to the wench's boy!" he shouts, scrabbling backwards in a crab walk. I loom over him, easily double his height and width. "We took 'im to force 'er to sign the papers, but I can take ya to where he is."

My chest swells as I inhale. "Her boy?" Her *boy*?

"Yes yes!" He seizes on the glimmer of hope I didn't mean

to provide. "The bitch whelped in prison—" he sneers briefly "—she tried to keep 'im under wraps, ya know? But when she sold 'im and my boss—"

"Take me." I've bribed prison guards for word of Tleia, but they hadn't told me *that*. Almost, I ball my hand in a fist and slam it into the wall.

She'd *had a child?*

"Get up," I growl, urgency swarming and pushing aside thoughts of my mate. "Take me."

The footpad pushes slowly to his feet, hands held up in the universal "don't kill me" sign. He's moving too slow.

I snap my teeth at him. "*Now!*"

He leads me to a wharf side warehouse on Pike Street, the location stoking fury that never goes away.

Pike. Haven't gotten to him, not yet. He'll meet my ax though; I'd Vow it if I had any Fae blood.

The dimly lit room is heavy with smoke despite the high ceiling, and the smell of spilled ale mingles with the usual stench of fish and questionable hygiene barely masked by rain. Rough wooden tables and benches fill the space, scarred by blades and charred in places by errant magic.

"Remember," I say quietly, "wrong move or word, you die first. All I want is boy."

"Roe."

Rat Face halts. We turn towards a Human woman. Sharp green eyes glint with menace and amusement in a scarred face surrounded by dirt yellow hair.

"Fresh meat?" she drawls. A match flares and she takes a

drag of whatever herbs are rolled in the brown paper between her fingers.

Rat Face clears his throat. "Buyer for the boy, Taye."

"Got a buyer already."

He shrugs. "This'un's payin' double. Ya want me to show 'im out?"

She weighs me. "Not seen you around before."

"Selling or not?" My voice is sharp. "Things to do. Not stay in stinking City longer than must."

"Don't look like ya got 'alf, much less. . .what did ya say, Roe?"

"Double, Taye," is his plaintive reply. The look she gives him is a warning that if it's not double, it'll come out of his skin.

"Where's the coin?"

I give her a baleful look. "Coin? No coin."

Pulling out a small leather pouch, I shake a couple of blood stained copper pennies onto the table. Technically coin, but they're worthless as cash currency except for this one use; the metal can absorb and carry the detritus of a bastardized Fae Vow.

Her eyes warm with greed. Each of these pennies represents a Favor owed, and I flip them over so she can read the marks of the individuals owing the Favor.

Slapping my hand over the small pile when she reaches out, I growl, "Boy first. Good condition only."

"As is," she snaps, "and yer lucky I don't have ya split from head to gullet for wastin' my time."

Sneer, I respond, "Can try. Good fun. Orc still eat Human marrow."

"Pay first."

Scowling, I eye her like I don't trust her—I don't. But I shrug and withdraw my hand. "Try swindle, will be back."

She scrapes the pennies to her, dumps them back in the bag and jerks a shoulder at Rat Face. "Get 'im out of here. And if the brat is dead, no refunds."

"Thought had buyer," I say with irony to mask my rage. "Can't sell dead boy."

Rat Face coughs and scurries forward a few steps. I stomp in his direction and am led into a small storage room. Muffled shouts and raucous laughter filter through the walls, but in here the only sound is the soft lap of waves under the pier outside. The room is empty except for a small boy huddling in a corner, with pale green skin and curly dark hair, too thin arms wrapped around his knees. He appears three, almost four. The night of his conception is burned in my brain.

Giving him one quick glance, I turn to Rat Face, handing him three Favors I'd reserved.

"Get lost," I growl. "Oh, wait." I swing my fist into his jaw too fast for him to dodge. "Spoke disrespect of my female. Be glad you live, rat. Git."

Clutching his jaw, he darts back down the hall. I don't overestimate his courage or his intelligence, so I have to get out of here quick. Once he convinces himself he's safe, he'll bring backup.

Stepping into the room, I shut the door behind me.

The boy jerks his head up, hissing and swiping baby soft talons, small tusks barely the size of a female's pinkie finger. "Want Mommy! I bite you!"

A thousand thoughts crash through my mind then coalesce into a single realization; I have a son. A son Tleia sold to the kind of refuse who would. . .I don't want to think about it. I don't want to think about what I'll do to her when she leaves prison.

I lower myself onto one knee, staying near the door, and speak in Gaithean again. "I'm your Pa. Do you want to come with me?"

He pokes his bottom lip out. "Don't have a Pa. I want my Mommy."

"Your mommy sold you." I want take the words back as soon as I say them because even if they're the truth—I have questions—he doesn't need to know that now. He's still a babe.

His eyes widen. "Mommy said she come get me. Mommy said—"

"How about we go get Mommy?" I need him to come with me willingly, or he won't remain silent while I carry him out.

"Are you a bad guy?"

"If anyone tries to hurt you or your mommy, I will hurt them first. But I won't hurt you." I grit my teeth. "Or your mommy." Unless what the footpad said *is* true.

"Look." I point to my tusks. "I'm like you. We are kin. *Uthilsen.* Orc kin do not hurt each other."

Tears well in his eyes. "I want Mommy boob. And I want oatmeal."

Opening my arms, I wait. "You can have oatmeal if you come with me, and then we'll get your mommy. . .boob."

Is he still nursing? I eye his teeth. Why would a woman sell a child she'd willingly nursed until he was old enough to ask for milk in complete sentences? I've heard my cousins yowl and curse when bitten by a toothy child at the breast. Nursing at this age, if there are other options, is an act of maternal love. The mothers remind their sons of this constantly.

He hesitates. "A pa is like a mommy, but a boy. You're a boy mommy?"

He was born and raised in a female only prison. Does he have a concept of males other than what Tleia might have explained to him?

"That's right. I'm your boy mommy, your *otema*. My name is Gethen."

He says the words, softening the consonants. I almost wince. Finally, he stands and walks towards me. "My name is Ethan."

"Ethan."

It's an Uthilsen name. I repeat it for him again with the proper pronunciation then swoop him into my arms and stand, wanting to kiss him, wanting to shed the tears pooling in my eyes. Time for all of that later.

"Can you be very silent for me? There are predators and if you make noise they will come for us."

He nods, patting my face, his eyes on my tusks. "Mommy

plays hide and seek with me. And I know how to bite. But my tusks not big as yours."

For him, I smile. "They will be one day. Now be very quiet for me."

————

Uthsha protects us; I emerge with Ethan from the warehouse and make my way to the cheap efficiency room I share with my cousin, who came for a visit a year ago and stayed when he realized I wouldn't come home until Tleia was out of prison.

We're not followed, and the boy falls asleep in my arms. He's not even a proper armful; his hair—which needs washing and braiding—weighs more than he does. If he's been fed a diet of gruel and mother's milk, then no wonder. The boy needs meat.

I lay Ethan down on my cot, pushed against the side of the wall, and contemplate whether I should wake him up to eat, deciding to let him sleep—he is an Orc. His instincts wouldn't have allowed him to rest in an enemy's lair.

He wakes once to whine about mommy boob, and I explain I have no animal milk, only water, and big Orcs don't drink from the breast once they have strong tusks.

My son gives me an arrogant, skeptical look I recognize and says, "Mommy give me boob when we get her," as if I'm clearly uninformed, then curls back to sleep.

He is definitely her son.

In the meantime, I make him a rough sandwich of dried

fish and the last of the seaweed and salmonberry I'd gathered from the shores of Paget Sunde, stuffed between two slices of black bread. It will take the edge off his hunger until I can get to the market at dawn. There are one or two fishwives I deal with; protection while they sell their morning catch in exchange for a fair pick of their goods.

Hathur returns home within the hour, staring down at the boy in astonishment. "Cousin, I commend you for your soft heart—" he says in a voice implying the opposite "—but we are in no position to mother orphans. Where are his kin?"

I wait for him to stop talking, partially because I'm going to enjoy seeing the look on his face. We speak in Uthilsuven when alone, which reminds me I must teach Ethan. "We are his kin. He is my son, Hathur."

Hathur blinks. "Repeat that once more."

"This is Tleia's babe."

"She. . .she had a child?"

I tell him of how I discovered Ethan, and what the rat had told me. The alarm on my cousin's face, and the growing fury, is only an echo of my own. It's enough of a failure that my female is confined by Humans, outside of my protection, but that she had my son and I didn't know it, and couldn't protect him either?

The debt I owe Tleia continues to grow. She will never be rid of me.

"What is he called?"

"His name is Ethan."

Hathur's expression softens. "Your grandfather's name."

Nodding, I am unable to reply. She'd given our son a good, clan name.

My cousin stares at the sleeping boy, then crouches next to him, tilting his head to study Ethan's face. "A fine looking boy." He glances up at me. "You're certain he's yours?"

I must keep myself from snarling at the implication. "He's the right age. She was with no one but me."

Hathur's gaze is steady. "You know that's not true."

I'm forced to amend my statement. "She was with no other Orc."

"And his father must be full blooded from how he looks. There's almost nothing Human in him." Hathur glances at the boy again then stands and turns to me slowly. "From what you've told me, she's a ruthless female. She'd use you for protection if she could."

He isn't wrong. I shrug. "She is Human. It is a good strategy. I would seduce an Orc warrior too if I were a tiny, clawless and toothless female. But I've known her for ten years, cousin. There are *some* actions she wouldn't stoop too." Some.

"You're certain, Gethen? What the damn graywings charge for blood testing—"

"I'm certain."

"Why would she sell him?"

"Only have the word of honorless scum that that is what happened. She's due to get out in a week. There could be a number of other explanations."

Hathur runs a hand over his face. "Maybe she was trying to get him to safety, if she knows there's bounty hunters waiting to jump on her the moment she leaves the prison. She'd want him secured first. She might have been betrayed. Our money hasn't stretched to smuggling a note to her in jail."

And if it had, we'd decided against it. My greatest use to Tleia right now is that none of our enemies know I am protecting her. I have to trust her to stay alive.

"Your conclusion is what I hope for," I say. I don't want to kill my best friend, my one-night lover in the flesh, the mother of my first and only son.

"If we're wrong?"

Even now, if it is true that she sold him to ease her own way, I desperately search for a reason to forgive her.

She was raised with no mother and father.

On Coho Street.

Taught nothing of honor, only of survival, enduring things that make my cheeks pale and I am over twice her age.

But at what point can a person no longer be salvaged? At what point is death the kinder option? I close my eyes. "I don't want to kill her. I love her."

Hathur lays a hand on my shoulder. "I'm sure it won't come to that. Wait before you make a judgment. We don't have all the information."

My cousin is kind; he wants to spare me the inevitable.

"If she must die, I will make sure she doesn't suffer," I say.

## TWO

## TLEIA

EARLY RELEASE FROM PRISON IS SUPPOSEDLY A GOOD THING. Since I'm certain *my* release is an execution, I'm minded that this is an example of too much of a good thing. I need muscle to survive, especially if Lord Seacliff of Pike Street is hunting me, but what I have is wits.

*Gethen, where are you?*

But Gethen is an Orc warrior, not a Fae Lord, and no matter how I throw my thoughts into the atmosphere, he won't hear them. If he's still alive.

"Here." Neteen, the guard I cultivated during my three-year prison sentence, shoves a small pack of supplies at me as she lets me out of my cell. She watches everything with that mile long stare of jaded prison guards everywhere, a faint perpetual scowl between her bronze brows. I suppress the continuous urge to look over my shoulder; a nervous twitch is a glaring sign of guilt to anyone who knows what to look for. "That's all I could get."

"It will do."

We begin to walk, though I'm limping—I haven't healed from last week's prison yard fight. Cracked ribs, a few sprained fingers, a mild concussion. I got off light, since I hadn't started the fight. If the Warden ordered me into solitary. . .I can't think about that.

It's well past lights out and everyone is sleeping, or pretending to. The women's prison is cold; inmates hunker under thin blankets in an effort to keep warm through breath and body heat. Incentive to keep their heads down and out of my current business. If that's not incentive enough, Neteen has a baton and a matching temper. She wields both generously.

"The package was delivered safely to its holder?" I can't help the ache of tension in my jaw or at the back of my neck as I think about the fragility of that package.

"I followed your instructions," Neteen says. "Can't guarantee what happened after the package left my hands."

"I'm in your debt then." My voice is a bit terse because it's true—and I loathe debt. It always rears its venomous fangs and sinks them into your throat at the worst possible moment.

But I force myself not to think about that package, or else I won't be able to focus on the here and now, and I'll make a mistake. On Coho Street, we learn young not to flinch, and not to look back. Not to worry about loved ones you leave behind to torture and death because sometimes the best help you can give them is to survive, and circle back later. Stronger.

It's harder to cling to that lesson than I'd thought. I've left behind more than family, more than blood.

I can't think about that either, not without loathing myself. Without starting to sink into that spiral of desperation, flinging enraged pleas into a night at a Human god who never heard them in the first place.

Or maybe a god had; I'd been imprisoned for debt, not murder, after all. Still, I should have listened to Gethen and switched my allegiance to Uthsha, his goddess of war.

"Get to the Sorting," Neteen says. "Get settled. Then pay me back."

Sorting is an interesting word. It's Gaithean, but when spoken in the Fae language has a cold, sinister inflection. The Orcish word has more pragmatic connotations since their version of servitude slavery is more benign.

Neither the Fae—Aeddannari, they call themselves—the Icarian Gargoyles or the Uthilsen Orcs with their incomprehensible guttural language, are native to my planet.

Despite not being its original occupants, the immortals now rule. Their wars, after their dreadnought crashed on our planet, nearly wiped out civilization as Gaithean Humans knew it. But despite the power of the survivors, what they don't have is numbers. Fortunately for them, Humans make good labor and breeding stock, especially the humans whose DNA has mutated enough to carry actual magic.

There are four Sortings a year, one each season, where Humans can offer themselves up for auction.

As I'm about to do, because the best protection from one immortal is another. I could try to buy protection, but then I'd be broke.

"You know I'm good for it," I say. "Have I ever failed a bargain?"

"No." We share a swift look loaded with history.

We both come from Coho Street, a wharfside neighborhood mired in the stench of poverty, desperation, and fish. We chose different paths but somehow ended up at the exact same point, at the exact same time.

Except on different sides of the bars. I can't quire decide if this irony is another subtle mark of some god's disfavor.

"Move fast, Tleia," my childhood ally says as we navigate the halls toward a discreet side gate, pausing now and again to avoid detection. "Don't know how many bounty hunters ya got on your heels, but the Warden was aiming for a payday." She shakes her head. "I still can't believe ya pissed off Coho *and* Pike Street dealers. You were always smart'n that."

"It was not I pissing on behemoths, but my dear deceased husband. I was a good little wife. Best acting I ever done. Good work ain't never rewarded." I'd made a miscalculation and I'd paid for it. I would continue to pay for it if I didn't get out of town by dawn.

Neteen grabs my arm and draws me into a utility closet as we listen to two guards approach, chatting.

"That idiocy why you killed 'im?" She speaks under her

breath, her dark-eyed gaze alight with curiosity. "Dabblin' with the Fae dark market trade?"

She's still trying to get me to admit to murder—she probably has money riding on the answer.

I shrug. "If I had, theoretically, it wouldn't be the main reason, but it would, hypothetically, have weighed in my decision to end his miserable existence."

The problem is my timing had been spurred more by a strong preference not to be gifted to another dear friend for the night for the sake of networking, and less by discrete strategy.

Discretion is everything to these high-class monsters. They'll sell their wives and daughters, trade in dark market goods, fuck hellhounds and make deals with the hounds' masters. . .but appearances must be kept. I'd been punished for breaking that wall of silence. I hadn't wanted to go to jail, so I'd taken my story to the papers to try and change the laws that held widows responsible for their spouses' debt. It had unveiled a slimy layer of Seanna City's Human upper-class society, and their financial dealings with Coho and Pike Street.

"Too bad," she says. "Ya had a good con going."

"It was comfortable, yes." In certain ways. In others, it was hells.

Neteen grins. "Ya still talk like 'em too, though ya been in the joint for three years. Don't sound like a Coho gal at all."

"Appearances must be maintained. It gives me something to amuse myself with."

I've worked very hard to ape the diction and manners of

the Seanna City Human upper class, who ape the Aeddannari Lords. I've even learned to *think* in their prissy grammar. I'm not going to waste all those years of self-inflicted torture by devolving into honest wharf cant now. It will take far more than three years in prison to break me—I've suffered worse accommodations, after all.

"Let's go," she says, and we leave the utility closet.

I can't go through the front gates, and it cost a small fortune in bribes for the guard posted at the side service door to look the other way long enough for me to slip out.

We share a last, final handclasp, a thing of the wharfs which if any of my high society former friends had seen, would expose me as a fraud. But I'd already been exposed three years ago, the darling of the papers for the weeks of my drawn out trial, my background and rise dissected.

Of course no one could prove I'd been the hand behind Herbert's death, or I would have been sent to an execution block, not merely a squalid debtors' prison. No, my trial had been for bankruptcy, a crime in Seanna City, not murder— only a crime if caught. Though I suspect my life is due more to the fact Herbert's creditors, including two Fae Lords, can only collect if I'm alive to be coerced into signing over what's left of his estate.

They may also assume I know the location of his hidden assets, and they are not stupid, so that's a fair assumption. Then they can kill me.

I make my way stiffly through the streets, slow from the injuries and several sleepless nights, my clothing smelling of mildew, wrinkled and not exactly clean, and probably three years out of fashion. Long skirt and frothy high-necked blouse cinched at the waist with a waspie, because three years ago Vittorian-core had been in style.

Almost there. I'll collect the package, praying to the deaf Human gods that it's been safely delivered undamaged, and then I have one more stop before we flee Seanna City for good, and head to the spring Sorting.

But I recognize the prickling along my spine as unease. The streets are quiet, too quiet considering I have a swath of bounty hunters on my heels. By now the Warden will have realized I slipped out of the wrong entrance. Truthfully, I'd assumed she was intelligent enough to watch all the exits, but Neteen must have come through for me.

Too quiet.

I can't quite believe I've managed to give Herbert's enemies the slip, and of course because I don't believe in it, it's not true.

I spend the next two days running in circles.

## THREE

## GETHEN

My prey is oblivious to my presence though I'm only a block behind her, slipping into the shadows created by gaps between flickering gaslamps attached to the crumbling brick buildings on either side of this narrow street.

Tleia glances over her shoulder, dark hair disheveled, face too thin, her pace a sliver too brisk for the casual stroll she began with.

The first sight of her when she'd emerged from the prison almost gutted me. She's always had a hard cast to her eyes, even when pretending to be a soft upper class wife, but she's never been brittle.

She's never been afraid—not until those last few nights. I scent her fear from the air, and every instinct in me demands I go to war. Against our enemies, but also against myself.

"Your female's fears are your failure, her security your success," my uncle said.

He's always in my head; he never shuts up. Sometimes he speaks through my mouth and those are the times Tleia just looks at me, scorn and pity in her gaze—but affection, too.

"Sweet country boy," she'd say, lounging on her bed in something sheer, a deliberate taunt for me to abandon my control. "This is Seanna City. You'll learn. The hard way, probably. Most of us do."

I close the distance between us, seeing the same threat she's now identified.

At age twenty-one, I'd just begun developing into an adult, losing the lingering youngling softness of adolescence. My mother and I traveled from the remote mountain village where she'd raised me, and handed me to my dead father's great-uncle, "He's yours now. He doesn't come home until he's a warrior," then left.

I did not see my mother again until the male's circle pronounced me trained, and the female's circle accepted me as an adult capable of providing for a family and contributing to the clan. My mother won't like Tleia. I suspect because they're too much alike, soft outer shells hiding inner krutzve'e.

"It's a fluffy pink mammal," Uther told me. "On our home world Orclings learning to track are instructed to run if they see tufts of pink fur in the bushes. There's no cure for the venomous claws of a krutzve'e, and they lure their prey in by appearing cute and harmless, then devour the victims alive while paralyzed."

I stared at him. "Then why let the species live?"

My uncle shrugged. "Eh. If you kill every species that presents a danger, you'll become weak. Besides, they keep pest species in check and experienced handlers can train them as weapons."

"What? Why?"

"The survival rate isn't good, so handlers tend to be wealthy," was the bland reply. "The point is. . ." he scratched his chin. "What point was I trying to make?"

"That females are cute but deadly, and you still have to protect and provide for them—but don't bother if you're poor."

Uther laughed. "Yes, that was my point."

"But the females are warriors too!" I'd protested. "Why are we responsible for them?"

"Because we will never birth children. We cannot enter that battlefield with them, and every time your mate takes you between her thighs she is risking her life, and the life of a potential babe. There is a price to pay for the privilege, son."

"You don't have a mate."

"Not yet, no. I will. I don't have to have a mate to understand the responsibility of a male, or to teach you. And, son, whether a female who takes you to her bed is your mate or not—you are accepting responsibility when you come inside her. This is the way of things. The females will say they prefer pleasure without strings attached, but the males know better."

Scowling, I respond. "Ratha never says anything like this. Because her mate is a female?"

Uther snorted. "No. It's because she is Ratha, and this is how all females talk. They don't want to be controlled or protected—until they want to be controlled and protected."

My head began to throb. "How do you know?"

"You don't. So we protect, provide, and control anyway. . .but we aren't obvious about it until she decides to marry you."

"I. . .see."

I did not.

His eyes gleamed with amusement. He was big for an Orc, shoulders broad and heavy with muscle, his chest and back scarred from decades of battle. Like any blooded warrior, he wore his hair partially braided during times when there was no active war or feud, and the beads clacked as he turned his head.

"If you're smart, Gethen, you'll never repeat any advice the male's circle gives you regarding females to the female's circle. That's a shortcut to getting your stones lopped off."

"Ooooh. So it's a male's secret."

Uncle patted my head. "Yes, son. Remember, stones lopped off. This is not an exaggeration."

In the present I steady my mind, focusing. We'll be home soon, I'll see my uncle and I'll offer penance for every hurt Tleia and Ethan ever endured. I will be cleansed of this, and then we will live our lives in peace.

I stop to make sure the girl Tleia robs is alive and covered, and briefly lose her trail. Tleia's wearing wide legged trousers when I catch up to her, her shirt tucked in, and because I'm male and know what she tastes like from clit to ass, I almost miss the next of her pursuers because I'm staring at her plump bottom. It's been too long.

Tueven understands.

Three years ago, I would have roared my challenge to anyone who attempted to hurt or touch her without permission. Now, I've grown cold, calculating, and let her be the bait to draw them all out so I can pick them off one by one. My uncle would be disgusted, but I don't think Ratha would mind. I'm conflicted. Coho Street will do that to you.

How many times has Tleia said this to me?

How many times have I given sympathy and a hug, but silently criticized either her character or her kin, who'd abandoned her at birth?

Even once I'd learned to keep my own counsel for the sake of our friendship, and leave Uther on the inside of my head, I'd been a judgmental prick.

Hard experience wears away judgement and reveals it as. . .I ponder the correct word as I watch another hunter close in on Tleia.

Hypocrisy?

She darts down an alleyway and the hunter follows.

Arrogance? No, wrong word too. Hubris maybe, but I abandon the search for the right word—Lei'a will tell me once we're reunited—as I turn down the same alleyway, closing the distance between myself and our enemy in seconds.

Tleia is climbing up a rusted, rickety ladder on the side of a building, having abandoned her stolen basket of shopping. She throws her leg over the roof ledge right as her pursuer begins to climb as well.

"Bad idea, Human," I call out in Gaithean, not bothering with grammar. First gen Orcish Gaithean has a syntax, and it tells Humans who they are dealing with. Someone old, and dangerous. "Come down now, and will not eat liver for dessert. Only kidney. Not miss single kidney."

He ignores me. I don't blame him, my threats aren't creative but it's been a long week. Ethan cries for his mother and refuses to eat when he's fixated on "mommy boob". He doesn't understand where she is, and I won't lie to him, so I say little. Because he's not stupid, he knows when I'm avoiding a question.

The pursuer is still climbing. The ladder creaks under his weight, and he pauses.

"Warned you," I say.

Because I have a new toy I want to try out, I take out my sling, load a rock and begin to spin it rapidly over my head, building up momentum. Releasing one end, I hurl the rock at the pursuer.

It whizzes in the air and makes a satisfying thud against the pursuer's skull. He topples backward and I pause to snap his neck, consider the ladder and my weight, and decide to go around. I have her scent; I can track her.

Because there's a pattern to the circles she's been running in the last day, and I already know her ultimate destination, I pick back up on her trail within the hour.

Worry bites at me. She's slow. She's taking more frequent

rest breaks, and she hasn't eaten. Everything in me rebels at treating her like this. No Orc would let the mother of his son go cold, hungry, exhausted, as well as using her as prey in a hunt.

I'm as angry at myself as I am at her. She doesn't know any better, but I do. I can't let what we've been through, or her betrayal, take me away from who I am.

A Bachdracht. A warrior with honor. A male who protects and provides for his female and young.

It's not until she approaches the back entrance of the orphanage that some of the tightness in my chest eases. Hathur spent several days gathering information, determining she hadn't sold Ethan but attempted to arrange for him to be delivered to the orphanage and stashed safely until she retrieved him. That she's coming here now is proof of her intention and strategy.

Forgive her for betraying me, I can and will, for fingering me as the guilty party when we tried to escape three years ago. But after knowing Ethan for a week, if I'd learned she'd tossed him away, I would have killed her.

I follow her into the building and wait outside the door until she exits, bending over at the knees and taking harsh, gasping breaths of panic.

It's proof how fatigued she is that she doesn't sense me in the shadows, watching her.

It's proof that she needs me to survive. That even if I am a sweet country brute, I add value to her life.

But if I don't, she's already mine, and I'm finally taking her back.

I step towards my female, I yank her against me.

———————

## TLEIA

My clothes are filthy. I don't dare stop to scrounge for scraps so I haven't eaten, and the only water I've had is rain falling into my open mouth—the weather here is dependable, if nothing else. We don't complain; in the outlands water is worth its weight in gold. Or would be, if gold was still a useful currency. I've huddled in alleys, in the ruins of buildings. I've run in circles evading my hunters, but those circles are tightening.

I'm being run to ground, flushed out. It's only because I know these streets well that they haven't caught me yet. It's only a matter of time before my odd luck runs out.

I'm two days late to pick up the package. *Two days late.* What will they have done with it? Disposed of it, sold it?

If I was ever sane in the first place, and I have my doubts, what's left begins to slip under the pressure of my own mind. I know exactly what can happen to that precious bundle.

I stalk a normal seeming girl my size and emerge onto the streets wearing clean clothing, the best disguise I can devise. My hair is rebraided and pinned up under her hat, her basket of shopping slung over my arm.

By some miracle I manage to make it to the orphanage unscathed, slipping around the back of the nondescript brick building, finding the back door open as I've been told it would be.

My jaw is locked, my hands shake from fear, hunger, stress. I have to get myself together, especially now. I won't be able to move as fast once I retrieve the package.

Neteen is owed a larger debt than I'd accounted for. The halls are quiet this time of night, and with the map of the interior still in my mind, I navigate them until I reach the designated room. Soon, I can stop thinking of it as a package because it will be in my arms and then I can afford to let myself feel.

"I'm coming," I chant, my knees jelly as I dart through the halls. "I'm here now."

There are no interior guards, not in a building like this. There will be guards posted outside, but they're bribable, which means they're for show. That angers me, but tonight it works in my favor as I slip inside the room, closing the door behind me, count down three cribs and stop.

Stop, as my heart stops. I grip the crib railing.

Empty.

*Empty.*

I spin, looking frantically in each one, but my son isn't there. "No. No no no no."

There are Human children, a few who look mixed species —no halflings, though, the Fae keep viciously tight control over the wombs of their women and Human concubines.

No green-skinned three-year-old child. No Orcling.

My knees buckle and I lean against the crib, then force myself to straighten. "Think. *Think,* damn you."

Maybe I've gotten the room wrong.

Maybe there was word of a threat and they've moved my son.

I note the thin, tangled blanket pushed to the side. I pick it up and shake it out. No note.

Panic and fear like I've never felt, not even on the day I realized I was pregnant and would be giving birth in jail, chokes me.

For once I don't know what to do. For once I have no scheme, no failsafe plan—I'd tried, but there'd been too many unknown variables and I almost sent myself into a tailspin before accepting the loathsome inevitable; I'm alone, with no allies and limited funds, and what assets I do have are stashed and inaccessible unless I find my child. If someone has taken him, it will be difficult to gather the resources to take him back.

If he's still alive.

Blackness creeps at the edge of my vision, and I pinch myself, then turn and tear out of the nursery.

I'm trying to think, trying to remain calm, clinging to the last shredded ribbons of what intellect I have left and not sink to my knees in the hallway and accept that my life is a miserable failure, I'm a miserable failure, and that it would have been kinder if my mother had drowned me in Paget Sunde the day I was born from her miserable womb.

I can't double back to Neteen, I'll be caught. I barely made it here in the first place. I don't know what to do. I have no idea at what point my plan unraveled.

*Think, damnit, think.*

I bend, bracing my hands on my knees and let out a long, guttural moan because if I don't excise some of this pain, I won't be able to function.

When I straighten, there's the barest flicker of sound behind me before a strong hand clasps over my mouth.

Instinct takes over. I don't scream; I try to bite. Kick backwards, but the hand is thick, and the muscled arm now locked around my torso pins my arms to my sides. I'm being dragged backwards down the hall as if I'm about as much threat as a stuffed toy.

The hand presses tighter over my mouth and nose, and for a moment of panic I think he might suffocate me. The only energy I have left now is the instinct to survive.

It's not just my survival at stake.

"Tleia."

My captor releases me, and I turn.

Hope wrapped around a nightmare is staring at me.

I want to cry out his name. I want to collapse into his arms and explain everything, beg him to forgive me.

Then I want to break his nose and tear out all his braids.

But I do nothing, because leaping on an Orc warrior with fury in his eyes as he silently challenges me would be foolish.

Especially when that Orc warrior is the father of my son.

"Why betray me, Tleia?"

Elation evaporates, the word betrayal slapping me across the face.

"Where is he?" The question tears from my throat. "Where is he?" I launch myself at him. "*Where is he?*"

"Tleia." He says my name sharply, snatching my wrists

and spinning me so my back is pressed against his chest, my arms trapped in a cross, bound by his strength once again.

I don't care. I rear my head back, hear his muttered curse, and with a harsh exhale his voice comes from a distance. I've snapped. There's a red-black haze over my vision.

"Tleia," he growls. "Safe. He's safe."

The words penetrate my mind and my knees buckle. Stupid, I'm stupid, I spent the last of my energy and after two days of no food, no sleep, barely healed while running in circles in a constant sprint with only snippets of rest. . .there's nothing left in me.

Relief snatches the last of my strength.

Gethen lifts me in his arms.

"Why betray me, Tleia?" The question is quiet, and in the syllables I hear my death if I answer wrong. I know because I've heard him speak to others like this, but never me. Not until now.

Now I know what I can do to Gethen to push him to that point.

"I had to," I say. "Or we wouldn't have survived."

"Ethan? Try sell him?"

"Sell him? Is that what you think of me?" I'm too exhausted for bitterness, my head limp on his shoulder. "I'm trying to keep him safe. I thought you meant something else." I assumed he's angry about me fingering him for murder.

That's the last thing I say.

When I wake, I'm floating, cradled in Gethen's arms. We're outside, and dense gray clouds blot out the evening sky. I close my eyes.

And open them, a thin cot under my back.

"Gethy." I think I say his name, but my throat is dry and tight.

A dribble of liquid passes my parched lips. Hot, salty, with slivers of beef and bread in it.

"Eat, Lei'a," is his gruff reply. "Don't choke. Reserve that right."

But his knuckles caress my cheek.

I let him feed me the soup, lifting my shaking hands to wrap around his and hold the mug steady, though it's not necessary. I drink it down, some of it dribbling down my chin, and sink back into sleep.

## FOUR

I OPEN MY EYES AND THIS TIME IT'S NOT ONLY GETHEN and me.

He's holding our sleeping son.

"We talk," he says, the fury he'd banked while taking care of me turning to something as desperate, as hungry as what must be staring at him from my face. "But no time. Can you walk?"

I sit up, flexing my muscles to test my strength. The food and rest have restored what I estimate is eighty percent strength. I feel bindings around my ribs. Had I told him I was injured? I must have.

Now that I'm sane again, and now that the question of my son is answered, I focus on Gethen.

Tall, well over six feet, with the broad shoulders and muscled physique of his kind. Green skin with a blue undertone, dark eyes with their slightly uptilted edges, a strong jaw and broad nose.

Gone is the tailored wool suit and pageboy cap he wore while employed by my husband. He wears supple leathers now, his muscled chest *bare,* Uthsha *bless,* arms and neck slung in clan ornamentation.

I stare. I've never seen his chest completely bare. He always dressed like a dedicated celibate.

So this is a good disguise. If anyone is looking for Herbert Lee's former head of security, when they look at Gethen all they'll see is a savage Orc. He's hiding in plain sight.

His chest should be illegal. Why in the world would any man with that chest *cover* it? It's a sin against—

"Can walk?" he repeats, snapping as if this is the second time he's asked. Can he blame me? Scowling brow and thinned lips. He's worried. I know his worried face like I know my own.

I drink my former best friend in, my gaze greedily caressing his face, his body, his weapons—his most attractive feature right now—as I grip my skirt like I'm about to faint from distress. I've absorbed too much of my persona the last two decades, turning myself from a wharf side street rat into a housemaid, then a lady's maid, and then an actual lady. It has been the longest, most successful con of my life, though there are those who might quibble with the word success.

We need to talk, he'd said. Too much in those four words. Worry, anger, the verbal translation of a visceral desire to wrap his hands around my neck and squeeze.

I face all of that unblinking, because I deserve it, though not quite for the reasons he thinks.

"Give me my son," I say. "I won't hurt him."

His top lip pulls up over his teeth, which is unnecessary considering his tusks are sharp, quite healthy, and therefore all the overt threat that is required.

"Two choices, Tleia," he says. "Come with me and I protect. Or stay here and do things your way. Take chances with Fae."

There's satisfaction in his gaze as he takes me in. He knows I have no choices at all, not with him holding our son hostage.

"Choose."

I stand, see my pack near the end of the cot and pick it up, adjusting it on my back after putting on my boots. He's right. Wherever this hidey-hole is, we've been sitting still like ducks too long.

"I have one more stop to make before we can leave the City." I pause, considering my words. "I intend to travel to offer myself at the Sorting."

His head jerks back as if I slapped him. "What? Why?"

"I can't stay in the City, especially not with Ethan."

"Looking for new fool to con."

I wait until he's done cursing at me under his breath in Uthilsuven, a language I understand better than I speak.

"Isn't that why any mortal goes to the Sorting?" I ask.

Looking for something. Food, shelter, protection. A new master to protect one from the old. A chance at a better life if you have nothing to lose anyway.

I have much to lose. And, unfortunately, my enemies in Seanna City outpace my ability to protect and provide for myself and my son.

"Take you to Sorting," Gethen says. "Watch you be claimed by stupid male if that's what still want. Son stay with me."

"How do you know he's your son?"

He sneers. I'd been testing him anyway. At least we won't be having an argument over paternity.

"Time is up," he says.

There's no time to quake over the unfamiliar hardness in his black eyes. The cold expression on his face that had once been tender enough to lull me into gentle dreaming again.

Shoving aside grief, I give him the same stiff coldness, and nod. "I'll carry Ethan. You need your hands free. I have a sling for him."

I drop my pack on the floor and take a long stretch of fabric out, wrap it around myself in a complicated fold, then reach for the baby.

I try not to show my fear, my desperation, but his nostrils flare; he can smell it. He starts to reach for me with his free hand, then forces it back down to his side.

"I can take him now," I say.

Gethen hesitates, protective of the boy.

The Orcs do anything for their mates, their children. Their families are their greatest weakness besides their honor. It makes them both exploitable, and volatile.

I hate their honor. I'd consign it to the hells if I could.

Not only because his son is in the circle of that protection, but not me. . .and he'd once called me his best friend.

I rein in resentment. "I would never hurt him, Gethen."

"Sent him away."

"You know why." My voice is sharp, because even if there's no point in arguing, I won't let him accuse me of placing my son in undue danger. "I smuggled him out to await me here. I had no way of knowing what would be waiting for me and if I'd been attacked, Ethan could have been taken or killed." I pause. "I couldn't find you on the outside."

"Tried?"

"Yes." I force my eyes to remain wide, unblinking. "Of course I tried. I didn't abandon you. I thought you were probably dead."

He exhales, shakes his head, and glances down at Ethan.

A whole week I've been separated from my son, and before that, the unsuccessful process of weaning him in preparation. It was a difficult decision, but in the end the best I could make.

No, it was better to get him out, to safety—such as it was—and come for him when certain I was safe.

Safe. I almost laugh.

I'll ask later how Gethen knew, if he's been watching us this entire time.

"Get proper basket for back at market," he says, tone more subdued. "That scrap of fabric is flimsy."

The Orcs strap their babies into upright woven baskets, like chairs, and put them on their backs. It don't make much sense to me, since when the baby wants to nurse you have to let them down. I prefer to carry the baby at the front.

He hands Ethan to me—I have to stop thinking of him as a baby, but it's hard—reluctance in his stance, watching with hawk's eyes as I slide the sleeping boy into the sling, and bounce a bit to make sure it's secure.

I wrap my arms around my son tightly, but not tight enough to wake him. He instinctively snuggles his head against my chest, and I want to cry. He's alive; he's unharmed. Even better, he's under the protection of his father and I can't realistically ask for a better scenario. If I'd known it was possible, I would have tried to arrange it myself.

"You braided his hair." There are a few braids along the sides of Ethan's head. Darling little Orcling rows, three on each side and the rest of his curls are left free. There are clan beads at the tips. My breath catches.

Gethen stiffens. "He is clan."

Did he blood my baby into his clan? He can't have, Gethen's clan is many, many days Northwest and the blooding doesn't happen until they are trained. He'd told me stories of his blooding multiple times, of how Ratha and Ilotha got him an older widow after to introduce him to sex and providing for young. The relationship ended amicably once the widow pronounced Gethen fit for "live" duty.

I gather myself. "Do you have his—"

Gethen jerks a shoulder, turning slightly to show me the battered leather pouch that holds Ethan's supplies. Another dear expense. Cloth diapers, his certificate of maternity, a few changes of clothing.

I don't move. "Is his baby Orc in the bag? He wouldn't be separated from it."

Irritation flashes across Gethen's face. "Try get him proper toy, but he bite me when try to take stuffed toy away."

"What's wrong with a stuffed toy?" *Are we really having this argument already?*

"It smiles. Should look fearsome. Not. . .cuddly." Gethen's bottom lip pokes out. He looks just like Ethan.

"It's a toy for a *baby,* Gethy."

He flinches. "My son will be warrior. Should have fearsome looking toy. Uthilsen start training warriors young."

"He's not even off the nipple, and you're worried about—" I stop myself. There is no time for this. "Can I have it? In case he wakes up, I'll need something to distract him. He might go for the breast and when he doesn't get his way, he'll morph into an unholy terror."

Something about that pleases Gethen, who nods and slips the pack off. I rummage through it and find the battered stuffed Orcling, discreetly squeeze its belly, and work to keep the relief off my face.

*That* had been a risk as well.

"We can go now," I say, shouldering the baby's pack. I intercept Gethen's look. "You need your movement unrestricted, remember?" I've tried to learn knife work over the years, but I'm terrible at it, mostly because I disdain pain, and pain disdains me.

Gethen's expression freezes into a death mask. "I know. Are ready? Useless with a blade. Learn nothing in prison?"

It's a verbal jab—Orc men like their women weapon trained. "I learned that I don't like prison. Will you let me explain, Gethen? Will you reserve judgment until we've had time to talk?"

He stares at me, flinty and unyielding.

"You owe me that much for your son. I didn't have to carry him to term, you know. I didn't want to." I firm my lips. "I did it because I knew you would want him."

"If don't want him, part ways now. I take care of son."

I shake my head. "Of course I want him. I've nursed this little gnawing brat for three years. He's demanding, fussy, messy, noisy, and he struts around the prison like he owns it and has every guard and inmate eating out of his palm. He's mine, and I'm not giving him up."

He turns to the door. "Come."

"No. You promise me you'll let me explain. That I won't have to endure your emotional bullying this entire trip. You owe me. Not just for Ethan. You know what Herbert did, and you did—"

"Enough." Another stream of guttural Orcish cursing.

"And you did nothing." Voice soft. Merciless. "Nothing. Nothing. But you don't see me blaming you. Because I understand the choices you made."

Gethen gently wraps his palm around the doorknob, his shoulders tense, his head bowed. He lets out a harsh breath and turns back to me. "Fine. If don't like fast talk explanation of *why*, make you suffer, Tleia."

"What more suffering do you want me to endure?"

Silence.

But I'm going to break this anger, this indignation, this false feeling of betrayal, and I'm going to break it now. "I'm done with suffering in silence. *Done* with it."

I did *nothing* wrong, not even when I betrayed him, and if he was caught up in the madness surrounding Herbert's death, that's nothing more than what he deserved for serving that monster. For letting that monster serve *me* on a platter three nights out of seven.

For standing outside the door, chained by his silly honor, then picking up my pieces night after night as if he had no power to do anything else. It's a paradox; he'd saved my sanity, but he hadn't saved me. I'd had to save myself.

Which I should have known in the first place because I'm a Coho Street girl. Like I said, I'd absorbed too much my persona. The moment it broke was the moment Herbert died.

"After the first year I spent cursing your name," I say, "I forgave you. You did the best you could at the time, what you thought was right. It wasn't enough, but it wasn't malice, and I've been expecting too much anyway. I'm only telling you this so you know I won't try to kill you as soon as your back is turned."

He stares at me, then closes his eyes a moment; when he speaks, his voice is rough. "I'm sorry. I think of nothing else in prison for year, then two while I wait for you. Think what should have done but didn't." He spits the word, looks at me

again, pain in his eyes as familiar to me as my rib. "Some
things more precious than honor."

I raise a brow. "Sacrilege. Are you sure you're Uthilsen?"

"Don't rub in, Tleia," he growls. "Females like to hear
males grovel. Shut up and accept victory."

"Win accepted."

"Instincts were. . .confused. You were another man's wife.
Didn't know what to do. If you'd been mine, would have
been no question."

There is no chance I'm letting him get away with that
excuse. "There wasn't a question when you fucked me,
*another man's wife*. When your cock was in my pussy spilling
the seed that made this baby."

"And would fuck you again, without question." His eyes
narrow. "But now, you are no man's wife."

It takes me a moment to respond. Are those words a
threat, or a promise? "Then you'll be nice to me?"

He steps forward and suddenly he's gripping my hair, his
mouth on mine though there's a sleeping child between us
and he can't pull me against him like he wants. My stomach
lurches. It's the first time I've been touched since—

The kiss is sharp with desperation, hot with want. I
freeze, heartbeat racing with the pace of a trapped thing, my
mind going dark as I let him take my mouth, not fighting the
hand painfully tight at my nape. His body hunches over mine
with pent up aggression and a hand slides down my back,
gripping my buttock, and squeezing.

I don't push him away. I don't move at all.

Gethen lifts his head and looks down at me, his brow furrowed. "Tleia?"

I hear the question in his voice, but I can't speak through my tight throat. I'd thought I had dealt with this in the last three years.

Gethen releases me and steps back. He seems to choose his next words carefully, pitching his voice lower, his tone softer. "Am Orc warrior. Am not nice. But you are my son's mother. Makes you *mine*."

After a moment, I can speak normally. "Until the Sorting."

A brief pause, a searing, searching look, then he turns and opens the door.

## FIVE

"WHAT DO YOU KNOW ABOUT MY SITUATION?" I ASK AS WE SLIP out of the building, our presence unmarked.

It's early evening, and for once it isn't even drizzling. The streets are still poured concrete in this neighborhood, broken by weeds and littered with trash—both inert and Human. The housing here isn't legally habitable, but it's better than nothing, and the landlords who've claimed the buildings are mostly Human. I suspect Gethen chose this location because it's one of the few territories in the City not owned by Aeddannari.

We skirt the neighborhood open market, blending into the dwindling crowd, and make our way towards a more dangerous side of town.

Gethen's sharp gaze scans our surroundings. "We owe money to Coho and Pike Fae. Price on head. Congratulations. Always liked to be center of attention."

*We. . .really.* "Hmm."

"You're worth cost of small homestead, in case wanted to know."

He's trying to provoke me, so I get my revenge the only way I can; indifference.

Gethen spares me a brief, keen look. "Rumor those owed expect to collect through a quick claim. Why they think? Herbert Lee left nothing."

I keep my expression neutral, doing nothing to draw attention to the baby bag strapped on my back, and debate whether or not to tell Gethen that the unsuitable stuffed Orcling is housing a small fortune in Icarian gems.

I decide to keep my mouth shut. Nothing will induce him to protect his son more than the fact that Ethan *is* his son, and if Gethen is somehow captured, he can't confirm what he don't know. Besides, if he knows I have the funds to eventually escape him, he'll take the stones from me.

He'll consider the act honorable, because it will be like protecting me from myself.

He thinks I didn't pay attention to any of his lectures or stories over the years. He's wrong. I pay attention to *everything.*

"I don't know why they think that," I say.

"Need find out why." We turn a corner and walk onto OakHorde Street, the one strip of land in Seanna City controlled by an Orc who styles himself Lord Cythro. "Hathur—"

"Hathur is in the City?" I've met Gethen's cousin a handful of times.

He grunts.

"Good. This is good." I need allies. All the allies I can get.

Gethen gives me a oblique glance.

We cross onto Dearrose, the florist district. Someone with a cute sense of irony named it, or maybe it's always been this way. The florists' block is the last bit of respectable real estate before we get to our destination. It's night, there's not a lot of foot traffic in this neighborhood.

I eye Gethen. "You're going to draw the wrong attention," I say, cupping my son's head. Ethan stirs but remains asleep. He must have eaten well, or maybe it's the scent of my breasts soothing him. He's an Orc male, after all. They're all fixated on boobs, maybe because their women are so. . .gifted. . .in that respect. "You walk like a warrior, and your death mask is on."

He relaxes immediately, his shoulders loosening, his expression softening. Now it's more of long-suffering husband at the end of a long day.

"Better?"

"Much. You've improved," I add, and pat him on the shoulder.

He'd been a bit of a common thug when we met a decade ago. Dangerous. But a country educated thug, one of those third generation Orcs born on Gaithea. He hadn't spent my years navigating the murky waters of the Human upper class. Murky with things filthier than mud, redder than blood. The monsters lurking in those depths all have pretty masks and you must learn each one—and then learn to don them yourself.

"I was taught by the best, Tleia," he says, his sudden City accent silkier than a rich virgin's bottom. "I knew there was something dark lurking under the society damsel exterior, but I never guessed at what I found."

"What of it?"

Gethen snorts, expression stony. "Deserve fat, placid wife and fruitful farm. Son running through fields waving first sword."

I can happily manage the fat, and fake the placid well enough. But somehow, I don't think that's what he wants.

"But best friend is treacherous," he adds. "So there's that."

"Treachery is an 'Annari word. You sound like a Fae poet." He begins to protest, and I hold up a hand. "We don't have time for this right now. If you want an explanation, I can give you one when we're safe." That much I can say to him now, especially if it will help him focus on his job.

"I spent year in jail, Tleia."

*Well, so the hells did I, Gethy.* My expression remains bland. "You were tried for Herbert's murder?"

"Tried, found innocent. Because *am* innocent." He says it with force, like he thinks I'm going to argue the point.

"I know that. When I gave them the tip, I knew they wouldn't be able to use it against you. They had no evidence, and you have no criminal record."

"Bought you time though." His voice is sour.

"It did. I didn't think you'd mind, all things considered."

He glances at Ethan, and his lips thin. Yes, it had been a little dirty to point the finger at Gethen, but it had been a misdirection, not a deliberate attempt at betrayal. The City Prosecutor had been about to hang me for Herbert's murder, before someone more intelligent reminded her what would happen to all Herbie's money if she did that. I'd just given her back a bit of face.

"I knew you'd want me to protect the baby above your life. You're an Orc warrior. Was I wrong?"

"No." Gethen blows out a noisy breath. "You are ruthless female. Suppose right. Good stock for son."

I pat him on the shoulder again. "See? It's a win win situation."

Gethen stops walking. "Not win win. Not when no punishment for you."

"Herbert is dead. Another dead monster. Why should I be punished?"

"It's matter of honor, both our honor. He died under my protection and was your husband. We owed him loyalty until honorably discharged from oaths."

"He didn't deserve your protection, or our loyalty." I keep my voice very, very even because this isn't the time to start shouting at him. . .or crying. "I belonged to Herbert, and you chose honor over me."

At least until the night Gethen's honor first broke. The night our son was conceived. The night I murdered my husband.

The Orc turns, stares at me. "It doesn't matter if he deserved his fate. I gave my service and failed. You gave your marriage oath. Penance must be paid."

I grimace. "How many times have I said you need to repudiate the Eyeless Priest. That sanctimonious prick."

"Not to Eyeless we will offer penance, but to Uthsha and Tueven."

"We?" I laugh. "I think not."

He's still staring at me, the expression on his face hardening into the same look Ethan gets when I tell him it's bedtime and his internal response is, "Bet?"

I sigh. "To return to the original discussion thread, you learned a valuable lesson about wasting your service on the unworthy."

"Now who sounds like Fae poet? Lesson must learn, Tleia. To honor word once given even if circumstances change."

"That's still the stupidest thing I've ever heard, and I hope I see the day where you *eat* those words. I hope you bleed." Ethan shifts, so I lower my voice.

We'd read the same poetry, the same tragic plays—often together. Herbert had trusted his Orc guard with his wife because of that stupid, pointless honor.

He shouldn't have. At the end, neither of us had been worthy of trust.

But I am the only one who doesn't feel guilt—not for that —and guilt oozes from Gethen's pores like anger does from mine.

"*Am* bleeding," he says, and steps toward me. "My blood is black."

More poetry.

"But Tleia," another step, "blood is also red. Fire burns on the water."

It's an old, poorly translated adage about the eventual fate of trying to combine things that should remain apart.

"Water doesn't burn. Only when there is oil on top, because the two cannot mix."

My voice is smooth, cold, even though a familiar pulse begins between my thighs because he's angling his body in a way that immediately makes me wary. I don't fear Gethen— or I didn't. But there's a look in his eyes now telling me he isn't quite the same man I used to know.

I won't be able to control him as easily.

"If say so, Tleia," he murmurs, and seizes the back of my neck, dragging me to him.

"Geth—"

His mouth swallows my cry, his lips slanting over mine with barely controlled lust, dominance spiced with anger and made bitter with longing.

There's a baby between us, but there won't always be. For the first time I'm afraid of *Gethen*. I know this taste on a man's lips, this clench of possessive fingers on my skin.

In his mind, I'm his, and he is owed.

The part of me that always craved a man's taste connects with the part of me that loves Gethen, and I want to kneel in the street, take his cock in my mouth and suck him till he spills down my throat.

I want to give him everything every other man I've encountered has taken, and I want him to look at me as if I'm as precious, as worthy, as one of his good, country bred Orc cows.

But I'm not quite ready yet.

His mouth roves down my neck, teeth grazing my skin and I whisper, "Please," hating that it comes out a weak plea and I'm neither weak, or a woman who begs.

*Ever.*

Damn him.

But I need him to let me go before I place myself in servitude to a man, again, as if I've learned *nothing*.

"Never again." I say it out loud, a bite of jagged iron in my voice. "I won't submit to you."

Gethen releases me, stepping back, his eyes wild. But he's in control and he glances away, focusing on some object in the distance.

After a moment, he turns his head to look at me again and says, inflectionless, "You will."

The baby stirs again and I look down, exhaling, shifting him in the sling a bit. He'll wake soon and either start screaming at me, or attack my breasts. Which means screaming, because I'll have to deny him until we're somewhere safe.

"And what will you do if they ever discover the identity of Herbert's murderer?" I ask.

Gethen is very, very still, watching my face closely. Sweet country boy. He's hoping with no hope that there's something in me worth protecting.

I did *nothing* wrong.

Gethen shakes his head, lowering his gaze to our son, then gestures to continue following him.

"What route are you taking us?" I ask his back once we begin moving again.

We pass an apothecary, and I make a mental note to double back. There are still some supplies that would come in handy on the road. Once I retrieve my stash, I should be able to take care of any magical wards that would prevent me from breaking into the shop.

"Made arrangements," he says.

"Did you? Normally I admire initiative, but how were you to know that your arrangements did not conflict with my own?"

He snorts. "Follow and remain silent. Be female for once."

*Really.* I lift my brows, though he can't see my expression. "Orc females are warriors."

"Be Human female."

Now we come to the truth of it. "You know, I may have seduced you for my own purposes, but you allowed yourself to be seduced. Don't lie to yourself that you didn't have a fantasy of taking the Human wife of your undeserving master. You wanted me beneath you, knowing I wanted you so much I would choose you over my own husband. What a tragic, star-crossed tale." In which I am the villain, but I'm fine with that. A damsel cannot save her child. I laugh quietly.

And stop on a dime, not running into Gethen, who froze.

"My darling Orc, we are going to have to work on talking and walking at the same time."

His shoulders tense, but then he resumes walking. "Will be a reckoning, Tleia. Promise you."

"Do you? I guess we'll see, won't we? You've made a lot of promises, but your follow through. . .well."

I shouldn't bait him, I know it. But he's beginning to get under my skin with his anger, his judgment, his self-righteousness. I didn't rape him.

The part of the City we're entering is worn down and definitely a little more on the seedy side, but working class enough that we can pretend to be honest. I hope his arrangements include some type of accommodation, because I'm tired, hungry, the baby is going to need to eat soon, and my neck is itching. The longer we're on the streets, the greater the chance one or both of us will be recognized.

My only disguise is the utter ordinariness of my features. Brown hair, brown skin, brown eyes. Short, still a little too plump for a woman who spent three years on jail rations, but I'm a mother. My people are native to this part of Gaithea, the old Paget Sunde region. There are thousands of women who look like me.

"Some of my things may have been smuggled out of the prison," I tell Gethen. "If there are Orc bounty hunters, they'll have my scent." The Warden would have done at least that much to earn her bribe.

"No Orcs." Terse, worried. "Intercepted Warden's message, threw bounty hunters off trail."

"Where are we going?" There's a moment of resistant silence. "Gethy, there's no purpose in keeping information from me simply to be contrary. I'm not your enemy."

"No, simply difficult keep alive." He mimics my tone. "We go to Hare and Stag."

"Wonderful."

I'm not being sarcastic. It actually is wonderful. The Hare and the Stag is where I made my own arrangements. "I have supplies stashed—"

He pushes me into an alleyway right as a knife whizzes past my head.

## SIX

I DROP TO MY KNEES AND CURL MY BODY AROUND ETHAN, flinging myself against a wall and making us as small a target as possible.

"Stay," Gethen growls.

"Take cover, you—"

But he's gone. I curse, then shut my mouth though I'm sure my position is already known. If they have an archer, it will be worse than stupid to take my chances running down the block to the inn.

No, I stay out of sight, trusting Gethen will get us out of this. If I didn't have a three-year-old strapped to my chest, I might chance running. But Ethan changes everything.

With his usual sense of flawless dramatic timing, my son chooses that moment to start crying.

I must have moved too suddenly, or maybe the fear scent

is now strong enough that it disturbs even a toddler. I try to shush him, rocking him against my chest as I listen to the din of fighting. A bright clash of steel, roars of pain and thuds of fists on flesh. The creak and crack of a bow and more hissing in the air, a scream after a buzzing sound that reminds me of. . .I tilt my head, frowning. A rock sling?

My back is to the brick wall, my line of sight obscured.

Ethan squirms, trying to get into the breastfeeding position, and clamps his meaty little hands on my breast, throwing himself backwards in my arms. His knees almost smack my chin.

"Mommy, you were gone! Bad!" I wince because each word is punctuated with his verbal outrage. "Want boobies!"

Of course he does.

His voice is angrier than normal, stronger, almost deeper, his grip on my hair yanking a wince from me as well as several of the strands. He's reacting to my absence, of course. I tried to explain to him that I would be gone for several days, but what can you really explain to a toddler?

All he must have known was that the enclosed four walls of the only home he'd ever known, and his mother, were both taken from him at the same time.

He won't stop screaming, so I give in and unbutton my blouse, yanking out a breast, and shove it in his mouth.

"Watch the tusks," I snap. They aren't very big, but still— not amusing when they get in the way. "Don't stab Mommy." I swear Orcs first learn to like the taste of blood at their mothers' breasts.

But shoving a boob in his mouth works like a charm every time, and I think I might have to learn to nurse while running.

The toddler nuzzling at my breast, settling down into a milk-induced stupor is familiar, comforting. I have to pry his hand away from the boob—he still kneads my chest like a stress toy, and I don't like it. Also, Gethen hasn't filed his talons. But my child is in my arms, alive and healthy and relatively safe.

I suppress my anxiety. It was only two weeks, I tell myself, and it was for the best.

I listen to Gethen roar. "Stupid male."

I'd try to explain to him why that was a particularly foolish habit of theirs, roaring in battle like a theater drama depicting the Hundred Year War. Maybe that's fine on an open field where there's no point in stealth, but not in a City street in the deep of night when we're trying not to draw any attention to ourselves.

I grimace.

Orcs.

Gethen returns, the look on his shadowed face wild, his teeth still bared. "Stayed put," he grunts. "Good. They didn't send enough warriors."

"They probably thought I'd be unprotected."

He snaps his teeth at me—though I hadn't intended it as a jab—then pauses, glancing down at Ethan as if he's never seen a nursing child before. His expression softens, something desperate and fierce flashing in his eyes.

I push to my feet, clumsily swiping up the knife that had missed my head. Gethen scowls and takes it from me, muttering. I don't blame him. I'll only cut myself.

"Can we still go to the inn? Were the hunters waiting for us there, or were they tracking us?"

He finally calms down a little. "Tracking. But will switch inns in case."

I nod. "The Hare is where my stash is. We have to retrieve it first."

"And mine."

"We make a beautiful team, Gethy."

He huffs, grabbing my upper arm and yanks me along with him. I hold my tongue as we approach. Gethen shares my love of back entrances because we slip through the alley to approach through the kitchen door.

Gethen knocks, grunts something to a half-Human half-Orc who pokes her head out, eyes narrowed, and we enter a moment later.

"I need to talk to Bethany," I tell her, pitching my voice low.

"I'm Bethany." Thick medium brown braids wrap around her head and her skin is that medium green with yellow undertones that indicates a Human grandparent. She's busty —they usually are—but she wears a full leather vest rather than the blouse and waist cincher waitresses all over use to tease more tips out of patrons.

"You have a package for Susanna Smith."

"Code."

"Homestead."

She squints at me, glances at Gethen. "You with her? Ya sure 'bout that?"

"You're being paid to provide a service," I say, "not to offer opinions."

Gethen grimaces. "Tell him come now."

"Him?" I glance at him sharply. "Hathur?"

He doesn't answer, crossing his arms. We wait in silence, Ethan detaching from the breast and wriggling so he's upright again. I'm shocked when he turns his head toward Gethen and all but flings himself out of my arms.

"*Otema!* Mommy, give me to Pa."

"What. Why do you want. . ."

I stare as Gethen takes the boy—there's a brief tug of war before I release Ethan—and cuddles him close to his chest.

"How long have you had Ethan?" I ask.

Ethan curls an arm around Gethen's neck and lays his small head against his Pa's broad shoulder. I don't quite know how to feel about that. I was his only shoulder, and now he has a much stronger one.

"As soon as you sent him away." He pauses, something dark flickering across his face. "Almost. Was sold. Bought him back—too risky to fight."

I open my mouth, then shut it firmly. "My relay failed." I'd pay Neteen a *visit*, but I don't think she deliberately betrayed me. "If you knew about him, why didn't you come for him sooner?"

"Did *not* know, Tleia. Learned of son when rat traded information for life."

For a moment I allow horror to shiver through me, my

limbs weakening from the residual stress of everything that had almost gone wrong—and I hadn't known.

I close my eyes. "Thank you, Gethen. I—I don't know what I would have done. I—" I shake my head.

When I open my eyes again, his expression is a blend of guilt, gentleness, and anger. "Do not blame you, Tleia. Failure is mine."

I don't argue with him. I've listened to Uther Bachdracht yap at me through Gethen's mouth enough times to know I'll never be able to counter-act that conditioning. Not that I want to.

Gethen sighs. "If had known of son, would have sent word to keep him with you. Orclings don't do well away from mother. Nurse until seven or eight—"

"*Seven or eight?* I think *not.*" I stare at my son in absolute horror. "He has *tusks. Talons.* I am *certain* he enjoys the taste of my blood when he bites me."

Gethen chuckles. "Less for half Orc. Four or five years, wean and begin to learn from male's circle." He sobers. "Why not tell me with child?"

"How? I didn't know I was pregnant until after I was charged with murder." It's. . .difficult to say those words without revealing the gut punch of shock I'd felt.

He narrows his eyes. "Managed to craft flight plan while still in jail. Could find me if wanted."

Maybe.

But. . . "It would have been too high a gamble. I had to call in favors, go into debt to smuggle Ethan out. I would have no way of knowing if you would accept my message, or care after I fingered you for the murder."

His eyes widen. "Not care about my young?" The pitch of his voice trails up at the end, as if I've offended him.

"You would have only had my word that—"

"Know this is my son."

Bethany—I highly doubt that is her name—returns with a larger pack of supplies and an Orc male I recognize in tow.

Hathur Tulekiyav, a distant cousin of Gethen's, is tall, muscled and bristling with weapons, wearing the same open but aggressive expression they always have when fresh off a farm because they know everyone is trying to swindle them. His eyes are dark blue, bright with curiosity and the awareness of exactly how handsome he is, and there's a hump in the bridge of his narrow nose. Skin a shade too blue for true green, rakish black hair brushing below his shoulders, his braids thin and slightly longer and tipped in clan beads.

Hathur exclaims, going to Gethen immediately and they embrace in a sort of side hug because Ethan is there, and I guess they don't want to squash him.

"Took long enough," Hathur says, then slides into Uthilsuven. "Did she come willingly, or did you have to threaten her?"

When he chooses to speak Gaithean, it's with an Uthilsen ori-gen dialect—I suspect he's second or third gen though, and mimics the elders to appear older and wiser. Gethen, who does the same, told me once that the Gaithean born generations often do that though they're native to the planet at this point.

"She understands you," Gethen says. "She cannot speak it much, but she understands."

He could have kept that information to himself.

Hathur gives me a look under his lashes meant to be charming. "Good to know. Was the journey here at least fun? How many did you have to kill?"

A fierce grin crosses Gethen's face. He catches the look on mine, and sobers up. "Some," he says. "Safety more important than fun, of course."

Hathur rubs his chin. "Of course, of course." He nods his head in greeting. "Mrs. Lee."

"I am no longer married," I say. "Tleia is fine. Or Mistress Shyncheia if you prefer formality."

"Widowed, yes?" Hathur switched to Gaithean, his tone a touch too pleasant to match the mischief in his eyes. "Seem to recall something about that."

I give him an equally pleasant smile, though I'm certain there is no mischief in *my* eyes. "Yes. I was tried for murder. Innocent, of course."

"Of course, of course." Hathur side-eyes Gethen.

"Is there a problem?" I ask.

Hathur blinks. "Nooo. . .the female's circle will like her well enough, cousin. Especially when she tells them why she slit her husband's throat. I'd keep one eye open if I were you. Are you certain you can handle this one? I thought you liked your females soft."

Gethen scowls. "Already said she understands you. She reminds me of my mother."

"Tueven's stones. That's what your mother gets for letting Ratha and Ilotha raise you. They'll hate each other."

Gethen winces.

Hathur doesn't have the nerve to look sheepish.

I glance at Gethen. "I'll take the baby. He needs to nurse some more."

There's nothing more visual than a nursing mother to drive home the vulnerable feminine visage I'm attempting to craft for the Orcs, and since Hathur has already decided I'm dangerous, I need to reframe my image. Two protectors are better than one and I don't want to give Gethen's cousin the wrong impression—that I am *any* use in a fight.

I am not.

The mischievous expression on Hathur's face softens as I take Ethan and settle him back against my chest.

"I'll need to check his nappy soon, too." I look up at Gethen like he's the sun and stars, my protector in this big, dark world.

He gives me a stink eye, suspicious. I turn to Bethany and she hands me the pack. I don't want to go through the contents in front of either of the males so I lift a brow at her.

"Is everything here?" I ask.

She props her hands on her hips and scowls. "Not the commission."

"Not the commission." I speak slowly, my voice sweet.

"Don't be gettin' snippy, girl. The building ain't warded and we have an infestation."

Spies for one of the Lords or the government. . .which means tax collectors.

"Where is the commission?"

I'm not leaving town without it. Even with Gethen and Hathur at my side, I'm not stupid enough to travel through the Pasifik Northwest forests to the Sorting with no weapons. There are monsters in those forests, and not the regular kind.

"It's at the Painted Lady," Bethany said, "with a working girl named Clary."

I tilt my head. "Is that a jest?"

She frowns at me. "No." Now she's the one speaking slow, as if I'm stupid.

"You gave my commission to my cousin? How did you know to do that?" Clary is probably the only person in the City left I'd trust. And trust is situational.

She scowls. "Had no idea she was your cousin. Good bit of luck, that. Unless y'all don't get along."

"We get along fine." I set aside resignation that I accidentally gave Bethany information she hadn't already had. I must be more tired than I thought.

I glance at Gethen, who's not trying to hide that he's listening to my conversation.

"Another stop?" he asks.

Good, it doesn't seem like he's going to argue. "The Painted Lady. Do you know it?"

He wrinkles his nose.

"Well, excuse me," I say on behalf of my cousin, who happens to make a good living in that establishment.

"Not modest place for Orcling," is the stiff reply.

"It's just a brothel." I shrug. "There are worse places."

## SEVEN

DOUBTLESSLY BECAUSE OF SOME MAN'S SENSE OF CITY planning, the brothel district is only a two-block walk from this section of the City. Someone was considering the ease of travel for visitors who might wish to seek evening entertainment. It works in our favor, especially since Hathur and Gethen are tense.

"How much your female owe?" Hathur mutters.

"Nothing," I say. Which is, of course, inaccurate. Also, I will have to speak to Gethen about discussing my business with his cousin. "My husband owed the wrong people money, and in this City a widow is responsible for a deceased husband's debts."

He lets out a soft breath, more of a hiss through his teeth. "Must be lot of money."

"It's enough. You could turn me in and claim the reward for yourself. I hear I'm worth a small homestead."

Hathur snorts.

Gethen must not be worried about that possibility because he doesn't twitch or blink. His gaze scans our surroundings as we walk.

"Mommy, I'm hungry," Ethan says. He's calmed down and must feel safer because he's resumed speaking in normal sentences again. Though that might be my influence. I doubt the Orcs bothered to speak in grammatically proper Gaithean around Ethan. "I want oatmeal. Otema said I could have oatmeal if I was good."

"Gruel not proper fuel for growing Orc," Gethen mutters. "Give him meat but wants only gruel."

I ignore Gethen. "Go to sleep, Ethan. When we get to where we're going, then we'll have oatmeal."

"Where we going? *Otema* says we can go to his house and I can play with other Orcings."

"Your Pa has more ambition than discretion. Go to sleep."

Ethan pouts but burrows back against my chest. Gethen placed him back in my sling once it was time to leave the inn. The males are best used to defend, not to carry babies. Not for the first time, I wish I have some skill with blades.

"What we retrieve from sexhouse?" Hathur asks me.

"You do like asking questions, don't you?"

"How else learn?"

"We're retrieving supplies."

"What kind?"

He's worse than Ethan. I'm not certain if Ethan's well-developed for his age, but I figure that years spent surrounded by women who did nothing but dote on him has benefited his verbal acuity. He began speaking in full sentences at two and I haven't been able to get him to shut up since.

"The kind useful for traveling through monster-infested forests." My voice is snappish, but he deserves it. "Instead of chatting, why don't you keep an eye open for patrols, and your hand on your weapon?"

"I can use my tongue and my fingers at the same time, dear cousin," Hathur replies. "There are any number of lusty females who—"

Gethen reaches out and smacks Hathur upside the head.

"There," I say, pointing my chin.

A gaslamp flickers outside an old townhouse, casting a golden glow over its weathered brick facade. A wooden sign with carved letters spells "The Painted Lady."

Inside, the atmosphere will be infused with the scents of wild rose, lavender, and musk. If the décor hasn't changed, then thick velvet drapes in rich green and deep blue will cover the walls and muffle the clamor of cobblestone streets beyond.

"I'll go in the service entrance," I say. "You two will have to go through the front with Ethan. They won't let males in the back."

Gethen shakes his head. "No. No split up."

"Even if they would let you in, and they won't, if a woman shows up with two Orc males and a baby, someone will notice. I can slip in the back by myself and find my cousin. Wait for me outside or in the front room."

Hathur is staring at me, both eyebrows raised. "With a baby?"

I shrug. "He's three."

"I'm a big boy," Ethan pronounces, proving he's listening. "I not a baby."

"Let me see your tusks," Hathur demands.

Ethan obliges, giving a little growl.

Hathur nods somberly. "No, not a baby."

"Just tell them your wife made you take the boy for the evening," I say. "This won't be the first time a father has brought a child with him. Sometimes it's safer."

With the increasing difficulty of all species, not just the immortals, in breeding, no one leaves their children alone these days. Which is a paradox, since children are left to run free on Coho Street. But those children are orphans, and we learn young to watch for predators.

"Don't like it," Gethen says.

"Do you have a better idea?" I ask. "It's vital we don't attract attention. I know the place, and I know where to find Clary. She's expecting me."

Finally, he nods, reluctant, then cups my jaw with his fingers, eyes slightly narrowed as he looks down at me. "Have our son."

The only reason to reiterate an obvious fact is if he's warning me not to take off. At least he understands I wouldn't ever leave Ethan.

His fingers press into my jaw, then slowly relax. "Will wait for you."

"That sounds like a threat, Gethy."

"Is. Don't be long, or I will hunt."

From the look flickering behind his eyes, I don't know if being an Orc warrior's prey will be as fun as it should be. Not if he thinks I'm fleeing him, and our child.

I glance at Hathur, who's wearing a smirk at the curve of his lips though his eyes are somber, and nod. As we approach the building the males veer towards the front entrance while I slip around the back. My clothing in this circumstance will do me good since I look a little run down, but not like trouble.

The back entrance is guarded from the outside, but I don't assume there won't also be security on the inside. There always is. To stop patrons or lovers from sneaking in, or indentured employees from sneaking out.

I give the name Bethany told me to use, and the guard waves me in. Inside, a Human woman carrying linens eyes me, her gaze traveling over my appearance.

"Clary is expecting me," I say, keeping my demeanor friendly. "I'm her cousin Tleia. Am I okay to go to her?"

I wait for permission, though I don't need it from a housemaid. But since I don't want attention, much less a fight, manners never hurt.

She jerks her chin toward the narrow hallway behind her. "Third door on the left."

"Thanks."

The layout hasn't changed in the years since I was last here. I find the door, knock the code, and a moment later it opens.

Clary looks me up and down, her expression stunned. "Tleia? You're alive."

She's an inch taller than me, brown skinned and eyed like I am, her hair a glossy raven's wing, half pinned up and half draped down her back. She's wearing the typical brothel uniform; corset, fitted mermaid skirt and enough layers of paint to make it clear she's working.

I give her a half smile, my body tensing because cousin or not, this could go poorly.

She shakes herself and seizes my wrist, jerking me into the room. Her room is small, decorated in shades of teal and gold. The scent of jasmine perfume lingers in the air.

"Do you know there's a bounty on your head?" she hisses.

"Yes, and I'm sorry you got involved."

"It's doubled since this morning. Three districts sent runners, and those are just the ones being open about it. The Banker's Guild—"

"I know."

She locks the door and turns to me.

But I've stopped speaking because we're not alone. A woman sits cross-legged on the draped bed in the corner, looking at me through a length of pale blonde hair, her dark eyes fixed on my face. She's too still, as if she's poised to run or fight but doesn't know which. She's about Clary's age, unless she isn't mortal and I have my doubts, and she's dressed like she works the front room.

Clary follows my line of sight. "This is Honoria." She sighs, catching my expression. "My wife. You can trust her."

I don't relax, at all. "When did you marry?"

"Two years ago," the woman says softly, her voice low and musical. "In secret. They don't allow couples here."

For obvious reasons. Jealous partners are a known business hazard, and expense.

But I recognize the look in Honoria's eyes, because I've seen it in the mirror. "Are you indentured?"

It's none of my business, but if she's kin now, I can't turn my back on her. I know what it's like to be trapped.

Clary shakes her head. "No, it's just that. . .this is the safest place for her."

"Explain."

Honoria gives me a slight smile. "I'm an untrained mage. Awoken too late. And I won't go to the Sorting."

Which means she's prey for any powerful magic user who stumbles on her. She's also breaking the law. Seanna City doesn't allow untrained and unregistered magic users. They kill them, imprison them, or match them with a "benefactor."

"Why are you telling me this?" I glance at Clary.

She lifts her chin. "You owe me for stashing your goods. I didn't know it was you when I agreed to it, but Beth said you could help me."

I wait.

Clary takes a deep breath and exhales, smoothing her hands down her hips. "You know Witch. I want you to get a suppressor from them."

I feel my brows creep up into my hairline. "That's permanent. Why not just seek training?"

"From who, Tleia?" Clary's voice is sharp.

I purse my lips. From who is the problem. Teachers who

won't take advantage of an untrained magic user are few and far between.

"That's fine. I'll go see Witch." It means another detour before I leave the City, but Coho Street folks don't abandon kin. "I'll do what I can, but I can't make promises. You'll be in Witch's debt."

Honoria nods, then glances at Clary and unfolds herself from the bed and walks towards the door. "I'll let you two talk. It's my shift anyway."

I wait until I don't hear footsteps anymore because I'm not certain how sharp Honoria's ears are. "Clary, she's bait. What were you thinking *marrying* her?"

Clary looks resigned. "I wasn't thinking. I fell in love. Help me protect her, please."

"I said I would. She's kin now." Some god help my cousin.

Clary nods, swallows, then gathers herself and refocuses on the business at hand. "I have your pack." She walks to the far end of the room.

"I didn't mean for you to be the one holding it. Does anyone know we're related?"

She shakes her head. "This isn't the first time Beth has used me as a courier. It's probably coincidence this time."

But her brow furrows, and I understand why. If my enemies think she knows where I'm at, or that she can be used against me, she'll be in danger.

"Give me the pack, and I'll leave right away."

Clary sighs. "I wish I could help you more. Do you have everything you need?"

"I'm fine, and I'm not traveling alone. My son's father and

cousin are with me."

"What! I hadn't heard you had a child. Word went out to look for a woman and child, but I thought someone got their info mixed up."

"In jail."

"Oh, hells, Telly."

I shrug, not showing my tension. "It's fine. He's healthy."

She purses her lips. "Well, that's good then. You'll have help on the road. Are they any good in a fight?" Clary straightens, pulling a pouch out of the chest at the end of her bed.

The supplies are a set of charms I also paid to be keyed to me. I donated enough blood and hair to ensure that, though having to do so is a risk itself. But the witch I'd chosen has a reputation for completing their job and not screwing over clients with unintended consequences. Still, I'm worried. The bounty on my head is enough to tempt anyone.

*Damn you, Herbert.*

"They're Orcs," I say.

"Your baby daddy is an Orc?"

"No rumors?"

"That you have allies? No. You know we couldn't come see you."

I wave a hand. "I know. Don't worry about it. You would've been in danger."

She approaches and hands me the pouch. "Don't tell me where you're going, but if you get there safe, try to send word? I'll know it's you."

"I will. We'll be out of the City the minute our business is concluded."

We've grown apart over the last two decades, having taken different paths, but we spent our formative years on the streets together, surviving, and that's not a link that can be broken by anything but betrayal.

Clary hugs me once, then pushes me out the door. "Go safely."

Walking down the hall, I mentally kick myself as soon as I register the din of a busy front room—music, laughter, conversation and other noise—proof the evening is in full swing. I don't know why it didn't occur to me to tell the Orcs to meet me outside. It's a bad idea to stroll into a crowd when there's a price on my head. We're all stupid.

I open the door leading from the employee quarters into the front room and I'm about to step through the threshold when someone seizes my arm.

"Telly," Clary hisses. She jerks me back and shuts the door with a quiet click. "There's Coho Fae in the crowd."

I turn and stare at her. "What? How do you know?"

"I went out for a smoke and saw them enter."

"That's not good. Clary. . .I didn't want to get you involved, but do you think you can find my man? He'll be the only Orc with a three-year-old with him. Probably."

She grins briefly. "That's not as uncommon as you think. I can find him, but they'll notice if I try to bring him through this entrance, and if the Fae are already in the crowd, then they'll be lookouts on all the entrances and exits."

But even as she's talking, I've sifted through the scenario. "Do you have clothes that will fit me?"

Clary's not stupid, and she thinks almost as fast as I do. She tugs me back towards her room. "I'm supposed to be on the floor, my supervisor will notice I'm missing soon. We don't have much time."

I'm already stripping as we reenter her room. She helps me strip then shimmy into a corset and skirt. I raid her cosmetics as she laces me up and swipe on red lipstick, three coats of mascara and enough blush and contour to shapeshift my broader nose and rounder cheeks. Even if I'm not a warrior, I can throw on a full face in five minutes flat, a skill that's come in handy more than once. She finishes pinning up my hair and hands me heels.

"You'll have to tuck the pouch in your corset," she says. "If anyone stops you, tell them you're already bought for the evening."

I glance at myself in the mirror. With my breasts plumped and my face contoured, no one will be expecting to see Mrs. Herbert Lee. They'll see what I appear to be; a middling priced sex worker. Sometimes it's better to hide in plain sight.

"This might work out better," I say, ignoring the fact that the corset isn't the reason I'm having trouble breathing now. My mind wants to yank on the memory of the last time I was dressed like this. I want my mind to shut up. "This way I can walk right up to him myself and no one will blink."

"Go in before me," she says.

I nod, we traverse the hallway, and I step into the front room.

## EIGHT

THE GLOW OF CRYSTAL CHANDELIERS GLITTER OVER THE inhabitants. Patrons—mostly Human and mixed species though there are a few immortals—wander the lavish parlor in varying states of refinement and dress. Or undress, if one happens to be working.

A young woman with warm gold skin and icy hair reclines against a fainting couch, her corseted waist accentuated to waspish proportions. I wonder if she still has ribs. Honoria meets my gaze briefly, but other than that, we don't acknowledge each other.

I put a hand on my hip and mimic the slow, purposeful gait of the other workers, scanning the crowd for anyone big and green. Then I wince, hearing a small child's delighted laughter. I suppose it's too much to ask that my son isn't enjoying himself. I suffer no delusions about the male of any species, young included.

Resigned, I saunter towards the laughter but don't get more than halfway across the room before I'm waylaid.

The Human man gripping my wrist is lean, the kind of lean that speaks to too much time on the road and not enough time to eat. The state of his clothing, a well-made but worn brown overcoat, navy blue woolen vest and dusty, knee-high boots mark him as a recent traveler. He isn't settled in for an evening of debauchery. Short brown curls frame a narrow face and hazel eyes focus on me—and I'm not nearly the most attractive person in the room.

He holds up a red token, its finish indicating what level of service he's paid for and requesting. . .a private experience.

I smile at him, tilting my head. "Apologies, darlin'," I drawl, inserting a hint of cant into my voice, "but I'm already spoken for this eve."

"Now I know for a fact that isn't true," he says, matching my tone.

"Allow me to find you a companion more suited to your station. I'm meant for a man more common than yourself."

Without turning my head, I scan the rest of the room, looking for Coho Fae or anyone with the patina of bounty hunter on them. I've garnered a few casual glances, but no more.

The hand on my wrist tightens and he rises from his couch, tugging me towards him. Then he lowers his mouth to my ear.

"Don't disappoint me by trying to run, *darlin'*," he says.

He begins to tug me through the room and I go along with him for one reason. . .Ethan. If it weren't for my son I'd chance starting a brawl and hope to get away while my captor is distracted by the scuffle. But Ethan could be hurt. I don't expect for one moment that Gethen won't get involved, though if he's smart he'd give the boy to Hathur and order his cousin to escape.

As he tugs me along I use the time to consider my options. As soon as he gets me alone, I can figure out how to get away from him. If he's not a bounty hunter and simply wants to redeem the token, then I'll steel myself for having to fall on my proverbial sword, even if nausea swirls in my gut and my muscles stiffen in fight or flight instinct. Not fight—fighting never made anything better. But that'll be the easiest way to get away from him. And by easy, I mean without attracting Coho thugs.

Another male steps in front of my captor, angling his shoulders in that aggressive way that indicates a fight is about to start. He has the mixed look of Fae and Icarian, dove gray skin with an underlying shimmer, and pointed ears.

"I'll trade you three red coins for the woman," the mixed-species says. It's a stalling tactic. Not even three of these coins is worth the bounty.

My captor chuckles. "If you know what's good for you—"

I twist my arm and bring my hand down, one of the few bits of self-defense Gethen was able to drill into me well enough to be useful.

The Human, having not expected me to fight since I'd come along docilely, loosens his grip just enough for me to yank. That, and the fist flying towards his face means I'm now free.

I drop, dive under a nearby table and keep low to the ground as the fight breaks out.

I'm fast, but a hand grips my ankle and yanks me from out underneath the table. I twist, landing a glancing punch against someone's jaw, and get the brief impression of a dark skinned Human face and cursing.

Then I hear a roar.

Oh, that *idiot.*

———

## GETHEN

"I don't like this," I mutter, shielding my son's eyes. Why did I agree to this?

We settle at a table and Hathur makes what I am certain he thinks is good use of the time to order tankards of ale because that is what he does. He never misses a bonfire when there is ale and dancing. I heard he tried to seduce my uncle's female and almost lost his stones for his boldness. I scowl at him.

Ethan shoves at my wrist, howling. "Pa, I can't see!"

I switch back to Gaithean. "That is point."

Heather clasps me on the back, still speaking Uthilsuven. "He has to see the world someday."

"Is not modest."

"You're mad because Ratha wouldn't let you see a pair of

tits before you were thirty, and then made you play house for Widow Salkoya for a year."

That distracts me a moment. "How are the girls?"

"Ianah had her baby."

"What? A baby?" Salkoya and I hadn't handfasted, but those girls I still consider my step-daughters. I've sent their mother money every year until I was arrested, since Sal'a never remarried. "She took a husband?"

Hathur is howling with laughter. "Nevermind that. Are you going to introduce Tleia to Salkoya?"

"Of course. They would get along. Nothing ruffles Sal'a, and Lei'a needs female friends with steady nerves."

My cousin gives me an odd look. "Human women are jealous, cousin. Be careful."

I shake my head. "I've told Lei'a about Sal'a."

"It's your stones on the chopping block." He switches to Gaithean. "Relax, enjoy ambiance. Don't be prude like Uther."

I sniff. I'm not shocked by a brothel after over a decade in this miserable City, but it doesn't mean I want Ethan exposed to this aspect of animal nature before he's had the proper years to develop discipline and decorum. Orc males aren't allowed to compete for lovers until they prove themselves worthy through mental and physical trials. Those who try to skip the proper steps are set down by the female's circle.

Set downs usually involve blood, but only rarely the removal of stones. A fool has to do something creative to earn that punishment.

Or cheating. Cheating almost always results in loped off stones, if proven.

Hathur tickles Ethan under his chin as a server brings our ale—and milk for the boy. "Let's wet our throats while we're here."

I tighten my arm around my son, who's now kicking and wriggling to get free.

"Where trying to go?" I ask him. He's as stubborn as his mother.

"Squeezing me," he complains, and bites down onto my wrist. "I want to sit in own seat. I a big boy. Mommy say."

"Mommy made career flattering foolish males."

But I put him in his own chair because there's no purpose in blunting his developing independence. He stands and begins stomping in time to the music, his eyes bright as he looks around.

"Boobies!" he shouts. "Time to eat." He pauses, and scowls. "Where's Mommy? It's eat time."

Hathur, having already spit out a mouthful of his ale at the first loud yell, begins laughing. "I suppose this'd seem like a buffet to a nursing child. Might betime he's weaned."

My back stiffens. "He's only three." As my son ogles a passing pair of breasts with hunger in his gaze, I admit Hathur has a point.

"Big boys eat meat and bread," I tell Ethan, and snatch him up as he's about to launch himself out of the chair and trail after an half-Orc female passing by.

"'Ware," Hathur says, voice quiet and eyes sharp though his posture remains relaxed as he lounges in his seat. "Fae bastards incoming, and they don't look like they're here for a good time."

My gaze I let brush across the thugs slinking through the room, spreading out. Some take tables, some go to the bar, others post up along a wall. There's a half dozen, which means they have a good tip their quarry is inside.

Tleia doesn't know it, but I'm not as angry at her as she thinks. In the last three years I've had to swallow my stomach to do things to survive. I don't know what she has that the Coho Fae Lord wants, but this isn't about a venal financial debt.

"We'll wait for her a little longer," I murmur. "Then you take Ethan and get out of the City while I go for Tleia. She's taking too long."

He nods, sipping, and there's nothing more to be said. Our travel arrangements are set, though I'm certain Lei'a has arrangements of her own she thinks we'll be following.

"Gethen." Hathur flicks his gaze towards a door opening in a far wall.

A Human woman steps out, her burnished copper skin glowing, silky dark hair in a simple loose braid around the crown of her head. Her breasts overflow a blue corset, waist cinched in before meaty hips flow out, a mouthwatering jiggle as she stalks through the room, dark gaze enigmatic, a smile curving red painted lips.

It stabs me in the chest; I haven't seen her dressed like this since the night she started her final spiral.

"You're a little slow," Hathur says. "That's your female."

Almost I snatch the tankard and dump it over his head. "Know who is. Keep eyes to self," I growl.

"You do know where we are, right?" he drawls.

Kill him later, I will.

I steer Ethan's gaze away from his approaching mother so he doesn't start shrieking her name and give us away. Because I'm watching him, I don't see the man grab Tleia.

Hathur stiffens, giving me a warning glance as I look back at my female and see her in conversation with a male holding up a coin.

A growl slips from my chest.

Not again.

Never again.

Darkness flickers behind her gaze though she smiles at the man and allows him to lead her away. She's turning her head, looking for me I can tell, and I stand, shoving Ethan at Hathur. Never again will she look for me and I don't come at her command.

Hathur grabs my arm, cradling my boy against his chest. "Don't do anything stupid. We can still get out of here quietly."

As soon as he says that, Tleia and the dead male who grabbed her are intercepted, and chaos breaks out.

"Get Ethan out of here," I snap, stride forward, and roar.

————

**TLEIA**

A blade presses against my neck. I still.

"Come without trouble or I'll slit your throat," someone new says, as if the blade isn't a clear enough declaration of their intentions.

"I know what your master is after," I say, "and it's worth far more than the bounty on my head. If you get me out of here, then I'll take you to the treasure."

It's utter horseshit, but I need to buy time. Gethen is coming, obviously, since he kindly announced himself, and I don't want the Orc to be forced to fight for me. He's a warrior, but fights are never predictable and we're already outnumbered.

At least I'm now certain he's willing to kill. Even after ten years as my personal guard, he'd never lost that brush of softness.

"Yeah?" the Human says. "You tell me what it is, and maybe we'll make a deal."

"That's not how this works. You escort me out of here unscathed, we get away from everyone else who's looking to steal your payday, and then I'll take you to the treasure."

The blade presses closer to my throat. We're moving at this point, interrupted because it's not as if everyone else doesn't have the same idea. We're all playing a game of capture the bounty, and with this many interested parties, keeping me isn't going to be simple.

A chair flies in front of us, and a woman in leather armor over denim tackles what looks like the establishment's security to the ground. The man holding me curses, startled, and I take that second where the blade isn't against my throat to—

Someone tackles him from behind, ripping him away from me.

"Get out of here!" Gethen roars in Uthilsuven. He's snarling, lips drawn up over his teeth as he strikes. "Meet Hathur at 21st and Drake."

Lord Cythro's territory.

I drop to the ground and dive under the closest table, my original strategy, to get out of direct line of sight.

If Hathur already left with Ethan, I'll have to trust that Gethen will survive and make his way to us.

The thought of their deaths tear at me as I make my way out of the chaos of the front room and step into the foyer—

—right into the arms of a Coho Fae.

## GETHEN

I watch Tleia dash out the double door leading to the foyer and front entrance.

It's a gamble to have her run. She's not weapons trained, and though she's willing to kill, the ability to execute is the other side of that coin. Once we're finally out of this stinking City, I'm going to make her focus and learn to wield at least a simple dagger.

Several Fae peel away from the crowd and follow her immediately.

They're tall and lithe to a man, their hair a rainbow of colors and textures but in a traditional waist length spill down each back, some bound with ribbons or other ornamentation. They wear bastardized Aeddannari livery, all black and tailored close to the body with short cloaks or longer overcoats to hide weapons; vassals of the noble Houses adapted for this planet and the circumstances to which we've all sunk.

I curse myself. *"If we keep reading Fae tragedies, we'll start to think like them,"* Lei'a used to tease. But if you want to know the inner mind of your enemy, read their literature. Listen to their music, watch their plays of love and death and war. Art will expose weaknesses the most stoic immortals refuse to reveal.

A swarm of mixed-species bounty hunters approach. I grab my sling, release—a stone slams against one's head, the others scatter as I continue to load and release.

Whirling, I launch again, crushing another foe's nose in a bloom of gore. They'd taken my obvious weapons at check-in, so now I rely on the sling, and fists.

Meadowland wants something from Tleia. He owes her a debt for his actions, and I'll take that debt by yanking out each of his teeth, then his nails, then his hair.

A Human tackles me.

Sidestepping, I grab his arm and swing him against the wall. Another takes his place and I whirl, landing a powerful kick into his stomach that sends him sliding across the floor.

The Fae are leaving.

Cold with fear, I go, because if they are leaving, they have what they want. Before I can follow, three more Humans run at me, wielding knives.

Cracking one across the jaw with my forearm before he can strike, I pivot and land an elbow in the throat of another.

As the third stabs at me, I catch his wrist and twist, hearing a snap as the knife clatters to the ground.

Launching towards the door, I barrel through the cannon fodder sent to slow me down and burst into the foyer. A half dozen Aeddannari guard the door, watching me.

Meadowland, Lord Coho, paid the brothel security off, because the Coho Fae are armed. One leaps towards me with a sword. I dodge, the air shrieking as his blade cuts through where my head had been a split second before.

A singing sword.

These are Meadowland's personal guard, no simple Seanna City born thugs.

"You are outnumbered, Orc," the Fae facing me says, his voice cool, his long black hair a temptation for me to grab and use as a noose to choke him with. "Our Lord desires speech with you. Come, and he may yet allow you to live."

"Meadowland can eat my cock," I snarl, knowing he'll understand my language.

He replies without blinking. "I doubt there is much meat on it to be had."

The swordsman unsheathes his blade and we fight. Aeddannari are faster than striking snakes, but Orcs are heavier, stronger. My fists sing their death song, each swing a note of rage. I think only of Tleia and Ethan's survival, of duty, of vengeance.

"Enough," one of the others calls out, and the male facing me leaps back, disengaging.

Turning to the one who spoke, I bare my teeth in a snarl. He looks at me, bored. "We have Tleia Shyncheia, her child, and the other Orc. You may come with us, or we can kill you now. Choose. Our Lord is not patient."

There's no way to infiltrate Meadowland's tower; I've tried. Figuring out how to assassinate him has been my other hobby the last two years.

Putting away my sling, I let them swarm and bind me.

———

The door of my cell opens and the threshold frames Meadowland. My cell is guarded and the only other way out is to walk off the ledge. Half the wall is crumbling ruins, and we're twenty or so stories up. Lord Coho likes to offer his guests a view of the setting sun.

There's nothing to distinguish him from his men, except he wears red instead of black. I eye his warriors with contempt, let him see my hatred.

*"Keep your enemies close, and your emotions closer, Gethy,"* Lei'a has said.

I am not Tleia. It's because of him, because he'd shown interest in her, touched her, that she was tortured and imprisoned.

"Already chained," I say. "Why need so many men? Fear me. Good. Not stupid Fae."

Meadowland's expression doesn't change, but the corners of his eyes tighten. "Gethen Bachdracht-kin. You are still far from your home. I was informed you fled the City once your former master's wife was imprisoned."

My shoulders stiffen at the insult, the implication I would abandon Tleia. "Where are they? If you touch them—"

"I have not. Nor will I."

He steps into the room, clasping his hands behind his back. The warriors don't come with him, and the door shuts.

"She and the child are unharmed," the Fae Lord says, "the Orc. . .well, his deportment is similar to yours." Meadowland shrugs. "If he is wise, he will survive my mens' tempers. If he is not, I will have earned their gratitude for this week's entertainment."

His taunting, I ignore. "Why detain her? For entertainment? She owes you *nothing*."

"I assure you, there is little I do these days solely for idle amusement. I have business with Mistress Shyncheia."

I was right. He wants something. "She isn't yours. Know where she comes from, doesn't make yours. Leave her alone."

Meadowland gives a pleasant smile that doesn't reach his eyes. "I intend to ask her to complete a small task, and you will assist. I bear you no ill-will, Orc. Business usually concludes faster when all parties cooperate."

Anger engulfs me, though I force it back, force my muscles to relax as I lean against the wall, chained like a dog. I spent the time stalking Coho and Pike learning. Meadowland has a weakness for females. Not sexually; he is celibate.

He doesn't hurt them.

He punishes any of his people proven to have harmed a female without provocation. Even female warriors he handles with a gentler hand, giving them a kinder death. It's a peculiarity his people should mock him for. They don't, which means he's more powerful than he appears.

"Do you know what happened the last time you involved her in your business, Fae?" I ask, switching to full Gaithean. "Do you know what Lord Pike did to her? The lacerations on her back, between her thighs? The bruises. Screams at night because in sleep she had to endure his torment. You were there for the first part of it. You *instigated* it."

Meadowland watches me, expression cold and still as a winter lake. "That was not my intent."

"Intent?" I snarl. "Whatever it is you want from her now, don't think you've done enough?" I lean forward. "She was kind to you. Offered you warning. You repaid by delivering her to *Pike*."

"The task," he says after a moment, his voice even, "she is uniquely situated to handle. She will need protection, however, and my people are being watched. The matter requires discretion."

He wants me to cooperate. What he wants from her is dangerous, and he can't use his own people. It benefits him in several ways to use me instead.

"And if I refuse?"

His lips curve in a cold, amused smile. "It's curious you think you're in a position to bargain. I have your female. I have your son. I have your cousin. Tell me, what do you have besides the paltry use you might offer me? Make your choice, Orc. I go to see Tleia next." He turns, glides towards the door. "She is one of mine, born and bred on Coho. I would take her oath of fealty if she ever gave it—I have watched her, and she would be an asset." Now standing in the threshold, the door open, he turns to me. "You? You are unknown, your only value in the dwindling potential of your bloodline. Tleia will do as I command. She is much, much smarter than you."

"Coho!" I lunge forward, rattling the chains.

He half turns, brow raised. "Yes?"

"Take me to her. Prove she and my son and cousin are unharmed and I'll help her help you." I hate the promise, but I taste magic in these chains. Even if I can escape, it will be too late.

Meadowland studies me. "I will take you to where you may await her while she and I converse." He smiles, because despite my stony expression he probably knows how much the thought of him alone with her, speaking to her, infuriates me. "Perhaps the exercise will be beneficial."

Three years ago I would have consigned us both to the flames before giving into the demands of an Aeddannari crime lord. Before enduring the dishonor.

But I have a son, and his mother.

Grim, I nod. I understand Tleia much better these days. I understand the price of survival.

## TEN

## TLEIA

"Good," a low, lazy voice says, "you're awake. No, don't pretend, Tleia Shyncheia, I have little time to deal with you. Findashir, encourage my guest to cease her playacting."

I open my eyes and sit up because I have no desire to experience said encouragement.

I know where I am. This tower is a crumbling skyscraper jutting up like a broken fang against Seanna's gloomy sky, enshrouded by dense vines and foliage clawing up and inside the gaping concrete walls. The lower floors have collapsed into a vast open pit, leaving the remnants of seventeen floors visible above, their walls mostly shattered to expose rusted steel beams and jutting rebar.

If I was allowed to walk to the edge of this room and look down through the crumbled wall below, I'd see streets. As it stands, a bird lands on the floor and emits a raucous caw before flying away. It's probably offering commentary on my intelligence.

Because the scent of fish wafts into the room, and I recognize the sounds of water lapping against boats, I know I'm on Coho Street. Only one Fae Lord rules here.

There are three Lords in Seanna's undercity who fight for dominance while the legitimate rulers officiate from the hills; Meadowland, called Lord Coho, Seacliff, called Lord Pike, and Cythro, called Lord OakHorde.

One of the three stands before me. An Aeddannar, Fae as they're called when you want to be mildly insulting.

His hair is long, the color of the heart of blood red rubies, his skin pale with a gold undertone. Eyes the same shade as his hair stare at me. He's wearing a three piece suit; trousers, dress shirt, lace corset vest accentuating the vee of his broad shoulders to his slim waist, all in shades of dark red.

He leans on the edge of a black desk, the only furniture in the room, his arms crossed. Behind him, the sky begins to lighten. It's almost dawn.

"Do you remember me, Mistress Shyncheia? It's been some years since we met."

Insulting him by pretending amnesia won't go in my favor. "Of course, Lord Meadowland. How could I forget our last encounter?"

His expression flickers. He straightens and gestures to a chair on the other side of his desk. "Come, sit. I have requested refreshments. Please, help yourself."

I've learned through hard experience the more pleasant

and hospitable a Fae Lord, the more cruel and dangerous. It's part of their culture, I suppose, that they hide their monstrousness under soft words and humble grace. But I've also learned if you play the game, it buys time. There's a form to these interactions, and Aeddannari bind themselves to the forms. And this one had almost, *almost*, been kind to me the last time we'd met.

I rise, walk to the chair and sit, crossing my ankles and placing my hands in my lap. "Thank you, Lord Meadowland."

He pours a glass of wine, hands it to me, then gestures to the tray of biscuits. I take the wine and sit, select a biscuit and nibble.

"There," he says, gaze contemplative, "there's no need for brutality. Your face is bruised, and I apologize for that. I asked my men to bring you along gently, if at all possible."

"I appreciate the consideration. But I admit, I'm puzzled why you felt it necessary. I'm unworthy of your notice."

He lets the silence stretch, holding my gaze. "Perhaps you truly don't know."

I tense, setting the food and drink down. "I wouldn't be stupid enough to deliberately do something to displease you. I have no reason to make myself your enemy. I want to live."

He smiles, the expression almost indulgent. But the smile is fleeting. "I'm glad to hear it. I admit I have little desire to treat you as an enemy, Mistress Shyncheia. Perhaps we might cooperate with each other."

My heart is beating faster. He's negotiating with me. By all rights, I should have nothing he wants, but he's treating

me as if I do. I don't want to have in my possession *anything* a
Fae Lord covets. Which is why I'm sitting here.

Because I *don't* have it.

Meadowland is watching me. "You say nothing of the
debt I owe you."

"I. . .how could you possibly be in my debt?" How can I
discharge it, immediately. The Aeddannari make owning a
debt more onerous than owing one.

"My lack of discretion that last evening, I believe, led to
some unpleasantness."

From the flair of scarlet in his eyes, he hasn't forgotten
that unpleasantness. Swallowing, I moisten my lips with the
tip of my tongue. "There's no debt. You had no ill intent, and
I wasn't yours to protect. I would rather forget it."

He picks a pen up off his desk, toying with it. "I
sympathize. There is much myself I—" Meadowland
straightens, setting the pen down.

I wonder what he stopped himself from saying? Much he
regrets, maybe? Or wants to forget? He could be three
hundred to my forty. I shudder to think of three hundred
years worth of regrets and nightmares that refuse to die.

It's why the ori gen are all vicious, of course. "Why am I
here, Lord?"

"You are direct. Very well, I suppose there's little time this
evening. You've inherited an item of mine, and I would be
grateful for its return."

I almost begin to laugh at the irony because I know
where this discussion must lead, but laughing would limit
the length of my life to about the next three minutes.

I wrap my hands around the arms of the chair to keep from bolting out of the room. I wouldn't get a foot, and he would then abandon his facade of civility.

Buying time, I prevaricate. "My apologies, Lord Meadowland, but I'm confused. If I had inherited any property of yours I would have been privileged to return it to you."

"I see. Perhaps you're unaware of the item? If that *is* the case, I would be happy to give you the opportunity to search, and return it to me without the need for further complication." He straightens. "Excuse me, I am remiss—Findashir, bring in Mistress Shyncheia's son. The boy was insistent he see his mother and I gave my word he would as soon as she awoke."

I keep my expression pleasant, though I know he must be able to hear the rush of my breath as if someone punched me in the middle.

"My son, Lord Meadowland?"

"Indeed. The half-Orc boy?" He chuckles, and I try not to liken his hair and eyes to the color of drying blood. "He's quite fierce. But I suppose that's to be expected, considering his parentage."

I say nothing more because anything I say is a potential trap, and the compliment unsettles me. The door opens and that beating heart of mine stops as a young boy howls.

"Mommy! Put me down, I want Mommy! I bite you!"

The Lord nods to whoever is behind me, and the patter of small feet precedes my son climbing in my lap, pulling at my hair and corset, trying to get to a breast. I doubt it's for

hunger. No, he needs comfort and reassurance. Lord
Meadowland lifts a brow and stares at us, looking slightly
aghast.

"I rarely see infants," he says after a moment. "I'd
forgotten how. . .feral. . .they can be."

I manage to get my son to stop trying to undress me and
cradle him in my arms, rocking him back and forth to soothe
him. He turns his head and growls at Meadowland, who
laughs.

"Your mother will come to no harm, little one. Will he
eat?" Meadowland addresses me. "Perhaps that might calm
him so we can continue our discussion."

I doubt the food is poisoned, there's no point. I hand a
stack of biscuits to Ethan who takes them from me and
settles down, shoving one in his mouth.

"Chew," I say. "Don't inhale."

"Findashir, bring water for the boy. Or milk, rather. Does
he drink other than yours?"

I nod. The more civilized and solicitous this man is, the
more the item's value skyrockets and my stomach sinks.

"Good, that should be along shortly." He gives me a
quizzical look. "Now we're all more settled, perhaps you've
had time to reflect? Do you recall the item to which I refer,
Tleia?"

If anything, his voice is gentler, the slight curve of his lips
sweet as honey. Stalling or lying further will get me killed,
but not before I have to watch my son being tortured.

"Your betrothal necklace, Lord Meadowland," I say. "If
my mortal recollection serves."

He rewards me by adding approval to his smile, and in any other circumstance it *would* be a reward. His smile is beautiful.

I loathe the Fae. But this one. . .

"Good," he says. "Good. I am gratified your recall is improving. Where is it?"

I'm not stalling anymore, I just don't know what to tell him.

"Tleia, I dislike torturing women, especially mothers, and you are very young. I will ask you again, and please consider answering my question. Where is the necklace?"

I swallow, the first crack in my facade. I've starved, I've been beaten, I've been gang raped. I gave birth in jail. That is the outskirts of what I've endured in my life, but I know from the look in his eyes none of it will touch what will happen to me if I give him the wrong answer.

"I'm afraid to tell you," I say. "You're not going to like the answer, but I'm also afraid to lie."

His eyes widen, and after a beat, he laughs softly. "You're an odd woman. I knew it when we first met, and I'm loathe to harm you, as I've said. I didn't expect such honesty, and because you've amused me I will offer you this. Tell me the truth, and no matter how what you say displeases me, you will not suffer for it this evening."

*This* evening. But despite there not being much left of this evening, it's still a reprieve. It's still better than nothing.

"I owe you something of a debt for what you suffered, even if you deny it," he adds, his voice quieter.

He falls silent when I hold up a hand. "I'm no child, and

no innocent. You owe me nothing." After a moment, I continue, "It was used to pay my husband for. . .my time. . .as well as some debts owed him. Was that why you were at the salon that night?"

He doesn't answer. I look away, reminding myself it's foolish to hold his gaze.

"Tell me, is that why you killed him, Tleia?"

My jaw loosens.

He picks up his pen and toys with it again. "I have a unique ability—it is no secret in my circle so I will tell you. When most people speak of seeing blood on hands, it's in the abstract." He sets the pen down. "When I speak of seeing blood on hands, it is not in the abstract."

It's obvious how, with a skill of that nature, he could rise to power quickly on Coho. Oh, the people I could blackmail if I had that ability.

"Yes," I say, "that's why."

He nods. "You did well."

With one simple, offhand sentence, he's won my cooperation.

"My Lord," I say after a long moment, "I'm grieved your property was taken from you and I wish the opportunity to make you whole, though I had nothing to do with the theft. But I accept responsibility as the widow of the man who accepted it as payment."

He's watching me, expression enigmatic. "Go on."

"The second part of the answer is that I sold the necklace to pay for supplies upon my release from prison."

"I see. To whom did you sell it?"

I slide out of the chair onto my knees, still holding Ethan, who having finished his snack is nuzzling my chest in a sly fashion, waiting for an opportunity to strike.

Taking a deep breath, I steel myself. I know what's required. Utter obeisance. It's the only thing that will save us.

"A witch. They coveted the item for some time and were eager to make the trade. I would assume it's still in their possession. I'm unworthy of your forgiveness, but please allow me to make amends."

"I'll allow it. You are one of mine, Tleia."

I come from Coho Street. In this world, that gives him a claim to my service. The world where power is the only right.

"Yes, Lord." This time when I say Lord, I give the word the Aeddannar inflection, acknowledging him. The acknowledgement is easy, a weight lifting from my shoulders.

Distantly, I wonder if I'm under glamour because my bent back is too supple, my desire to please too eager.

But if this is the worst he'll do to me tonight, I'm very, very lucky. The squirming child in my arms reminds me it could be much worse. And I have no idea where Gethen is.

"Very well. I accept your service in this matter."

I hear an almost silent scuff of feet and then he's kneeling in front of me, sliding fingers under my chin and raising my head so our gazes meet.

"But it will be dangerous, and it's my judgment your son shall remain with me for his protection." His voice is sibilant, sliding around me in a silken rope, binding me to his will.

"You cannot take a young child with you into the bowels of that district."

Almost I break free of the glamour, but I'm merely mortal. "Yes, Lord." A single tear trails down my cheek.

Meadowland sighs, his gaze following the tear, then he leans forward. Soft lips, the tip of a tongue, catch the bead of moisture. He pulls back.

"I do not harm children in my care, though it is my right. He will be well looked after, and as happy as we can make him as I have no desire to listen to an Orcling express displeasure. Return to me in three days, Tleia, no more. You know the consequences of failure. You know among my people, children inherit the failure of their parents."

"Yes, Lord. I will not fail you."

The fingers on my chin tighten and he claims my mouth in a kiss, sealing our deal. It's not sexual; it's a binding.

He draws back and stands. "I taste strength in you, something worth saving. Prove yourself, and I will aid your escape. I will detain you in this City no longer than I must."

Meadowland turns away, dismissing me.

Then he stops. "There is one other matter."

## ELEVEN

"As you can see," Lord Meadowland says, arms crossed as we gaze at the arena pit three stories down, "his decision making process requires refinement. He was informed you and his son were well, but he is an Orc. Those on the dreadnought with us were barely more civilized than those born on Gaithea." He shrugs, as if to say, "what *can* one do?"

"He is of Commander Bachdracht's bloodline," he adds, "and it's for the sake of my sentimentality that I had him thrown in the cage rather than treated as his behavior deserves."

If Lord Meadowland has one drop of sentimentality left in his blood, I'll slit my own throat.

It hits me what Meadowland said. "You know Gethen is from the Bachdracht bloodline?"

He glances at me, quizzical. "You didn't know the bloodline of the male you allowed to seed you?"

Of course I did. But Gethen hasn't made that information public. "I was thinking of other things at the time."

Uther Bachdracht's name is known, though supposedly he hasn't been seen in decades, having retreated to some remote area of the Pasifik Northwest to farm. There's some political value in a direct line to the Commander's ear, and Gethen hadn't wanted to deal with that. I'd agreed, and kept my mouth shut.

"Lord," I say, bowing, and wait.

"Yes."

"It will be easier for me to retrieve your item if your portion of the bounty on my head is rescinded." I speak in my humblest, politest tone, still bent in a bow.

"Perhaps, but discomfort usually increases one's sense of urgency."

"And one's mistakes."

"I would think you have incentive enough to make none. Am I wrong?" The rich tenor voice is a touch deeper now, chill.

"No, Lord."

There's silence, then he sighs with the air of a man overburdened by even this small show of indulgence. "Very well, I will issue a three day stay. But no more, Tleia."

He walks towards the stairwell, indicating the discussion is over, and I rise and follow after him.

We descend to the first intact floor, converted into a fighting arena. Meadowland stages fights both for the amusement of the City's patrons, and to punish those who anger him. It's one of the punishments I fear because in an arena, pitted against almost anyone, I will lose. My only advantage is the small pouch of charms tucked into my cleavage, but each one is single use.

Gethen roars, his chest bloody. He flashes his tusks in a menacing snarl, this glimpse of him proof that whatever happened in the last three years burned away any lingering squeamishness. He looks at his opponent as if he's eager to rip out a throat and feast.

Good.

Only children and recluses can afford self-righteousness.

Someone lands a blow and spectators roar as bookmakers work the crowd. Guards keep the blood-hungry mob in check, preventing anyone from toppling into the abyss below in their frenzy. I glimpse Icarians patrolling in the sky outside.

"With time and training he would be a valuable asset," Meadowland says. "I believe he will go where you lead."

It's a subtle invitation and I incline my head rather than insult him by ignoring it. "It's my intent to leave the City, but if we were to return, we would consider placing ourselves in your service."

An hour ago, my words wouldn't have been true. But now I see in him a glimpse of something I think I can serve, if all other options are exhausted.

He's the first person who hasn't judged me for Herbert's murder and that means something. But then, even more than Gethen, Meadowland can probably guess why. He'd been there when my husband gave me to Pike.

Lord Coho says nothing else and then we're on the first

floor. The crowd parts as he walks through and as I'm on his heels, I have no trouble either. I intercept a few speculative glances, but I doubt anyone thinks I'm the woman Meadowland has chosen for his bed this evening; it's rumored he chooses none, and considering the necklace, I believe it. The Aeddannari are not adulterous.

The fight ends and from the sound of Gethen's triumphant snarls, he's the winner. I suppose it's too much to hope that winning has earned him a purse of some sort; we can use the extra income on the trip to the Sorting.

A Human scrambles to open the chain link fence separating the fighters from the crowd and Meadowland steps through, gesturing for me to follow him. The gate slams shut behind us.

Gethen whirls, facing Meadowland, his large hands curled into fists. His black hair is wild around his face and shoulders, and his teeth are still bared.

*Bow,* I urge him silently, stepping from behind the Fae. Gethen's gaze shifts to me and he lurches forward, his eyes widening.

Meadowland holds up a hand. "As you can see, Tleia Shyncheia is unharmed. I have brought her to you."

"My son," Gethen snarls.

Meadowland glances at me.

"He's well, Gethen," I say. "He's a guest of Lord Meadowland and under his protection while we undertake a task on our Lord's behalf."

"He is not my Lord." The words are ripped from Gethen's throat.

"I have sworn us to his service for three days. Our son is under his personal protection during that time."

Gethen assesses me, his eyes cold. "Why?"

"I owe Lord Meadowland a debt. It's my desire to repay it." Because otherwise neither of us will leave except through death.

I'm afraid Gethen doesn't understand what I'm saying, but then he nods, and bows to the Aeddannar.

"She is the mother of my son, and widow of the man to whom I swore my service," Gethen says, "so in this I will allow her to speak for us."

I blink, my brows creeping up at the smooth intonation of his words. He's still speaking Gaithean, we all are, but with an Aeddannari cadence.

"I'm pleased to hear this," Meadowland says, and smiles, the picture of graciousness.

"Lord," I say quietly, "if we're to undertake your task and succeed in the time allotted, we should leave now."

He nods, dismissing us, and Gethen and I are allowed to leave, though not unobserved. I can't help my tightening jaw and the prick of tension along my neck as we emerge onto the streets.

We pass an alley and before I can react, Gethen whirls me into the darkness and pushes me against a rough wall, his hands pinning my wrists above my head.

"*Gethen.*"

"Let him have our son?" There's an edge in his voice. Not quite contempt, and not quite threat. Almost disappointment.

I am tired of being judged by people who haven't lived my life.

"This isn't a Faery tale," I snap. "Do you know the number one lesson *we* learned growing up? Survive first. Let me go."

He shoves a thigh between my legs, leaning his weight into me, the line of his shoulders aggressive, his eyes slightly narrowed. His heat reminds me of the night I took him to my bed, the night he pressed me into the mattress and fucked me like he wanted me to die on his cock, screaming.

Throbbing begins between my thighs, though the timing is stupid, and my mind rebels at stupid timing. My body doesn't care.

"What good would it have done if I'd fought a Fae Lord, and died?" I continue. This is a new side of Gethen—he's never been aggressive with me before. "I would have died, you may not have known where Ethan was, and Meadowland may have disposed of him as useless. Maybe he would have raised him as a servant. Gethy, please." I whisper the last word.

He shifts, releasing my wrists, but slides his hands around my waist. After a moment he exhales, and leans his forehead against mine. "Don't blame you, Lei'a. Should have protected you both. My failing." He pauses. "Are you hurt? Did he touch you?"

"I wasn't injured."

"He wants you."

I stare up into his face when he leans back. "He does not."

His lip curls up. "Don't see what I do. Never be alone

with him, Lei'a. Remember how this started. You wanted him too."

"That was three years ago, Gethen."

Gethen's eyes search mine, his gaze dark with anger, growing lust, worry. "Lying to me. I know you. Did he touch you?"

He's spacing his words out now, his tone too calm. He's on the verge of turning around and marching back to the tower if I don't confirm what he's somehow guessed.

"When we sealed our bargain, he kissed me."

He moves, and I throw my arms around his neck and go limp. He doesn't even feel my dead weight.

"Gethy, don't be an idiot! It wasn't sexual." I release him and step back.

"And never will be. With you, or any other once I'm done with him."

"You'll endanger Ethan."

He roars in frustration, whirling, and a fist slams into the wall next to my head. Startled, I flinch.

"Knew he touched you. Smell him on your skin." His eyes are wild now. "Could smell him, then Pike. Every time another man touched you, their *stench* in your skin. Listened to you cry after, and did nothing."

If he breaks down so will I, and we don't have time for this. There's never time for anything but base survival.

I slap him.

Gethen stares at me, then turns and steps out of the alley. I throw myself at his back, grabbing handfuls of his shirt.

"You idiot! What will happen to Ethan if you barge in

there on some brutish need to mark your territory? If he'd wanted me, he could have had me already. Get ahold of yourself."

He whirls and slams me against the wall again. He's never been rough with me. Never.

Gethen shoves a hand between my thighs, cupping me. "Called him your Lord." He's pulling my skirt up now, shoving his hand against bare skin, his thick fingers sliding between my slit. "Wet. For him?"

"Have you lost your goddamn mind?"

He presses against my clit, the flick of his fingers deliberate, nothing warm or romantic in his eyes. I don't care. I bite my lip, going limp.

"Gods," I breathe.

He wraps his free hand around my throat. "No, call on *my* name. No other."

The hand tightens, his mouth taking on a cruel edge. I don't care, because my core is pulsing, tightening, and I'm riding his fingers for a release I hadn't known I was still capable of.

In a dark alley on Coho Street.

This is far too close to old times for my comfort.

I let my eyes drift closed.

"Open," he snarls, then his mouth is on mine, his tongue invading my mouth, his kiss bruising as he all but gnaws at my lips.

Fingers plunge inside me as he works my clit, and I'm digging my nails into his shoulders, frantic.

When I come, my knees collapse and he holds me up,

muttering hoarse Uthilsuven in my ear. Curses, probably, because he'd refused to teach me those and I don't recognize all the words.

"The only Lord you will ever serve is me," he says, and these words I do understand. "The only fingers you will ever ride are mine, and the only cock that will ever spill in your body again is mine. I'll kill to defend my claim, Lei'a. Don't test me."

Slowly, he pulls his fingers out of me and lifts them to his mouth, sucking each digit. "Next time you come, will be on my cock. This was freebie."

I give him a withering look, straightening my clothing. "Do you feel better now? Can we go on about our business?"

He bows.

I stalk out of the alley. Then I stop, and face him, speaking slowly in his language. "If you ever slam a fist near my head again, you will have to kill me because I will take Ethan and you'll never see either of us again."

Gethen lowers his gaze and nods, mouth tightening. "Forgive me. Would never hit you, Tleia. Am not myself."

I nod and turn, resuming travel. I don't think he'll ever hurt me, but he's a little different. . .and it's not that far a leap from fists in walls to fists on bodies. If I stay with him, he'll need to take time to deal with his pain.

"Where we go?" he asks, falling in at my side and slightly behind in his unconscious bodyguard role.

"We're going to see Witch."

He stops.

I continue walking. "We have to retrieve Lord

Meadowland's betrothal necklace. That's the price of our lives."

Gethen catches up with me. "Tell me didn't steal betrothal necklace from Aeddannar Lord. Tell me not that stupid, Tleia."

"Do you think I'm a fool? No, I didn't, but it doesn't matter. Through a chain of unfortunate ownership, I'm now responsible for returning it to Meadowland. We have three days, Gethen, so let's continue to practice talking and walking at the same time."

———

A pall of coal smoke and dark magic hangs thick over the entire city block, graying the rising sun. Rusted gaslamps flicker, and they almost seem to cackle and hiss as we approach.

"This grimdark industrial witch vibe is definitely a point of view," I say. "I admire their flair for setting."

I'm not being facetious–I'm taking mental notes. Setting is as important to pulling off a character as costume, make up and mannerisms, and all the other aspects of a long con.

"Have you been here before?" Gethen asks.

"Yes. I've made it back too."

Witch is my go to for mag-tech of a more ambiguous nature, where ambiguous means neither quite legal nor what a gal would consider entirely moral. Partly because one must be crazy to approach them in the first place—if they don't like the deal, they'll make use of you in unsavory ways for the insult of wasting their time. Partly because they're also something rare; honest. Once they strike a deal, they uphold their end of it in a straightforward fashion.

That doesn't mean they aren't dangerous. As we step across the invisible demarcation into their territory, I feel a warning trickle of magic. Like dozens of eyes on me, and unfortunately, I know that's literal.

We skirt the barrier of the witch's domain, a crumbling warehouse of soot-covered brick and rusted iron. Windows like shattered black holes gaze down on the narrow weed-choked sidewalk.

Only the desperate come here, and the foolish.

"Must not want visitors," Gethen mutters, "except to stew in big pot."

I give him a sidelong look because it's been some time since I've heard him crack a joke. "Come on," I say as the front door opens. "We've been invited in."

## TWELVE

THE DOOR SLAMS BEHIND US WITH A METALLIC CLANG AS SOON as we step inside. Witch has a sense of theater.

"Tleia," Gethen growls, grabbing my arm and shoving me behind him.

"You're allowed to defend yourself, but don't start a fight."

"Are you *expecting* a fight?"

"Witch won't see us until they've been sufficiently entertained."

"Were you going to warn me, Tleia?"

I'm only indulging his hysteria because I'm waiting for my eyes to adjust. Once they do, I pick out that the warehouse is a cavernous chamber filled with rusting machinery and crates stacked up to the ceiling. Dim light filters through grimy skylights, catching on sharp claws and jagged knives as goblins pour in, the clatter of nails on steel and concrete making my teeth itch.

A high-pitched, screeching chorus fills the air, their collective voices a swarm of angry cicadas.

Gethen roars, leaping in front of me with an ax in one hand, his other outstretched in readiness—the talons are weapons as well.

"Oh," I say, peering around him. "Good. Just the standard welcoming committee. It's fine if you kill a few, but be polite. They're cheap to make, but tedious."

"We're going to have a *talk*," he snarls.

"I don't see what your fussiness is about. It's only a few dozen goblins. You're doing such a good job," I add, and pat his tense shoulder because sometimes undeserved praise motivates Ethan too.

The creatures hiss and cackle, waving weapons cobbled together from scavenged metal and bone. It's all very theatrical. They charge with jaws slavering, and I watch as Gethen dives in and goblin bits begin flying in a flurry of limbs.

"Over here," I say sharply when a handful break off and get too close to me. "Pay attention, please and thank you."

Gethen whirls and intercepts them, but I sigh and with a grimace dig into the pouch of charms tucked between my breasts. I feel along the etched runes until I find the one I want then withdraw it, muttering the activation word.

A long bladed club appears in my hand.

"Know how to use that thing?" Gethen yells. "Hit goblin on head or stab in neck. *Don't* swing at *me*, Lei'a."

He must know I'm tempted.

"I understand, thanks." I'd recognized the need for some

type of mundane weapon and had decided a bladed club was the shortest learning curve, and the least dangerous weapon to wield for someone who isn't trained. "Hit the enemy on the head, stab the pointy end preferably in their direction."

"Uthsha bless," he mutters. "Was I unfilial son? Why me."

"You're killing too many." I raise my voice. "Don't be rude."

As for myself, I'm aiming to knock them out or encourage them to attack me slower. If we destroy too many of their creatures, they won't talk to us. Bargaining for the necklace is already going to cost me, especially since I'm going to have to do some fast talking on both sides. I haven't forgotten Clary's request, but I've already decided to. . .modify it.

I swing my club, cracking a goblin across its skull. I spin and jab, driving them back. A knife whistles past my ear, thudding into the wall, and I jerk in the opposite direction.

"That is no way to treat a lady," I snap at the creature.

"No lady present," someone mutters. "Only krutzve'e."

I ignore Gethen, for now. I'll make him pay for his attitude later.

Once he sees I've got my back against the wall, steadily defending myself, Gethen wades into the thick of the fray with a roar, swinging his massive fist.

"Good fun," he chortles.

Bones crunch as he pummels the goblins, sending bodies flying. They swarm over him, stabbing and biting until he shakes them off with a savage yell.

I whack another goblin, ducking its claws by a hair's

breadth. A blade slashes my sleeve, drawing blood. I stumble back, clutching my arm. Gethen grabs a goblin and tosses it into the mob, bowling over the others. He rushes to me, inspecting the wound.

"I'll live," I say.

His lips curve as he squeezes my shoulder. "Good girl," he says before turning back to the fight with a bellow. Gethen upends a massive crate and sends it skidding into the goblins. Several are crushed beneath it, but the rest scramble over and continue their advance.

He's enjoying himself. I've watched Ethan corner and toy with roaches or mice the same way.

Suddenly, the goblins turn and flee into the shadows, leaving behind their dead.

Gethen halts, lowering his ax. "Come back," he says mournfully. It's almost a wail, if his voice wasn't so deep.

"I'm delighted," a scratchy contralto voice says. "I find Orcs who have been freshly exercised to be much more mannerable. Come upstairs, Telly, and bring our guest too. I have tea and cake."

Damn. Tea.

"Be wary," I murmur to Gethen as we ascend rusty metallic stairs. They creak under our weight. "They're offering us tea and cake."

"Poison?"

". . .nothing fatal. They feed off memories. The explanation was deliberately vague."

"So don't eat," he growls.

"Do you want to offend a witch in their own territory by refusing their hospitality?"

I want to slap him upside the head because he knows better. These second and third gen Orcs act as if they've had no training sometimes.

He huffs and falls silent, his air a peculiar blend of danger and sulkiness that makes me wonder if this is what Ethan will look like when he's a big boy too.

Witch's office is a chamber of oddities and arcane clutter. Meticulously dusted bookshelves sit under the weight of leather tomes. Specimen jars holding preserved creatures line the walls, strange organs and herbs floating in murky liquid—I know for a fact some of the "organs" are pickled vegetables.

Witch sits behind a massive oak desk carved with alchemical symbols, its surface strewn with quills, ink pots, crystals and candles. A skeleton in the corner seems to follow my movements with hollow eyes, a sinister sentry guarding its master's secrets.

I've seen it all before, though I think some of the props are new, so I step inside and bow my head without blinking, though next to me Gethen is looking around, his eyes slightly wide.

"Tleia," they greet me, already pouring tea into tiny iron cups in the shape of dragons. "Who's the bumpkin?"

Their complexion is a warm sandy brown with green undertones, their angular features and piercing yellow eyes making their species and race indeterminate. Lavender mermaid locs shimmer in a cascade to their waist, adorned with metallic charms. Their age is impossible to discern; they could be a youthful forty or a long-lived four hundred.

"Witch," I say. "This is Gethen. My friend."

"Bit more'n that, I think, but you be you. Gethen, dear, welcome to my abode."

He nods stiffly.

"I thought you'd be dead by now, Telly," Witch says. "Shanked in prison, or jumped once ya had the nerve to show yer face. Bold to make a deal with Meadowland. Come, sit. Have some tea and cake. It's lemon and rosemary today."

"My favorite," I say, resigned to our fate. We might as well enjoy the lemon loaf. "Glazed?"

"Of course."

Gethen looks at me askance but says nothing, following my lead as I take a chair and face Witch, who slides a plate of cake in front of me and hands me the tea they poured.

There's no way of knowing what surprise Witch chose for us. I sip the beverage and break off a bite of the cake, putting it in my mouth. Lemon and sugar burst onto my tongue, and I shrug, taking another, bigger bite. Gethen doesn't touch anything.

"Not very well trained, is he?" Witch asks, sipping tea. The lavender satin robes they wear slither as they shift in their chair.

"Gethen, have some cake," I encourage. "And a sip of the tea. Good boy."

Gethen turns his head slowly and pins me with a look

that says he's going to show me how good a boy he can be, and I probably won't like it.

I don't really mean to be insulting or facetious. I'm so used to dealing with Ethan that it rolls off my tongue.

I flutter my lashes and take another bite of cake. There are bits of candied lemon rind in it. They always were a good baker. They'd tried to teach me to bake bread when I was a child, but I'd proven too feral to stand still in a kitchen long enough to learn.

"This terrible idea," Gethen mutters, but sips his tea and eats a bite of cake, then pushes it to the side and glares at us both.

"I don't think he's been in polite society for the last three years," I tell Witch. "Please excuse him. You know how I was when I was first learning."

Witch waves a long-fingered hand tipped with pearly pink nails. The lacquer is a minor illusion, since Gaithean factories haven't been able to produce nail polish for centuries now. The immortals don't like the smell of it.

"Hmm," they say. "You don't look none the worse for wear after having run into Meadowland's thugs. Where's your boy?"

It takes me a minute to reply because I think the enchantment Meadowland laid on me to keep me calm and cooperative is starting to wear off.

"Lord Meadowland has him."

Witch winces. "Then he's as good as dead if you don't give that blighter what he wants."

"I know."

Gethen wraps his hands on the arms of the chair; the wood whines in protest. Witch gives him a look and he takes a deep breath, relaxing. The chair purrs, then settles back into silence.

"How are the charms working?" Witch's smile is sharp. "You know there's no refunds. If you don't like my work, ya shouldna hired me."

I shake my head. "Your work is exemplary, as usual. That's not why we're here." I set my tea down. "Are you still looking for an apprentice?"

Their hunt for an apprentice is notorious in certain circles. There are a handful of others whose fate is undetermined. Three—that we know of—have died. Two more were graciously set loose, albeit minus their sanity, and one died of old age. . .allegedly.

Actually, I think that one is the skeleton in the corner squinting at me. I suppose that is, technically, old age.

Witch blinks at me, their finger tapping the rim of their teacup. "What are you offering?" they ask after a moment's scrutiny.

"We have kin-by-marriage of middling talent who is unclaimed by any other master."

"Bloodline?"

I shrug. "A mutt as far as I know. But lovely, so there may be an ancestor or two of quality there."

Witch blows a raspberry. "Don't care about looks. Are they stupid?"

"They've survived as an unclaimed magic user in Seanna

City. They're a legally employed adult, and they currently maintain a functioning relationship."

All of those facts add up to some level of sanity, responsibility, and emotional health as well as interpersonal skills. Witch could do worse.

"Kin, you say?"

I fold my hands in my lap. "Yes. I don't offer them lightly. It's not as good as if they were blood, but next best thing."

"You bring me this kin-by-marriage who I've somehow missed and if they're suitable, ya got a deal."

It's lovely not having to deal with stupid people. Of course Witch understood without me having to say why I offered.

"What did you want with the necklace anyway?" I ask.

Their smile is vulpine, and inscrutable. "Got what I wanted. He can 'ave it back."

I hope I'm well out of town when Meadowland figures out whatever it is Witch either did to it, or with it.

"I'm gratified we have an understanding," I say, and stand.

Or try to stand.

Blood rushes to my head and my knees collapse beneath me. I sit down hard in my chair.

I also realize why Gethen has been silent, and not because he's being quiet while I focus on the negotiation. I slump in my chair, shifting my gaze to him because now that's all I can move.

He's out cold.

Witch lifts their teacup, inspecting the brew. "Must 'ave

got the formula wrong," they mutter. "Knocked 'im out
before you."

"What game?" I manage.

"A little nip of lunch, that's all. I *am* fond of you, cousin."

That's the last I hear before everything goes dark.

## THIRTEEN

A ROUGH HAND SHAKES ME AWAKE. I JERK MY EYES OPEN, recoiling, silk sheets slithering across my bare skin until the last of that very odd dream leaves me. Gethen and I in Witch's office negotiating. . .for something.

The dream slides away. I prefer it that way.

Myrtle stares down at me with dull grey eyes, her expression flat.

"Master ordered I get you ready, Mrs. Lee," she says.

When I first married Herbert I tried to befriend her and several of the staff, but they rebuffed my advances. It became clear after a short time why.

I push aside the covers and climb out of bed. I'm naked, my skin clammy with sweat despite the ceiling fan. I walk to the copper bathtub already filled with steaming water and get in, pulling my knees up and resting my forehead on them as she begins scrubbing my skin and washing my hair. She isn't gentle; it's been a long time since I've felt gentle hands on my bare body, but she isn't deliberately rough either.

She's like the rest of us. Afraid of the consequences of screwing up her job. Since I know what the consequences are, and the kinds of opportunities out there for Coho girls, I don't complain and I don't give her extra work.

"Do you know who the guests are tonight?" I ask once I emerge from the tub, slipping into the robe she hands me.

I walk to my vanity and sit down on a padded bench, docile as she begins detangling my long, thick dark hair. An older maid, Baylen, comes in, tackling makeup and wardrobe. I'm a married woman, mistress of a grand house, but on nights like these I'm nothing more than a sex worker.

So nothing is new. I *do* appreciate the irony.

"Coho Fae," Myrtle says.

I tense. "Fae?"

"Lord, by 'is looks."

"Fuck me." It can't be. Not *him*.

Baylen snorts, the brush she wields on my face steady, but otherwise she doesn't respond. They keep my secret and I keep theirs.

Myrtle shoves expensive alcohol into my hand and I down it like water. I don't dare take something stronger because I need my wits about me. A drink or two is enough to dull the edge and help me convince myself I'm here because I want to be, and not because I walked myself into a pretty trap.

But not nearly enough to delude myself that I'm anything but the pretty trap to lure others.

"Y'all did good," I say, rising, and inspect my appearance critically.

I'll never be beautiful, but with the skillful makeup applied, the costume accentuating my curves, and my glossy thick hair in an elaborate half up, half down style, I'm something better than a boring beauty.

I'm alluring.

A little mysterious.

And forbidden.

Unless you can afford me, and only the highest echelon men in Seanna City can afford the wife of Herbert Lee.

Everyone waits for a few minutes, but this isn't going to be one of those nights when I throw up lunch and they have to fix my makeup.

Excellent.

I eye the bottle of alcohol on my dresser. "Make sure to lay in a stock of that vintage. That there is quality, evidently."

"Because it ain't regular alcohol," Myrtle mutters.

I pause at the bedroom door and glance over my shoulder, lifting a brow. "So?"

Baylen looks defensive. "I sprinkled a little somethin' extra in it. A new blend on the streets."

I stiffen. "You know how I feel about drugs."

She shakes her head. "Tested it out myself. I wouldn't give you anything that'd put any of us in danger."

Unless there was profit in it. I consider her, then shrug. If they want to poison me, or have me otherwise make a fool of myself, they wouldn't warn me.

"What is it?"

Her shoulders relax. "It relaxes you, makes ya think everything is all hunky dory."

"So it's a hallucinogen."

This time there's a duo of snorts.

I step out into the hallway, glancing at the guard who falls in at my side.

The Orc wears a charcoal wool suit hugging his muscled frame, precision tailored with razor sharp lapels, a pristine white shirt underneath, obsidian cufflinks flashing at his wrists, and a black tie knotted tight at his throat. If we were in the streets, a newsboy cap would cover his shaggy dark hair, shading eyes cold as steel—except when we're alone, then they melt into a boyish warmth I find intoxicating. His appearance is stylish and sinister, a testament to his master's wealth and power just as I'm the ornament on the other side of that coin.

Herbert Lee's infamous Beauty and Beast.

His hand brushes mine as he paces behind me. Once we enter the parlor, there will be too many eyes on us, and the last thing I want is for anyone to know what Gethen means to me.

He's my protector, my jailer. He's also my best friend. And I think, in this hell we've both sworn ourselves to because we're idiots, I'm his as well.

"Are you alright?" he asks quietly. "Your pupils. . ."

"The maid gave me something."

"Lei'a."

"Hush."

He subsides into unhappy silence. Baylen will get the

edge of his tongue later if I don't remember to tell him to leave her alone.

I'm already feeling out of breath because this corset is cinched tight enough to make even my waist look tiny. I swear to the gods, Herbert orders these things like lungs and ribs are removable. The bones cut into me, and I suck in a deep breath.

"Breathe any deeper and might as well forget corset," Gethen mutters, my breasts all but spilling over the top of the red satin.

Red.

No matter how hard I've tried to convince Herbert how vulgar the color is, it's his favorite on me.

And I'm supposed to be the common one.

Speaking of the hells' damned devil, my husband appears around the corner, a man of medium height and slender build, round spectacles on his golden brown face, silky black hair cut to perfection framing a small head.

His gaze shifts from me to Gethen, and I still. Herbert made very, very clear early in our marriage what would happen to me and my guard if our relationship ever "went the path of cliche." When he chose to make an example of one of the staff to demonstrate his point, I'd received the message loud and clear.

Gethen, slightly behind me, doesn't move and Herbert dismisses him, focusing on me.

He kisses me perfunctorily on the cheek. "You look ravishing, my dear."

"Is that the goal this evening?" I ask

"Perhaps, perhaps." He touches his spectacles with slender fingers. "We'll use you to sweeten a deal I'm negotiating."

Use me.

But my lips don't twist in a bitter sneer. I knew what I signed up for.

"Who are we entertaining?"

"Meadowland and Seacliff."

I stare at him. "Lord Meadowland of Coho Street. Lord Seacliff of Pike." Two of the three. *Those* two. They hate each other. Has my husband gone insane?

Herbert frowns at me. "Is there a problem?"

Yes, there damn well is, but Herbert doesn't know I'm a Coho girl, and he never will if I can help it. But there's no reason for Meadowland to recognize me. I ran a few griffs, a few errands for his men over the years when I was younger with multiple layers of separation between me and him, thank you very much. I know his face, but there's no reason to think he knows mine. Or to think that, if he did, he would give me away. What advantage would there be to him in revealing my identity?

I steered *well* clear of Pike.

I force myself to smile. "No problem, husband."

He pats my shoulder. "Good. I don't have to tell you the consequences of embarrassing me tonight."

"Have I ever embarrassed you?" Please. I hate when he questions my professionalism, though he doesn't know that's what he's doing.

"No," is the amiable reply, "but there's a first instance for everything." He glances at the Orc at my back. "Guard her well tonight. Allow no one to touch her unless I instruct otherwise."

I'm to tease a room full of dangerous men so he can put them in a slightly better mood so he can possibly gain a sliver of an edge in whatever his latest scheme is. He still doesn't understand that these are the sort of men who only take the bait when they want to—amused by the fun of springing the so-called trap before displaying their own, superior, teeth. Herbert assumes if he has a weakness, then everyone else does.

I hope this isn't the night he gets me killed.

Taking a deep breath—or trying—I follow my husband into the salon.

It's thick with fragrant cigar smoke and muted laughter. Ornate clockwork fixtures cast an amber glow over velvet-upholstered tables where Herbert's guests play cards or dice; men in satin waistcoats or corsets, the only women present clad much as I am—in next to nothing. One of the women is already splayed out on one of the tables though the night is young, another's mouth between her naked thighs as the men watch, fondling themselves and each other.

My gaze slides over the tableau; I feel nothing.

A servant proffering wine tours the room, though alcohol isn't the only delicacy available.

The Aeddannari touch nothing.

My foolish husband still doesn't understand it's an insult.

He abandons me after a round of introductions in which I pretend to be the sexually bored young wife of a Seanna City Human banker. I fall into the role, observing my marks.

I steer well clear of Meadowland, and watch Seacliff. If Herbert brought me here for the latter, I might shank the bastard myself tonight. My husband, not Seacliff. If I tried to kill that particular Lord, death would be a mercy.

I've heard about the things Seacliff likes to do to his sex partners.

"Do you know what this deal is?" I ask Gethen, my lips not moving as I sip water.

He's tense and watchful at my side, discouraging interest from the men at the card tables I drift towards. I'm not the only spouse in the room; others have brought their spouses, some even their first or second born; a relative of worth is the required offering to enter this circle.

We're all here for the same reason. To be dangled like bait, sold or traded or given as favors for a night. One of the uglier secrets of Seanna City's well-to-do folk—that the spouses and offspring of this wealthy set are no more than high-priced courtesans; not all of them, of course, just this subset that dabbles in things it shouldn't. Fortunately for me, wealth doesn't always correlate with brains.

"No," Gethen says, his voice a short rumble. "Seacliff. . ."

"If he wants me, Herbert won't tell him no."

"Stay out of his sight."

I sneer delicately. "Thank you very much for the obvious advice, Gethy," I say in Uthilsuven. He's the only Orc in the room; unless and until Lord Cythro buys entry to this circle, no other Orc in the city will insult him by cutting in line.

From across the room Herbert meets my gaze. I set aside my water glass and weave towards him, the sneer morphing into a sweet smile. I sidle up to him, posing my body to make it less obvious that I'm slightly taller.

"Husband."

He kisses my temple. "My dear, I was telling Lord Meadowland what a delight my wife is at gambling." He chuckles. "Can you imagine? A gently born girl having mastered Pistons and Pinions?"

I'm too well practiced for the smile on my lips to strain. I turn in Meadowland's direction and bow, altering the form to make it look like something a gently bred girl with an average education would give. Cute, but imprecise. He wouldn't expect flawless, though I can serve that if required.

His garnet gaze brushes across me, disinterested though not impolite. He's wearing his signature red suit, though it's closer to black tonight, and his dark blood flame hair is styled half on top of his head, then left to fall down his back.

"A pleasure to meet you, Mrs. Lee."

The courtesy of his response surprises me—and he hasn't ogled my chest once. A feat, since there's plenty of it to ogle and it's more or less in his face.

I'm impressed.

"Why, she can even beat me three games out of five!" my husband continues.

A toddler could beat Herbert at Pinions and Pistons. The expressions around this card table don't change; if Herbert wasn't completely lacking in empathy he'd feel the amused contempt.

"My husband is modest," I say, lowering my lashes. "He lets me win because he doesn't like to see me cry."

"I'm certain that's not true," Meadowland says, voice light, bored. "What man wouldn't enjoy a woman's tears?"

"Hush hush, don't say such things," Herbert says, chuckling. "I don't choose to expose my wife to the games men and coarsely bred women play."

I've heard it all before. If only he knew how coarsely bred I am.

"Certainly no man would," I say, matching Coho's tone.

I lift my gaze to see Meadowland watching me, a slight twist on his lips. He's one of the few Lords who's harder to offend, and once you do. . .

But I have no more intention of tugging his tail tonight.

"Husband," I begin, "I should go and—"

Herbert squeezes my shoulder. "Nonsense. I must tend to our other guests. Entertain Lord Meadowland."

That's code for crawl onto Coho's lap and if his cock happens to slip into my pussy under the table, even better to entrap him with.

The smile freezes on my lips this time. "I would be honored."

"I am graced by your presence," Meadowland murmurs, again with that impenetrable courtesy.

*Herbert, Herbert, I think I will shank you tonight.*

Except I have yet to find a copy of his will and see if he kept his promise. There's more than one reason why my husband is still alive.

I've heard nothing about Meadowland that indicates he enjoys having his prey served to him on a platter, so I take my seat and deal the next hand of cards, flicking my gaze to his once or twice, coolly coy. Ignoring him would be an insult, as if I found him undesirable or worse, boring. He doesn't pretend not to be watching me, but he's not overly interested either.

What's Herbert's game? It's clear Meadowland doesn't want me. I know that look in a man's eyes when I see it, and no one bothers with subtlety at these types of gatherings.

Two of the men bow out after I win three hands, scooping more winnings over to my side.

"If you are cheating," one of them begins.

Meadowland clucks his tongue. "Don't be vulgar. The gently bred wife of Herbert Lee would never cheat at cards."

"Indeed," I say. "Just as an Aeddannar never lies."

"Truly spoken, Mrs. Lee." There is open, if gentle, mockery in his voice now.

He knows. My face, my first name, or he recognizes the lingering stench of the wharf. He's mocking me—still, the warning in his voice is real. I have no idea why he's defending me.

Both statements are on the surface absolutely, scrupulously, true. The gently bred wife of Herbert Lee wouldn't cheat at cards. And a Fae Lord cannot lie.

Except I'm not gently bred, and the Aeddannari circumvent the truth all the time with skillful deceit that satisfies whatever species magic they're cursed with. Or maybe it's technology, not a curse. I wouldn't know, since when the immortals crash landed, their dominance war wiped out planet Gaithea's tech, sending us back into the Vittorian era.

Another perfunctory seductive glance in his direction and I see I have Meadowland's full attention now, though it still feels relatively benign.

Gethen must not think so because at my back he shifts, and moves forward. He doesn't sit, but suddenly he makes his presence known. I glance up at him. He's staring at Meadowland, his dark eyes cool.

Meadowland glances at him. "Peace, Orc. I am not her predator tonight." He's a little amused, a little curious, but not offended. Not yet.

"My husband casts his lure to see what he can catch," I murmur. "But I'm more sunfish than salmon."

Sunfish look sweet and delicious, but are poisonous when ingested. Gaithea's version of a krutzve'e, I suppose.

"You would be, wouldn't you?" Meadowland says. "Is the warning meant as a courtesy?"

I lift one shoulder. "I was raised on Coho salmon, and Herbert is a poor fisherman."

I don't know why I'm prompted to warn him against falling into Herbert's schemes. Maybe because not once tonight has he given me that particular brand of contempt the men in these salons usually do.

He's been. . .courteous. Granting me the same bland, indifferent respect he would the claimed Human of an Aeddannari acquaintance of equal rank or status. It's thrown me off balance—and also revealed a weakness in myself I hadn't recognized before now.

Soon we're the only two left at the card table and I begin losing each hand, one after another.

"So," I say, after I finish sliding the last of my winnings towards Meadowland, my voice dry, "you weren't truly playing before."

He chuckles. "I was bored. I no longer am."

Gethen pulls up a chair and sits.

"Then I'm gratified to have done my duty," I say.

"I hope it's not entirely duty. Though yes, I feel the hospitality has markedly improved. I wonder to what extent it will improve this evening?"

"It will not," Gethen says, laying a closed fist on the table.

I glance at him sideways, and clear my throat. The men ignore me, focused on each other now.

"Gethen?" I speak his name in a tone that says "have you lost your mind?"

Meadowland's toying with his full wine glass, having already brushed aside his winnings indifferently. "Is that what your master would say?"

"My master charged me with—"

I lay a hand on Gethen's tense forearm. "You forget yourself."

"Oh, no no, Mrs. Lee," Meadowland purrs, "let the Orc speak. When they bestir themselves to garble in *complete* sentences, one always pays attention."

Gethen snorts, wide shoulders still tense, but settles back in his chair, accepting my rebuke.

My stomach clenches, and I lower my gaze to avoid Meadowland's stare. I don't know what has gotten into Gethy—or the Fae Lord. But this is my function tonight, and I'll end up in bed with someone here whether I want it or not. It's rarely I do want it, but every time I think of getting out, every time I calculate the pros and cons, I come up with the same answer.

Whatever's waiting for me out on the streets will be just as bad—but there will be less food and far uglier clothing.

I steel myself to pretend like the evening won't once again end the way it will.

"Please disregard Gethen," I say, "he has his duty, and he takes it seriously. But it's my husband's goal to be famed for his hospitality."

"Ah. Is it yours?"

How quaint. He's asking if I'm willing. If his fucking me tonight will be consensual. "Naturally, my Lord."

He pretends to sip his wine. "You're one of mine, Mrs. Lee. You know how I feel when my own lie to me."

The words are spoken gently, but my hands jerk anyway. I settle them into my lap so they can't betray me again.

"I am Herbert Lee's wife," I say. "My wants mean nothing."

"I see."

I don't like the look on his face, neutral, piercing. I've offended him. Quickly, I regroup.

"But if I had desires of my own," I say, softening my voice, "as you have said, I am one of yours."

A Coho Street girl. There's not a single one who would deny her Lord anything he asked of her. The consequences of refusal are known, but so are the rewards of graceful service.

"I hope my wife has been entertaining you properly," Herbert says, approaching the table with his easy smile.

"She's a credit to you," Meadowland says, and once again I see the brush of contempt in his eyes when he looks at my husband. And then it's gone.

One of these vipers-in-wait will kill my husband one of these days, and Herbert doesn't even know it. I wonder why they keep him alive, what use they think he has.

Herbert bows, then glances at me with a smile that crinkles the corners of his eyes. "I'm pleased. Are you having fun, my dear?"

"Of course."

He pats me on the head. "I leave you in good hands, then."

## FOURTEEN

"I'M CURIOUS TO KNOW YOUR STORY," MEADOWLAND murmurs when Herbert wanders away.

I shuffle the deck of cards, then cut it. "Another hand, my lord?"

He shakes his head, watching me, waiting.

My lips curve in an empty smile. "I have a feeling you know more about my story then I'd like." Our voices are pitched too low for any but determined ears to listen in.

"What I know," Meadowland says, "is the mettle of my people. It surprises me a man like Herbert Lee has earned your loyalty."

I don't say anything. It's a tricky line to walk. The Fae, especially the Lords, prize loyalty—odd, considering how treacherous their cultures are. If I openly betray one for the sake of another, I'll earn contempt, yet it would be stupid to refuse even this desultory salon overture.

"If you know the mettle of Coho born," I say, my voice light, "then you also know our ambition."

He chuckles. Gethen watches us, perfectly silent, dangerously still. There's something about Meadowland he doesn't like—well, apart from the fact that my Lord Coho is a Fae who crashed with the original dreadnought.

"I do. And what's the scope of your ambition, Mrs. Lee?" He gestures. "I feel this place has little to offer you."

"I've had no better offers. While I remain Herbert Lee's wife, I'm content to further his goals."

Meadowland's lids lower slightly as he settles back into his chair. "Goals." There's scorn in the word. "Men such as your husband know nothing of goals. They're children, pursuing venal wealth and empty status as if those things hold value." He softens his voice. "Come here."

I rise, round the table, and settle onto his lap as he slides an arm around my waist.

Meadowland lowers his mouth to my ear. "You may be a sunfish now, but you once swam in my streams. You know who spawned you."

I tense.

"I won't ask you to betray your husband, Mrs. Lee. I place little value in servants who bite the hands of their masters." His hand slides up my back, squeezing the back of my neck and the gesture is oddly. . .affectionate, almost paternal. "You think I don't know you. I know everyone who has ever worked for me, Tleia. Especially the ones with ambition. You never came to me for help. You never needed it."

Gethen's chair scrapes against the wood floor, a deliberate warning.

"When you're ready to return to the home stream, come to me."

Meadowland stills. I hadn't realized that the body beneath me was almost relaxed until this moment. I glance over my shoulder and stiffen, the hand I'd placed on his shoulder digging in for a second before I release him and begin to rise.

He tightens his arm around my waist—then lets me go a moment later.

Seacliff bows, leaning on the head of his engraved cane. "Lord Coho."

"Lord Pike." Meadowland's voice is short, neutral.

My heart rate immediately spikes because standing in between two feuding Seanna City Lords is not where any intelligent Human wants to be. But I also don't want to move and draw attention to myself.

Too late, and I curse Gethen as he rises because that prompts Seacliff to shift his gaze to me. His eyes are blue with striations of green like poisonous, creeping vines, his lids smudged in smoky gray. Copper-gold hair brushes his shoulders in styled waves, all the more bright because he wears unrelieved black, except for the ornate gold head of the polished cane he leans on.

He bows, lifting my hand to his mouth and brushing my knuckles with his lips. "Mrs. Lee. I've heard from others how enchanting you are. I've heard other things as well." His gaze flickers back towards Meadowland, and Seacliff gives a sweet smile. "About fish jumping streams, swimming in lakes that were never their own."

It's clumsy prose, but the meaning behind his words is clear enough. Both Meadowland and Seacliff, somehow, know the con I've been running on Herbert. I wonder then if I've been as discreet as I thought, moving in and out of under and upper world circles for the last twenty years. I hadn't thought I'd gained anyone's attention.

Now I worry.

People like me are useful to have planted throughout the upper-class houses—we can be blackmailed. There's not a self-deprecating bone in my body, so I don't brush aside the thought, demurring that I'm not important enough.

Herbert is important enough, and I'm Herbert's wife.

My husband walks up, rubbing his hands as if he's delighted his guests are having such a grand time. "Lord Pike!"

Unfortunately, the mistake is genuine. Meadowland and Seacliff, Aeddannari of equal status, may refer to each other by the names of the territories they rule, but a Human doing so is a minor breach of etiquette. If Herbert is going to host these sorts of gatherings, he should know better. He should know better than to have Lords Pike and Coho in the same room.

Can he really be this stupid? I'm never quite sure because he wasn't born to wealth. Not to poverty, either, his parents were respectable enough. But Herbert worked his way up into the upper echelons of society, proving he has to have some measure of canniness.

Herbert turns to me. "I can't allow any of my guests to monopolize your attention, my dear," he says, his eyes sparkling. "Lord Seacliff has expressed his admiration. Perhaps you'd enjoy getting to know him a bit more?"

I rise and give a short bow, though my heart is sinking. What is Herbert doing?

Meadowland says nothing, his gaze glancing off Pike's face. Despite his apparent disinterest, something about his reaction has pleased Lord Pike. Seacliff turns to me, holding out an arm, and I have no choice but to accept it, Gethen an unhappy presence at my back.

"And of course you'll keep an eye on our lovely one," Herbert says, glancing once at Gethen, his voice cooling. He's noticed my guard isn't happy about this turn of events. Guards aren't supposed to have opinions, especially when said opinions indicate criticism of a guest. I don't look at anyone as Lord Pike leads me to a seating arrangement in the corner of the room.

Velvet couches and a low table. Refreshments set out, and the usual selection of dice and card games.

"You can stand over there, Orc," Lord Pike says, not looking at Gethen.

I don't look at Gethen either, who posts himself in the corner, his back to the wall, his attention on us.

I settle next to Seacliff, crossing my legs, and angle my body towards him, a practiced smile on my lips.

He drapes an arm across the back of the couch, eyeing me, then clasps my jaw in his fingers, turning my face from side to side as if he's examining the goods.

I detest Aeddannari.

"Meadowland usually avoids the wives and daughters in the salons," Lord Pike says. "But he spoke to you. You caught his interest, Mrs. Lee."

The flattery is meant to make me simper—and run my mouth. "He was accusing me of cheating at cards."

Seacliff laughs. "I doubt it. If you had truly cheated him at cards, you wouldn't be alive, little spawn."

I say nothing. I don't understand enough about the undercurrents I sense, but when I glance instinctively at Meadowland, his gaze is on us. Lord Pike makes a low, contented noise in his throat and I realize my mistake as I glance at him, then Meadowland.

Damn Herbert to the hells.

He's playing the Lords off one another, and somehow I've become the rope they're tugging between them tonight.

"He's seething, watching you in my arms," Seacliff says, smoothing his hand over my bare shoulder and down my arm, then wrapping his fingers around my wrist. "Shall we give him a bit of a show?"

Gethen steps forward and I glare at him. He can't do anything but make this worse. I turn my head, searching the crowd for Herbert and locking gazes on my husband, who's watching obliquely, and gives me a small nod.

There will be no help there.

"A show, my Lord?" I say.

"What do you think it will take to pry him from his seat? Will he approach if I fuck you on the table, do you think? He has this peculiar weakness—he dislikes seeing women bruised."

I'm not fooled by his idle tone. He slides a hand under the top of my corset, squeezing my breast. I force myself to breathe slowly, not to react. This is nothing new.

Lord Pike pulls me into his lap, at the same time tugging my breast free and lowering his head to capture the nipple.

I shudder, and not from desire. Herbert is usually more discreet; in the last five years he hasn't allowed a man to play with me openly in a salon. He has them take me into private rooms.

But Herbert 's doing nothing.

I don't look at Meadowland because making Lord Pike think I hope for rescue from that quarter will only make this worse.

Seacliff's hand is between my legs, slipping under the scrap of satin that covers my mound and he begins caressing his fingers up and down my slit.

"Spread your legs wider," he murmurs in my ear. "I want him to see you come on my fingers."

He means, he wants Meadowland to see me fake coming on Pike's fingers.

"I think he needs more incentive," Seacliff says, and my breath comes faster. Let him think it's from desire, not disgust.

I don't want him using me as an incentive, but there's no choice. Not even Gethen will interfere, not when he's given his oath of loyalty to Herbert and has to abide by Herbert's orders.

Lord Pike jams fingers into me and I cry out, then bite my lip.

"I also think you need more incentive, little spawn," he says. "And I want to watch Meadowland's face as he watches me take one of his girls."

"I'm not his, or a—" I begin, but Seacliff tosses me on to the low table in front of us.

My teeth sink into my lips because I bang my kneecaps and elbows against the floor and wood, and it hurts. It hurts enough that I'm pliant as I feel Lord Pike behind me, spreading my legs, tearing aside my panties.

"Don't move," he says sharply as I begin to rise on my knees. A hand to presses on my back, pushing me against the cool wood of the table. "If you want to please your husband, little spawn, then please me." He pauses. "Wait, what's that quaint Human custom—oh yes. Do you consent?"

Is he joking? My voice trembles, but I smooth it out. "What do you want to do to me?"

"I will penetrate you, and I want you to scream. Look at Meadowland as you do." Lord Pike's voice is silken. "But if you deny me, of course, I'll release you."

Out of the corner of my eye, I see a flicker of movement from Gethen. I turn my head, catching as much of his gaze as I can, and narrow my eyes at him. Too little, too late, for both of us.

If I tell Lord Pike no, Herbert will make my life hell for weeks. It's easier to get this over with, here and now.

"I consent." The only reason any of them bother with this

farce is so they can look their victims in the eyes with plausible deniability.

I hate them all. And this is what I worked hard to become a part of. I should have set my sights on a farmer.

Something smooth, round, hard and cold nudges that my entrance. I close my eyes.

"Open them," Lord Pike says.

The cane pushes inside me and I cry out. My body is cold, and tight. He jerks my head back and turns it so I'm looking in Meadowland's direction.

Coho's expression is bored as he pretends to sip his wine, but there's a spark in his garnet eyes, a growing fleck of bright ruby red.

Behind me, Gethen growls. "If you injure her—"

"Don't force me to reprimand you, Orc," Lord Pike says. "I see you're not fit to serve your master."

That shuts Gethen up.

But I can't pay any attention to what's going on behind me, other than the feel of Pike's cane pumping in and out of me.

"You're not very enthusiastic, are you?" Lord Pike muses. He stops working me. "Fuck the cane. Keep your eyes on Meadowland while you do. Moan for me, little spawn. Your husband desires that you please me."

And I know the consequences if I don't.

I begin moving my hips, obeying, forcing fractured sounds from my throat.

"Hmm. Perhaps a little assistance," Lord Pike says, then gestures. A server approaches and Seacliff plucks a glass of wine, sitting it next to me. I listen to the crinkle of paper, watch in growing horror as he tilts crushed herbs into it.

"No," I say, my voice rising at the end of the word, "I don't want drugs."

"It will make you more receptive, little spawn." He shoves the glass against my teeth and when I don't cooperate, fingers slide into my mouth and wrench open my jaw. He tilts the cup and I splutter, half choking, half drinking the drugged wine. Then he sets the glass aside as I pant.

Being raped isn't the worst thing—pardon me, consensually raped. I've endured far worse than this bastard's cane in my pussy—he probably uses a cane because he can't get it up, this tiny limp dicked piece of shit. It's the drugs, him forcing the liquid down my throat and making a lie of everything I tell myself. That I choose this. That I choose it every time I don't pack a bag and walk away. What little illusion of power I've cobbled together disintegrates as he forces that drink down my throat.

Slowly, my body warms, my head spins. I don't have the choice to withhold my pleasure from him, because the drugs take over.

I'm nothing more than a bitch in heat; powerless, licking his feet.

"Now fuck yourself," he says. "With some enthusiasm, mind."

I let it overtake me, this artificial lust, burning away anguish and humiliation.

Meadowland isn't the only one watching now. I close my

eyes and orgasm, shuddering, and don't dare wipe the tears off my cheeks because I already know Pike likes them.

"Good girl," Seacliff croons. "He's infuriated. I believe I'll entertain myself with you some more this evening—perhaps I'll even consider your favor repayment of some of your husband's debt. You'll be rewarded, little spawn."

He wrenches the cane out of me, and wraps his hand around my upper arm, tugging me to my feet. I stumble a little, ankle twisting, and he tugs me towards Herbert, Gethen at our heels.

I can't help but glance over my shoulder, once, and meet Gethen's agonized eyes before they go hard and indifferent again.

I won't leave Herbert, and Gethen is bound by his oath. We're both trapped, and even if I let myself feel better by hating him for a few minutes, there's no point. It's not his fault.

I barely listen as Seacliff informs Herbert that he desires my company in private for the rest of the evening.

I think of nothing as Lord Pike takes me to one of the empty rooms.

## FIFTEEN

My hands shake as I wipe makeup from half my face in an exact vertical line down the bridge of my nose, one side gilded falseness, the other side weary truth. Without the plump red lip, the thick kohl, the bronzing powder that sharpens my round face, and the ground colored minerals on my eyelids, I look like every other working class girl on Coho. Tired, a little worn down, a little grim, and a whole lot mean.

I keep looking in the mirror hoping that one day I'll see something different. Something worth saving.

On the heels of that thought I viciously pinch my inner thigh.

I'm worth saving, but I have to save myself.

I take a deep breath and let it out, blinking away tears as I remind myself the situation I'm in is twenty years of my own making.

My hand curls into a fist, my nails biting into my palm.

*Don't cry now, minnow.*

After the makeup is gone I unpin my hair and brush it into a simple braid, then struggle out of the corset I'd loosely laced back up over skin that burns. The panties are gone, of course. I don't know where my shoes are, and I'm not going back to that room to look for them.

I stand and turn away from the mirror, ignoring the bruises, the welts. I cross the room and sink into bathwater gone lukewarm, hissing. Tonight is one of those nights where I can't stand the thought of attendants, not even the women who grew up in the same streets I did.

I don't want any hands on me.

Though I'd take a certain pair of arms at this point. Gethen has learned, over the years, how to hold me so that my pieces stay inside the meatbag shell of my skin.

I stare blindly out my bedroom window as the sun rises, and barely register the click of the door opening, then closing and locking.

Silent footsteps approaching.

A large, comforting presence kneeling at the side of the tub.

Gethen doesn't touch me. He doesn't say anything. He waits for me to tell him what I need.

"I'm fine," I say after a few minutes, my voice brusque.

"You're not fine," he replies, his voice softer.

There's no anger in it, no growl, no edge of murder. It's a balm and I close my eyes, shivering because the bath water has gone cold now.

"What do you need?" he asks.

I laugh. "I need Pike's head on a pike." I cackle again, because even if he doesn't think it's funny, I do.

I feel his shallow breaths against my ear, and slowly, he rests his forehead against my temple. "Lei'a. When will enough be enough?"

"You bastard. That is *not* what I need."

"Don't think you're capable of seeing what you need."

Oh, he's pissed. Normally he's careful with his words after a night like this—he doesn't want me to think he's judging my choices. When he'd first been assigned to me, there had been plenty of judgment.

We'd both been miserable, butting heads, slicing into each other until over time, we settled into a stalemate.

Until over time, we settled into understanding. It was hard won, and now he's going to ruin it.

"You let these males abuse you three nights out of seven—"

"Let?" I twist, glaring at him.

He sits back on his heels, his gaze steady. "That's what you always tell me. That is your choice. That you worked hard to get here."

My chest rises and falls with my rapid breathing because now my rage has an outlet. His gaze doesn't leave my eyes, not once.

"As usual," I say, "you still don't know what you're talking about."

"You have to leave, Lei'a. When it was just a few nights of

simple sex, that was bad enough, but Mr. Lee is letting these men hurt you."

I turn away from him. He doesn't have to tell me what Mr. Lee is allowing. I'm the one who's enduring it. I'd honestly thought Pike was going to kill me. I don't know why he hadn't.

"I can't make you leave," Gethen says, "because you're right. You chose this situation. You tell me over and over you knew what Mr. Lee was. You've stayed for a decade."

"Where am I supposed to go?"

"I know what you want from me." His voice hardens. "But I'm not going to pick you up and take you out of here. You have to walk out on your own. If you go, I'll follow you when my contract is done."

I surge to my feet, the water splashing, and step out of the tub, reaching blindly for a towel. It's in my hand a moment later.

"Aren't you an Orc warrior?" I spit. "Aren't you all supposed to be protective of your females, of those weaker than you? Why won't you just—"

"Because taking the decision away weakens and dishonors you. Because I gave Mr. Lee my word."

"Your stupid fucking honor. We'll set aside the issue of you using my own words against me—"

"You want me to choose you over my honor. But I want you to choose me too. Over your fear. Or greed. Not sure which you have worse."

I turn, and our gazes clash.

This is an old, old argument.

"You are wife of man I gave oath to," he continues softly. "Until you leave him and are divorced, I can't help you any more than do now. Would be wrong, Lei'a."

I shake my head. "You're stupid and impractical, and you live in fantasy land. A result of your happy, two parent upbringing on a farm, I suppose." Ratha and his uncle count as two parents.

Instead of getting angry, he stands and closes the distance between us and carefully slides his arms around me. Careful of the welts on my back. It stings anyway.

"This tear me apart inside," he murmurs. "I hate to see you hurt, and worse, hate to see you in trap you've made with own mind."

I wish I was wearing heels. I would grind them into his toes. I wrench out of his arms.

"It's not a trap of my own mind! You've never been hungry, you've never been hunted by gangs, you've never had to sell your body for a crappy roof during the winter. You've never had to suck the doctor's cock so he would set your broken arm. You've never had to—" I try to rein myself in, bending over at the waist and resting my hands on my knees to calm myself down. "There's nothing out there for me better than this."

"Nothing out there better than rape and torture?" His voice starts to warm with anger, and with an edge of contempt. "You're a coward. If you divorce, I come with you, you'll have me. Even if we sleep under the stars and live off the land—"

I straighten, laughing harshly. I sound like a seagull with

a nose cold. "Live off the land! I will never, ever be poor again. Ever. I would rather—"

His eyes are dark, and I stop talking, seeing the look in them. "You would rather be raped and tortured than trust me to take care of you." He curls his lip up over his teeth. "An Orc female would never allow herself to be used like this. She would never—"

I launch myself at him, shrieking, distantly aware that the noise is going to draw the attention of the household. . .but Herbert is frequently gone by dawn anyway.

I swing my fists, kick, try to tear his hair out at the roots, try to get my fingers around his tusks and rip them out of his jaws.

He grunts, and lets me rage for I don't know how long until he whirls me around, trapping my arms against my torso, and walking me towards the bed where he flings me onto my stomach and drapes himself over me.

I buck and shriek, trapped beneath him, and he just lies there, saying nothing.

"You're going to destroy what little is left of you," he says when I finally exhaust myself.

Tears are leaking into the sheets. "Then why don't you take me out of here? Is your honor more important? Your principle? If I don't have the strength to leave, and you say I don't know what's good for me, then why don't you be what's good for me?"

He says nothing.

The argument, and my disappointment, leaves me drained. I'm certain he feels the same. This isn't the first time we've fought like this, but it's the first time it felt like we were on the edge of breaking.

Part of me knows he's right, but part of me also needs him to accept that it's not that simple.

\* \* \*

It takes two days to put myself back together to something resembling normal, and Herbert must know more than I think because during that two days he leaves me alone other than to have the staff bring me flowers and meals in bed. He even hires in a masseuse.

Any other silly woman would think it a sign of affection, or even respect, but I know what it is. He's protecting his asset, and you can't expect an asset to yield a return unless you invest in it. He's just as stupid as Gethen. What advantage does Herbert really think he's going to get by pimping me out? I'm pussy, nothing special. I really hope I'm not a major part of his overall strategy, because he's going to be disappointed sooner or later.

I snort to myself, stirring a silver teaspoon in a cup of strong black tea. I've joined Herbert in the parlor as a subtle signal that I'm ready to go back to work.

He folds his paper in half and sets it down, peering at me through his spectacles. "You seem to be feeling better today."

"You take very good care of me, husband."

He reaches out and pats the back of my hand. "I'll have to buy you something special. Pike asked for you."

My heart stops pumping as my blood freezes in my veins. "What?" My voice is hoarse.

"He's requested the pleasure of your company at a

house party this weekend. Don't worry, it'll be respectable. Some of the other wives will be present. I have business, but there's no reason why you shouldn't go and enjoy yourself."

"I would rather—I would rather. . .st-stay home." I'm stuttering, unusual for me.

His eyes harden. "You will attend, and you will make yourself pleasant." He picks up his paper. "I think I'll give Gethen the weekend off. He's been working hard lately, and it's impractical to abuse the servants."

\* \* \*

I ask Myrtle to bring me the wine and the powdered white stuff Baylen swore she tested on herself.

Turns out you aren't supposed to dump the entire packet in a bottle of good red, and down it in one sitting. A little is supposed to do the trick.

I'm splayed out on my bed, staring up at the ceiling alternating between resignation, rage, and forced pragmatism.

I have good shelter, servants. High quality clothing and the best food. I have most of the toys I want within reason, and Herbert doesn't disrespect me in public. In fact, he almost dotes on me. The fact that any husband would sell his wife is loathsome, but if I make myself think of it in terms of a business arrangement, that helps.

Maybe I'm the problem.

Maybe this streak of romanticism, this yearning that I bring out and dust off every once in a while for a tarnished warrior with a heart of gold and a sharp double edged blade to come lay the heads of my enemies at my feet, needs to be obliterated.

I'm not a girl anymore, I can't afford fantasies.

The door opens and I push myself up into a sitting position, my silk robe falling to either side of my naked body.

"You should be dressed by now," my husband says, strong disapproval in his voice. "I see I'll have to discipline Myrtle."

I grimace, swinging my legs over the bed, and try to rise. Stumble, and catch myself on the bedpost.

"Ish not her fault," I slur. "Dismissed her."

"You're drunk." Now the disapproval has frozen into something more dangerous. "You know I despise intoxicated women. It's vulgar."

*Oh, I'm way past drunk, you cunt.* I snicker. "But your favorite color is red, Herbie."

There is a moment of silence. "I see. I don't believe Myrtle and the other servant wench are a good influence on you. I'll dismiss them immediately."

"No!" I take a deep breath, staring at him through blurry eyes and try to smile. "I'll order coffee and sober up. There's still time to get ready." The house party guests aren't due to arrive until this evening.

He approaches me, surveying my form. "The marks are healing nicely. Why are you drunk?"

My bottom lip trembles. "Pike is vicious. I'm afraid." A tear leaks down my cheek. Because I'm drunk, I let it. I never show this much vulnerability when I'm sober.

"You've demonstrated amazing resilience until now, my

dear. I hope you won't disappoint me. Perhaps I've indulged you. My mother always believed that a touch of deprivation does wonders for one's constitution."

My numb fingers open and the bottle of wine drops to the floor, shattering. He leaps out of the way, muttering, and I fall to my knees, hands trembling as I try to pick up the shards.

"Don't be ridiculous!" He almost snarls the words. "I'll summon the servants to clean it up. And to bring you coffee. This is *unacceptable* behavior, Tleia."

Oh, hells. He said my name. He never says my name. One of the girls is going to pay tonight.

I close my eyes. "I'm sorry. Herbert, I'm sorry. I'll do better. You've been good to me and I'm grateful."

His icy stare bores into the back of my bent head. "Well, we all require correction. To err is to be Human."

I take a deep breath, release it. "But please. . .may I arrive at the house party in the morning? Be fashionably late?"

I need him to say yes more than anything. A cup of strong coffee isn't going to sober me up. Or rather, it might, but I have other issues. I don't think I can play the high-class courtesan tonight.

I'm too close to the edge.

"You will go, and you will do your duty tonight. You will not insult Lord Pike by—"

"Don't call 'im Lord Pike, you idiot!" I scream at him. "It's an insult, don't you know any better? Ya stupid fecking—"

Pain blooms on my cheek, blood in my mouth. Once, and then again. The third time he swings, my arm arcs in a half circle. There's a shard of the bottle in my still mostly numb palm, and I hadn't even realized I'd cut myself.

I'm bleeding, and the screams I'm hearing aren't my own. I stare in shock at the glass embedded in Herbert's groin. It's pumping so much blood.

*You've still got it, minnow. You're still one mean fishy.*

Herbert is screaming, and I need him to shut up before he brings the household down around my ears.

He's probably going to bleed out and. . .I don't think that's good for some reason.

Oh, right. Murder. They frown on that sort of thing here.

Lurching to my feet, I swipe out again, catching him in the throat.

## SIXTEEN

THE SCREAMS STOP AS HE GURGLES, HIS SHOCKED EYES STARING at me as he clasps his hands around his neck.

"Just shut the fuck up already, you cunt," I say, a little surprised at how clear and pleasant my voice sounds. Cheerful, almost.

Interesting. Well. . .we all learn things about ourselves in times of acute stress.

He stumbles back—alright, fine, perhaps I trip him—and goes silent as the back of his head hits the floor.

Finally.

Staring down at Herbert, I try to wade through the sluggish cheer of my mind. It's unusual. I feel on top of the world but also like my thoughts are pushing through chin-deep mud in order to emerge.

Contemplating the puddle of red—the good red—on the floor, I can't quite decide if I still think this is a fine vintage.

Stepping forward, I trip over Herbert's body, stumble to the floor and hit my forehead, biting my lip at the same time. Cursing, the pain clears a little of my madness, and the appropriate emotion rears its head.

Panic

Hot, slicing panic and a strong sense of self-preservation.

They're going to hang me.

Murder isn't technically a crime because the immortals would be in and out of court their entire miserable, drawn out lives, but oath breaking *is*. Killing my husband counts as breaking our marriage oath.

I crawl to the bedroom door and use the knob to pull myself up, then open it a hair. How in the hells has no one heard Herbert screaming?

I poke my head out; there's no one in the hallways. I close the door, lock it, and go ring a bell for Myrtle.

She's the least likely to snitch—I know where her sister lives. I'll be certain to remind her of that fact.

There's a knock on the door and I walk in a mostly straight line towards it, crack it open, and clear my throat. "Myrtle. Get Gethen."

She frowns at me. "Mr. Lee gave him the—"

My voice rises. "Go get Gethen!"

Her eyes widen a little and she rakes me with a quick look, then cranes her head to try to see inside the room.

I slam the door in her face—then open it a crack a second later. "Stop being nosy. Get Gethen or you're fired. And if you say anything to anyone, I'll pay your sister a visit."

She stares at me, the stupid dull cow-eyed expression going flinty. *Yes, minnow. I knew you were a fake fishy.*

"Don't be a bitch," she says.

"Uh huh, right. Just get Gethen."

Myrtle blows out her breath. "What the hells happened?"

"It's better for you if you don't know. Trust me. Let me keep you out of this as much as possible."

She's not stupid. She fixes the cow-eyed vapid look back on her face and shuffles away. I love working with competents.

I lock the door and go sit cross legged at Herbert's side. The least thing I can do is keep him company as his corpse cools. The blood will wash off. Maybe I shouldn't have been so quick to send Myrtle away.

I jerk awake, having drifted into a sitting dose, when there's a sharp knock at the door.

"Lei'a?" Gethen catches himself. "Mrs. Lee?"

I stand up, stumble—ah, still not sober I guess—and open the door enough for a massive Orc to squeeze through. Which means, it's pretty wide open. But there's no one else in the hallway.

After closing the door and locking it, I turn and almost bump into his back.

He's utterly still, and I assume he's looking at Herbert.

"Tleia." He draws the syllables of my name out. "What did you do?"

I walk around him. "Possibly I found him like this."

I'm jerked to a halt by his strong fingers around my upper arm. I wince, because the bruises haven't healed completely.

He whirls me around and when I look up into his eyes, they're wide and panicked.

That won't do. I frown. "You have to calm down."

"They'll hang you," he says hoarsely. "We have to—we'll summon authorities. Explain—"

I slap him. Hard. "You just said they would hang me, Gethy."

My slap didn't faze him; he doesn't blink. "We'll tell them everything. About abuse, about—"

"Are you a fecking idiot?" Why are all the men in my life morons these days? "If you tell them about Herbert, then you'll pull the lid off two dozen of the top families in this City. You think they'll hang me? They'll strip *you* into pieces and feed you to the fish, my green guppy."

There must be an underlying unintended long term side effect to that cocktail I drank down, because the energy and peppiness remains, but the muddy mind feeling is dissipating, leaving my thoughts razor sharp. Or it could be the adrenaline and my strong preference not to hang, who knows?

I feel more like myself then ever.

"This is what we're going to do," I begin, but he shakes me. Not hard, but enough to shut me up.

"We get you out of here. Did anyone else see?"

I pause. It's a good question. "Myrtle will put two and two together. But she's not going to say anything."

Maybe from loyalty, maybe from fear that I'll make good on my threat—but mostly because if she answers one question, it will lead to a host of others, and she'll be killed to force her to keep her silence too.

"Don't worry about Myrtle. What we're going to do is—"

He begins to drag me towards the door. Then he stops, whirls. "Bathe first. Get dressed. Something. . .yellow. Baby blue. Need to look innocent. Can you pull that off?"

Not since I was a cute sixteen-year-old pre pubescent. I know my limits. "Gethen. It doesn't matter how innocent I am. I'm a liability. If you go to the authorities they'll arrest me, take me to jail, and I ain't gonna survive."

I don't think my words are making it through his thick skull, the skull with the amusing—under other circumstances that don't involve my death—thought rattling around that the law will actually help us.

How can he work for Herbert and still be so naive?

A two-parent upbringing, that's how.

Farm boy.

It's going to take more to convince him. I grab two handfuls of Gethen's shirt and tug him towards the bed and shove him down.

"Sit, darling. You've had a shock."

Defensiveness, anger, or a hostile challenge will only make him set his heels in. He's a man and an Orc warrior, after all. I need to circumvent his instincts.

Entering my closet, I rummage for my hidden stock of emergency brandy—no glasses, because in an emergency who bothers—then return to Gethen, who's staring at Herbert.

I shove the bottle at him, stepping in his line of sight to block his view of my dead husband.

"Take a drink, a long one. It will help you settle your nerves and decide what to do."

It's utter horseshit. I need him malleable so he'll do what I tell him to do. Having an Orc for a best friend is like owning a double edged blade—if you don't know how to wield it, it will cut you, but it will be your fault.

He obeys, which tells me he's more rattled than he's letting on. "Tleia, if we do this your way, we end up right back where we were, in worse trouble."

I place my hands on his chest then slide them up to his shoulders, squeezing. As if absently, I unbutton the first few buttons of his shirt and slip my hands underneath onto bare skin.

Gethen has strong collarbones, and this peek of chest is intriguing. He always keeps his shirts buttoned all the way up to the collar, even the times I've caught him relaxing in the kitchen with the staff. One day he got drunk and rolled his sleeves up, all wild and crazy like.

"You know the kind of people who come to the salons, Gethy," I say softly, leaning forward to place a soft kiss on his now bare chest because I've been busily unbuttoning his shirt and then his vest, pushing the cloth aside. "They'll kill to protect their secrets. They'll kill me."

"They aren't the only power in Seanna. There are—"

"For every good man or good judge in power, you know there's one that the evil of this City have in their pocket. If I go to jail, they'll move fast, they'll send someone to kill me.

They'll take you to jail too. You won't be able to protect me locked away."

I trail kisses up the side of his neck, along his jaw, then fasten my lips over his. He tastes of the brandy and I'm sure my taste is of wine and blood. His mouth. . .I've fantasized about his mouth. About his hands, about his eyes staring at me as he finally gives in and fucks me. He wouldn't because I was married. Everyone else would, but not Gethen. Throbbing begins between my thighs, my breasts tingling.

"I'm afraid they'll kill me before they know the truth," I whisper against his lips. "Do you think I deserve to die?"

He grabs my hips, his hands squeezing. I open my eyes and his are gazing at me, his expression fierce.

"Of course you don't deserve to die," he says.

I rest one knee on the bed, then drape myself across his lap, my open legs a cradle for his groin.

I begin to grind, slipping my hands into his hair. "We can clear our names. We can seek justice the right way." I kiss his jaw, slide a hand down his chest, down his taut stomach, and begin fumbling with his belt. "But we should go somewhere safe first, where they can't reach us. Just in case. So we're safe from the corrupt men."

He still looks skeptical. I undo the belt, undo his trousers, and grip his hard length. If I can get him thinking with his cock, this will be easier.

He inhales abruptly. "Lei'a, what you do?"

"I'm afraid. Everything is confusing." I stroke his length, up and down with slow, even strokes. Harder, and faster, clamping around him. "I've been so unhappy. I can't sleep because of the nightmares."

His chest rises in a deep breath. "Lei'a, get clean, then we must—"

I grab his hand and bring it to my breast. His fingers close around my flesh, squeezing reflexively. For the first time he looks, and I wonder if he fully realized before that I'm naked. That I'm naked, splayed open on his lap. He takes another, hitching breath, and his eyes flash, then darken.

"They'll kill me," I breathe, and kiss him again. And again, slipping my tongue into his mouth as I work his cock.

He's gripping both my breasts now, his touch almost painful, growing urgent.

Gethen pulls his head away, but not his hands. His thumbs caress my nipples into pebbles. "I'll protect you. We—"

"Fuck me. I need to forget everything. I'm yours now. Take what belongs to you."

I've deepened my voice into a sweet, husky croon, and I lift up slightly on my knees, position him, and then slide down.

He jerks, and a groan slips out.

I gasp, riding him, my hands on his shoulders for leverage. "Touch me, Gethy."

He's not thinking about anything but his cock in my pussy now. And I let thoughts go as well, because as twisted as it is, this is our first time together. I move faster on his cock, my breasts bouncing, and he slides a hand between my legs, touching my clit and rubbing. I gasp, moaning his name, and close my eyes, giving myself over to the pleasure.

Suddenly his hands are around my waist, and he's lifting me off him.

"Gethen! No, don't stop—"

But he throws me on my stomach on the bed, his weight shifting behind me as he pulls my hips up, spreads my legs, and plunges inside.

Before, I was fucking him, but now the tables have turned. He's pounding into me, his hands on my hips and I try to meet the speed and strength of his thrusts, grabbing the bedspread.

None of the noises coming from my throat are civilized, and the noises coming from him sound nothing like a Human man.

"Yes, hells, Gethen," I moan, twisting so I can watch his face. "Fuck me. Harder. Make me yours. More, I need more. I need it to hurt." I need the pain, I need his cruelty. I need his fingers bruising my hips and his cock tearing into my pussy.

"Mine," he pants, his voice harsh and ragged. "Finally mine. Not his. No other touch you."

Now that's more like it.

"Promise me you won't go to the law, Gethen. I'm yours now. Promise me."

"*Lei'a.*"

I meet his dark gaze, let him see my fear. "If they put me in a jail with other men, they'll take what belongs to you. They'll rape me."

The growl that comes from deep in his chest is guttural, savage.

"Don't abandon me, Gethy. Take me somewhere safe."

He breaks. "Promise. I promise."

My walls tighten around him and I orgasm, crying out. He thrusts another minute then swells, stretching me, and with a shout I feel his hot seed flooding my body. I grind my buttocks against him, claiming every last drop, and my voice trembles.

"Gethen, do you think I could be pregnant?" For ten years I've tried to give Herbert an heir, and failed. I use protection with Herbert's. . .guests, but even so I've never gotten pregnant.

But Gethen goes utterly still, his breath ragged, his hands still gripping my hips.

And then he curses.

Sliding out of my body seconds later, he flips me over onto my back. I stretch my arms above my head, a pleasant soreness between my thighs, and drape them open to ensure he has a nice view of his baby batter dripping out of my unprotected pussy as he stares down at me.

His expression is hard, and cold. His body is *magnificent,* and I drink it all in. "I know what you're doing, Tleia."

I blink up at him. I guess we're not doing aftercare. "Do you know why Herbert sent you away for the weekend?"

Gethen flicks an eyebrow up, but doesn't move.

"He was sending me to Pike's house party. My orders were to hand myself over to that sadist on a silver platter." I stare up into his eyes and drop all my shields, letting him see my fear and horror. "Do you want me to tell you what he did to me, Gethen? With his cane? Next time it will be knives, and chains."

Gethen closes his eyes, his jaw tight.

"Do you know why he uses a cane? Well. . .I won't be indelicate. But a man like that, he won't be satisfied unless he has an audience. Is that what you want?"

Gethen's shoulders bow. "Lei'a, I'm sorry."

I don't want to hear it. "Herbert sent you away so Pike would have freedom to do whatever he wanted to do to me. He sent you away so I would be unprotected. I begged him, Gethen. I begged him to give me one more night to heal, to gather myself. And he hit me."

Gethen jerks his head up, his gaze glancing off my face where he must see the bruises. He looks away.

I scramble off the bed and grab his chin, wrenching his head back towards me. "Don't look away! I didn't intend to kill him, but I broke. Do you blame me?"

"No." His voice is soft.

"But everyone else will. Gethen, the moment he died, you were no longer bound by your oath, nor I mine."

He sighs, the sound defeated.

Then his gaze hardens again and he slides his hand around the back of my neck, clamping down. "I know you're manipulating me, Tleia. You think I'm stupid. That's fine." He kisses the tip of my nose. "Love you anyway. But when we get to my clan, no more. You will learn honor. I will teach you."

He'll try, poor man. "I'll only be fucking you. Though, of course, if there's some advantage in giving me to—"

His look is withering. "Will be no more seducing. No more murdering. Except if I murder male who touch you."

"It was self-defense. You always blather on about how fierce Orc women are. You whine that I refused to make a choice and walk away." I spread my arms out wide, mocking him. "I would say this is a definitive choice, wouldn't you?"

He curls his lip up, then dresses. "I get help for corpse." He glances at Herbert, and there's nothing but detached calculation in his gaze. But he gives me the same look a second later. "Bathe. Dress. Pack. Kill no servants if come to room."

"Am I insane, Gethen?"

"No response."

When he leaves, I laugh and laugh as I bathe and dress, because Honorable Warrior Gethen fucked me as my murdered husband's body cooled on the floor.

The next time my Orc starts bleating about honor all I have to do is remind him of this night, and that he's no better than me.

I think we'll make a fine couple.

Gods help our children if we have them. Maybe I should start praying to Uthsha.

## SEVENTEEN

HERBERT'S BODY BLINKS OUT OF EXISTENCE

Pain shoots up my knees and I gasp, my head spinning. I close my eyes, riding the wave of dizziness, chill seeping into my palms as I swallow hard, fighting the urge to vomit, and not only from having re-lived the start of the worst weeks of my life.

"Damn you, Witch," I whisper, hoping the stinging in my eyes isn't tears. My entire body shudders as I struggle not to cry, not to give in to sobs I haven't allowed myself even when confined to solitary. Not even when Meadowland took my son from me.

"Tleia!" A deep, hoarse voice shouts my name seconds before hands seize my shoulders, yanking me into a strong, familiar hold.

I slap my hands against his chest, instinctively trying to push away, but his face is buried in the curve of my neck, his arms squeezing tight as if he's Ethan taking comfort from the stuffed baby Orc.

Gethen whispers my name over and over again, his voice cracking on the final syllable. "What—what was—"

I know what he's trying to ask. How the hell had we ended right back in our nightmare.

"Witch," I say, weariness sinking bone deep. "We were lunch. Let me go."

"Never again. Never let you go again. Never watch you hurt again. Never."

I know I'm not the only one suffering, though his is less visceral. I think. Resigned, I let my body go limp in his arms as he rocks me, wetness against my neck, mine or his I'm not certain. Grudgingly, I admit we both need the comfort. After some time, his frantic rocking slows down, then ceases. He takes a deep breath, lifting his head.

"What the fuck, Lei'a?"

I stare at the floor. It's no longer polished wood boards, but cold concrete. My bedroom has been replaced with the four walls of a familiar gray cell. The fun isn't over yet.

I shift, remembering where my body really is—and when. "Let me go, please."

This time he obeys, watching as I rise and turn in a slow circle. I shake my head and head to the cot pushed against one wall and sit down.

"I don't know how long we'll be trapped here," I say.

"Where is here?"

"Witch spiked the tea. They do this occasionally." I

grimace. There's nothing we can do about it except give Witch what they want.

"Tleia," Gethen growls, as if he knows I know more that I'm saying. He stomps toward me and drops down onto the cot. It doesn't creak, further proof this isn't reality. "What do they want us to do?"

"Talk."

"Talk."

The one word says a hundred.

"My son is in hands of Meadowland," he says, "and Witch-cousin wants us to talk?"

"That's about it. They say conversations make good snacks." I'm not happy myself, and I have to shove the thoughts of my son away or else I won't be able to function.

"Talk about what?"

"Don't use that tone with me. This isn't my fault. And considering the hellscape I re-endured, I can deduce what they want us to talk about. That night."

Gethen is stone. Unmoving, unspeaking. I wait. I'm certain I've processed the events of that night, and what led up to it, but I don't know if Gethen has.

I'm tempted to slap Witch when I see them next.

"This is stupid," he says.

Maybe I'll slap Gethen first. "This is what it is. Either we cooperate, or we allow Lord Meadowland to decide the fate of our son."

He fixes a flat stare on my face. "What we do now?"

I *am* going to slap my cousin when I see them again. If they're stupid enough to let me get close. What kind of conversation will provide my dear cousin with the snack they want? Something that will stir up a table of emotions, but not a buffet.

"I wronged you," I say. "I wronged myself, and I wronged Herbert."

"This talk or confession?" His voice is dry. "I am not priest."

"This is me graciously not blaming you for being yourself and getting us both locked up."

He doesn't protest, which tells me he's thought about the series of events after that night as much as I have, and come to the same conclusions. He'd trusted the wrong person, had been in too much of a hurry and gotten sloppy. And we were caught. A bit more time and care, and we would have gotten out of the City before we were hunted down.

Closing my eyes, I say, "I was never a good person. I won't say I'm evil, but I've never cared much about how my actions affect others. I have my goals, and I focus on achieving them."

"Not so different from anyone else."

I lift a hand, waving his words off. He's always made excuses for me. "I'm not concerned with anyone else. I'm concerned with myself. I'm not a good person. I think I'd like to be, if I can find the right opportunity. It's likely that that opportunity is best found away from a City where I can be tempted."

Tempted by so many opportunities, so many vices.

"Herbert was a decent husband," I continue.

"He was bastard. Deserved his death."

"He didn't. Not really. Maybe if I'd been some innocent sheltered miss, he would have—"

"He thought you were."

"I'm uncertain. Besides, it's irrelevant what he thought. He thought that because I wanted him to think that. I manipulated him and I lied. It led to his death."

His lips tighten. "Take too much on yourself, Lei'a. He had goals too, didn't have to use his wife to achieve them."

"No, he didn't. I'm not saying he was blameless. I'm saying I contributed to the situation. You were right, you know. I valued comfort and perceived safety more than I valued the peace of a simple life. . .and you."

Gethen shifts slightly. "You weren't ready."

"Maybe I never would have been ready if it weren't for three years in jail. That changes a girl's perspective."

He snorts. "Being poor with me better than prison."

"Vastly better. Perspective is a wonderful thing." I keep my voice light. It's a truth, and a hard truth. But it's not the entire truth. "Instead of killing Herbert I should have walked away. I overestimated my ability to eat shit for years in a row."

"What you ate not taste like shit."

"How would you know?" I give him an arch look. "Have you ever swallowed come?"

"Not a man's."

I shrug. "All I'm saying is that I'm not mad at you. I'm bitter, and a little resentful. But I don't blame you for what happened."

He turns his head to stare at me. "I didn't protect you."

"It wasn't your job."

Gethen starts laughing. "It was exactly my job!"

I guess it's his turn for hysterics. "No, your job was to follow Herbert's orders, which you did. And you're right—I wanted you to rescue me. I didn't want to make a difficult decision. I didn't want to face that I was wrong, and I spent all those years chasing my tail for *nothing*." I clench my teeth, my chest constricting. "Telling myself there was a plan, a goal, a *reward* made it easier to accept the hurts, the indignities. It was all for nothing."

The need to break something, someone, is a jabbing hot poker in my throat. But no one in this room deserves my cruelty. Not even Gethen. Especially not Gethen.

I make a mental note—be nicer to him. He's doing his best. Have I ever done my best at anything but breaking my own life? How can I mother Ethan and I can't make healthy decisions for myself? I'll ruin my baby. Maybe I already have, and how do you *fix* that? How do you fix trauma that began before a child is born, hurts that started in the very womb? I don't know. I'll try, but as usual, I doubt my efforts will be enough.

"Don't let me hurt him," I say, suddenly frantic. I rake my nails down my arms, needing the outlet of this small violence. Some days I think I might actually go insane. "Don't let me destroy my baby."

He captures my hands and tugs me into a sitting position. "What is this? He's a good boy. Intelligent and as well-behaved as can be. You have not ruined our son."

"But what if—"

"Baby." His hands squeeze mine. "Ethan is fine. You've done well. Have me. Have Hathur. When we return home, will have everyone to help. Uncle Uther and Ratha. He will have good life, promise you. We won't let you ruin him."

After a moment, I nod. "He'll be fine."

Gethen slides an arm around my shoulders and I lean against him. "You're still young, Lei'a. Learned hard lesson, but not broken yet. Should have protected you."

Then he sighs and switches to Uthilsuven. "In the clans we live or die by our honor. Too few of us left after the crash, and then the wars that followed. My mother, and then Uther, used to tell me stories."

I know better than to speak against Uther, though I dearly want to. It's not that Uther is a bad man, but he overcompensated when raising Gethen.

"I learned to fear breaking honor," he continues. "We were taught there's nothing worse, except to allow death or destruction to come to your clan or your female and young."

"And I'm not clan, and I'm not your female."

Gethen squeezes my shoulders. "You were always mine. I should have understood protecting you was a higher principle than not breaking my word to scum. No, don't say it, Lei'a. That you knew what you were getting into. Doesn't matter. A male protects his female. Even from herself."

I sniff.

"If I'd done what I should have, you never would have been hurt," he says. "You wouldn't have had to kill Herbert."

"Because you would have killed him first?"

His voice flattens. "No. I would have picked you up and

taken you away, like you asked. I won't make the same mistake, Tleia. This time, I'll take you home with me."

I turn my head and nuzzle his shoulder, smiling. "Oh, really? I said I want to go to the Sorting. Shop around for a strong male."

He curses in Gaithean. "Fine. Want me prove worth. Just like a female. Take you to Sorting, kill all challengers. Then only games play are on my cock."

I lean back on my hands. "I look forward to it, darling."

He tracks my movement with a dark, simmering gaze. "Can eat pussy now. Make come on my tongue every night till reach Sorting." His voice deepens into a gravelly purr. "Addict you to me. Will enjoy when you submit."

It's been three years since a male has touched me like that. I spread my thighs open in silent invitation. "Prove your worth then."

## EIGHTEEN

GETHEN'S EYES MOCK ME, HIS PLAYFUL SIDE SWIMMING TO THE surface. "Want something from me, I want something in return."

I wave a hand. "I'll suck you off once I come. Me first."

"Ah. . .great to know. What I mean is, I want you to remove the corset. Now."

"If you insist." I sit up, making short work of the hooks.

He kisses my knee, then replaces the kiss with the tip of his tongue, and licks up my inner thigh.

"What do you intend?" I ask, voice unsteady.

"Only intention is marry you, get more baby on you, keep you fat and shrill."

"*Shrill*." I've worked *hard* to modulate my voice and tone.

"Like now. Sound like wharf-wife. Your tits bounce when mad." He lowers his gaze, and smirks. "I like. In my best interest keep you angry."

"Have you forgotten what I did to the last man who made me angry?"

He pauses. "I reconsider my statement."

"Thought you might, darling."

Gethen straightens as I finally unhook the corset and toss it away, then yank the soft, low necked chemise that was underneath over my head.

He's staring at my breasts, an expression I've seen in another variation on Ethan's face. It's feeding time, except Gethen is a grown man, not a baby.

He flicks his gaze up to mine. "I touch?"

I don't bother stopping the soft smile that curves my lips. "Of course, Gethy." Not that he asked in the alley. "Touch me however you like."

He cups his hands around the heavy weight of my breasts, his talons a light prick into my skin. I let my head fall back, closing my eyes as I attempt to control my breathing as he massages me. They're sensitive, and after several seconds I feel the prickle of my milk letting down. My breasts think they're being primed to nurse a baby, but no, they're being primed to pleasure a grown Orc.

"Tits are gift from Svaratu," Gethen mutters. He squeezes again, a bit more firmly, than buries his head in my cleavage.

"The Uthilsen Allfather?"

"Yes."

"Wouldn't it be gift from Allmother, then?"

"No."

He spends the next several seconds playing, batting them

back and forth, or attempting to put both nipples in his mouth at once.

"You have the same expression on your face Ethan gets when he finds a pretty new rock, or a roach," I say.

Gethen grunts. "Ethan baby. In twenty years, will exchange rock for tits too."

"I'm almost certain he shares your joy and love for breasts now."

"Won't share, not even with son."

"Well, don't you get the father of the year award. You know breasts were made for infants, correct? Not for adults."

Gethen ignores my mockery, and takes one nipple into his mouth—it must have been hard to choose which one, poor baby—and begins to suckle.

I fall back onto the cot, my clit roaring awake. "My milk is for the baby, Gethen."

He ignores me, even lifts his head and squeezes my breast so a stream of milk squirts into his mouth. Of all the kinks, it's relatively benign. "I'll have to drink more if you keep this up."

"Will feed you, Lei'a," he murmurs. "Good food, good drink, good cock. All you want to eat. Cake too."

"If you want to eat something sweet, why don't you bury your face in my cunt. My cum is sweet like candy."

He releases the nipple with a pop. "No need to rush. I'm growing Orc. My female feed me hers, then I feed her mine."

My core clenches at the image of him shoving his cock in my mouth, filling my throat with seed. "Oh, hells. *Now.* I don't know how much time we have left."

He chuckles and slaps the breast he isn't feeding from. "Impatient. Be good girl, will give you everything soon."

As he's suckling, he slides his hand up around the back of my neck to cup my head, the gesture proprietary and tender. I stretch my arms above my head and lift my heels to rest them on the edge of the cot.

He obeys the silent encouragement, abandoning my breasts with a sigh, and begins to kiss and nibble down my torso, pausing along the slight inner curve of my waist, then kissing across to my belly button where he pauses and leans his forehead.

"My son was here," he murmurs, and I don't think the words are meant for me. "My female was big with child and I could not protect her." The hand cupping my head tightens. "Never fail again in this way. Only failure is death."

"Kiss me, Gethy. I'm here right now, and right now I'm not going anywhere."

He kisses my stomach, his free hand trailing along the light stretch marks over the curve of my hips. Gethen removes his hand from my hair and grips my hip as he lowers his head down to the juncture of my thighs, spreading my lips and finding my clit.

I tangle my fingers in his thick, slightly coarse hair, my fingertips teasing out a few of the braids. I smash his face against me, and a rumble of laughter shakes his shoulders.

"We'll see who's laughing when my mouth is on your cock," I say, my eyes fluttering closed as I gasp. "Oh, hells. I'm coming—"

"Not yet," he snarls.

"What?"

*"Not yet."* He squeezes my hip.

I barely register when a finger enters me. Slowly at first, as if he's testing his welcome. I want to tell him to go ahead and have a party, but I can't speak.

He's fucking me with his fingers and my walls clench around him. "Now you come. Now you scream name."

I give myself up to him, up to the pleasure. My body obeys as soon as the words leave his mouth. Arching my back, I cry out. His mouth on my clit, his hand back on my breast.

I can barely hear myself think around my moans as he brings me to one climax, and without releasing my clit, continues to suck and lick and stroke until I reach a second.

My world centers on the man between my thighs, pleasuring me as if every orgasm is a link he's forging in the chain he wants me to wrap around my own neck. In this moment, I'm not certain I won't strangle myself with it.

Gethen rises, mouth stained with my release and I lay still, letting him look his fill; glaze-eyed woman, heaving chest and slick thighs, trembling from the aftershock of the orgasms he gave me.

And, of course, my gaze lowers to the erection pressing against his trousers. . .I lick my lips. "Come. Please me again."

He grins, unbuttoning his trousers and leaning a knee on the cot. "Please you, or please me?"

"Oh, it's definitely to please me, though I suppose you'll enjoy it too."

Gethen frees his cock and scoots up me so his knees are

straddling either side of my head. It's what I want, him above me, his hand braced on the wall, his other hand holding the back of my neck as he positions himself above me and shoves his cock into my willing mouth.

There's nothing sweet in his eyes now, nothing but hungry Orc male, but the hand cupping the back of my head caresses my scalp gently.

I choke on him, relaxing my throat to take as much of him in as I can and still breathe. He thrusts, using my mouth with the same desire I used his.

I dig my fingers into his thighs, and give myself over once again, offering him the submission he wants. The mindlessness.

"Dark thoughts in eyes, Lei'a," Gethen says, his voice a harsh rasp. "Only thoughts should be of my cock."

Soon there's nothing of thought left in his gaze either, his dark eyes glazed over, his lips drawn up over his teeth and his tusks gleaming. I wince at the sound of talons scraping down concrete.

He comes with a roar, his groin mashing into my nose and almost cutting off my air passage, the hot jets of his endless come spilling down my throat. After a few moments I begin to struggle because he's bracing against me and I actually can't breathe anymore. I can't breathe, and my clit is pulsing because I want him to do this to me while his cock is in my pussy. Take my breath. Take everything.

As his cock slips out of my mouth, I inhale big gulps of breath, coughing and spluttering. "Were you trying to suffocate me?"

"You like it," is his calm reply.

"Maybe I want it slow and sweet and gentle for once."

He gives me a look.

"When did you become so cynical, Gethy?"

"When my female sent my son away with strangers because she think I not come for her."

It takes me a minute to speak. "I told you. I didn't think you were alive."

"That's what you said. But maybe you just think I am weak." He jerks a shoulder, his gaze steady on mine. "Not trying to fight, Lei'a. Understand. Already said would prove myself to you."

"Don't you want me to do the same?"

"No, Lei'a." His dark eyes are gentle. "Always knew your worth. You have nothing to prove to me."

It's too much. I curl up on my side, and I weep.

## NINETEEN

I DON'T OPEN MY EYES RIGHT AWAY WHEN I RECOGNIZE THE leaden weight of my sluggish limbs, the dusty herbal scents of my distant cousin's office. The brief time I had with Gethen trapped in the cell of my mind, something in me eased and rearranged itself. Like lancing a wound, I still bleed, but the blood is untainted by puss.

I truly have forgiven him. I'd wondered if I was just fooling myself.

"Lei'a?" Gethen's raspy voice, the sound of him stirring next to me.

I take another few deep breaths then open my eyes, forcing my body to get back to work.

Talons wrap around my upper arms, helping keep me steady as I look up into his face, orienting myself in the present.

"Lei'a," he says again, this time a hint of a growl in his voice.

"Well," a disembodied voice says quite cheerfully, "you two have pressing matters to take care of. You know the way out. Don't come back until ya 'ave my apprentice."

Gethen and I exchange a look.

"Can I trouble you for a change of clothing first?" I ask.

It's early morning and because of the nature of the enemies on our heels—Lord Meadowland's amnesty only takes care of his people—we're cautious on our way back to the brothel.

I'm in travel clothing—sturdy brown trousers, a cream blouse, and brown corset vest. Clean, nondescript, and in good repair. I hadn't been looking forward to traversing the streets in broad daylight while in brothel wear without so much as a cloak to divert attention.

It takes longer than I'd like to reach the Painted Lady. It's noon by the time we arrive, tense and exhausted since it's been hours since real sleep or food—though the exhaustion is mostly mine. My injuries are still healing despite the day of convalescence Gethen forced on me.

"What plan if cousin say no?" Gethen asks, an edge in his voice.

I pause in the alley and turn to him. "You'll let me do the talking, Gethen. It's going to take diplomacy to convince Clary to give Honoria to Witch when I was supposed to be negotiating for a suppressor."

"Diplomacy." The irony in his tone is exquisite.

I shrug. "Fast-talking, a subtle threat. Diplomacy."

"Meadowland has son and cousin."

"I know better than you what will happen if we fail." I hold his gaze, steel in mine. "You will let me do the talking. If she refuses initially—she will—you'll remain friendly."

Gethen steps towards me, taking my upper arms in his hands. "No allies in this City, no kin other than Hathur. Have called in every favor owed me to keep you alive in jail."

I rear back. I don't want to hear this.

"Don't say this to make you feel guilty, or to put you in my debt. You're mine, the mother of my son, it was my duty to protect you as best I could. If she refuses to help us, I'll have no choice."

I shake my head. "You can't force her to accept an apprenticeship, and Witch won't take an unwilling apprentice. What do you think you can do?"

"Will make offer costly to refuse, Tleia. You will not interfere, or I deal with you too."

His voice chills me at this point. He doesn't sound like himself, he doesn't look like himself.

"You would hurt me?"

"Never. But will ensure you can't intervene. Have duty to my son as well as you."

He's speaking this way, slow and measured, to make sure I understand what he's saying. I stare up at him. "The man I knew never would have hurt a female."

"I'm not quite male you knew." Gethen releases me. "Tleia, you've not grown a conscience now."

No. No, I haven't. But I also won't give up my cousins to a wolf. I close my eyes. My son. . .my shoulders slump. "If there's a point where I know nothing I say will overturn a refusal, then I'll signal." I exhale. "And then you can intervene."

Gethen nods, brushes my cheek with the back of his knuckles, and we continue down the alley.

During day hours it should be a skeleton staff—maintenance, security, laundresses and whatnot. When we approach the back entrance, there's a half-Orc male leaning against the door, smoking. Tall for a Human, broad shouldered, his skin a light gold-green and his hair closer to medium brown versus the full-blooded black.

Slowing to another stop, I glance at Gethen, placing a hand on his arm. His gaze is cold, focused on the man who drops the cigarette and crushes the butt with his heel and then straightens, glancing in our direction. He's alert, but not yet alarmed.

I paste a bright smile on my face and stride forward. After all, we're just a couple visiting during the day to see my cousin. Nothing to be alarmed about.

"Good afternoon!" I say cheerfully, relaxing my voice so my natural wharf cant comes through. "Here to see Clary. I know she and Ria are sleeping, but I owe her money and I'm leaving town today. Thought I could drop it off now 'afore she hunts me down. She's ugly as sin when's she's angry."

The Orc casts Gethen a wary glance, then replies to me. "Clary didn't say she was expecting visitors."

"No, I didn't tell 'er I was coming today. Can I just go inside and knock on her door? Unless you got paper and I can write a note."

"Who are you?" he asks Gethen.

Gethen grunts. "Hers."

After a moment the guard shrugs. "Fine, but I gotta pat you down for weapons first."

"No problem," I say cheerfully, and spread my feet shoulder width apart, lifting my arms.

He crouches, beginning at my ankles, his touch brisk and professional. He swipes his fingers between my legs and—

I don't blink before Gethen has him slammed against the brick wall, a hand wrapped around the guard's throat, showing his teeth. The guard is snarling as well and even knowing it isn't a good idea, I grab Gethen's arm, hanging my weight on it, which must be nothing to him 'cause he don't twitch. It's aggravating.

"What are you doing?" I shout.

"He—"

"He was patting me down, not feelin' me up. What is wrong with you? I'm sorry," I address the guard. "I had a baby and he's sleep deprived. He knows you were just doing your job."

Gethen lets me pull him back, the snarl fading from his lips. The guard is a professional—he glares but doesn't reach for a weapon or escalate the situation.

"Keep your female at home if can't control your instincts," he growls. "Feckin' new fathers. The hellsdamn worst."

"There no weapons between her thighs," Gethen retorts— and I beg to differ—but his tone is more huffy than angry, his glare flat. "Next time I break fingers."

"*Gethen.*" I curse myself a minute later. I shouldn't have

said Gethen's name, but he'd rattled me with his shift from alert to violent in the space of a second.

"Meet disrespect with broken bones," he snarls at me.

Taking another deep breath, I slide in front of him and give the guard a thin smile. "He has issues. Don't mind him. The sooner we can—"

"Yeah yeah. Wait here."

He returns minutes later and jerks his head. "Ya got ten minutes."

We quickly traverse the hallway until we're at my cousin's door. It's already partly open.

"I didn't expect you back so soon," Clary whispers as she ushers us into her room.

Gethen leans against the door, brooding.

My own internal time clock is ticking, pushing at me. We've only used maybe eight hours of the three-day time frame Meadowland gave us, but I can no longer push aside my worry and impatience. I've distracted myself with the task at hand up 'till now, but those distractions are running out.

"I've found Honoria a protector," I say.

———

"No," Clary says.

Her dark hair is wrapped underneath a bed scarf, her face clean of makeup. She looks younger, softer—until you look in her eyes.

Honoria sits on the bed, legs crossed, saying nothing, simply watching her wife.

"What are your objections?" I ask. I expected the hard no, I'm not yet discouraged.

"I don't know, let me think, Telly. Maybe the fact that out of the last five apprentices, exactly none have survived?"

"That is a concern, I admit, but when you look at each case on an individual basis you'll find there are mitigating circumstances. And I believe only three are confirmed deaths."

Clary crosses her arms across her chest. "You'll do anything to save your son."

I shake my head. "No, the Orc will do anything to save my son." I wait a beat, let that sink in and watch as my cousin stiffens. Honoria doesn't moved. "I'm attempting a fair negotiation. I have no desire to see you or your wife harmed. I really do think the above cases are simply a matter of mismatch. Or stupidity on the part of the apprentices. Honoria is an adult, and she's kin. That will protect her somewhat."

"Will I be in servitude?" Honoria asks.

I could lie to her. I have nothing in particular against lying. But I do have something against deceiving kin.

"They will be your master. You'll be bound to obey their will." I smooth my hand along my thigh. "They were kind to me as a child. I have no reason to think they'll abuse you."

"And no reason to think Witch will accept Honoria," Clary says, her voice still hard.

"What other options do you have? Honoria is past the age

where she'll be accepted by a more. . .conventional master. If her talent is discovered by anyone with ill intent—and let us not kid ourselves, that's the majority of magic users in this city—then she'll be in a far worse circumstance than she would as apprentice to a witch with the power and reputation to protect their territory and their apprentice." I shake my head. "You know this living situation here is only a matter of time. You've been lucky thus far."

"I won't do anything unless my wife and I are in agreement," Honoria says. "But I see the potential benefits of going, as well as the potential risks of staying." She glances at Clary. "My sisters. . .if I'm ever discovered, they'll be in danger. Sajena is on the road all the time and can't protect them. My mother just remarried. She's having another baby."

"That's why you cut off contact with them," Clary says. "So if you're discovered—"

Honoria shakes her head, lowering her gaze. "I'm afraid it won't be enough."

"I'll be in your debt," I say softly.

"What is your debt worth, when your Orc over here is going to cart you off to some farm in the mountain where you can't be reached?" Clary retorts.

Gethen, who's remained silent until now, straightens from his crouch against the door. "On my honor, we'll provide you with means to send word if we are needed. Will both be in your debt."

Clary weighs him, the line of her mouth grim. The word of an Orc holds a little more value then the word of a Human street rat. I'm not offended.

"You know I wouldn't ask this if it was anything less than my son," I say. "And technically, Witch didn't say Honoria had to accept them as a master, or that they had to accept her as an apprentice. Only that I bring her to them, and they would give me the necklace."

Honoria slides off the bed, standing. "I want to go, Clary. It makes no sense to not at least speak with your cousin. They have no reputation for harming those who don't bring trouble to them first. They aren't evil."

Oh, Witch can definitely be evil, but no. . .they aren't, at their nature, evil. I've never known them to attack innocence. Stupid people who ignore all the warning markings around their territory, yes, but that's not the same thing.

"Fine," Clary says. "We'll go. We'll talk. But that's it, we make no promises, Tleia."

I bow. "It's enough."

## TWENTY

WITCH PROVES THEIR KINDNESS—THOUGH I KNOW BETTER
than to ever discuss it with outsiders—by accepting my
introduction of Honoria as the fulfillment of our bargain.

They give me the necklace without any further games,
and surprise me by pulling me into a hug, their green tea and
jasmine scent embedded in their robes.

"Leave the City and never return," they whisper, voice
fierce. "If you come back, it will swallow you. Let nothing
take this opportunity, even if you must excise pieces of your
soul. You won't miss them."

Because I understand their message, I don't scoff. At this
point, well almost at this point because we haven't cleared
the City yet, I'm my own worst enemy.

I was born here. Raised here. Almost died here, and
brought life into the world. Leaving is harder than I thought
it would be.

Once we're on the road, it will be kindest to tell Gethen he doesn't need to prove himself. We have enough to be miserable over. Except, I think he needs to do. . .whatever it is he thinks will suffice. Fight for me, kill for me, show he's willing to die for me, for Ethan. If this journey to the Sorting is a trial and penance he's laid on himself in order to earn absolution of some kind, then I won't take it away.

"I don't know if I'll see you again," I say, pulling away from their hug.

"Good," is the reply.

It's meant as a blessing.

When I glance at Clary, her eyes are shimmering, but she smiles. Honoria clasps my hand for a moment.

"It was good to meet you," she murmurs. "And I hope we *do* meet again."

Gethen slides an arm around my shoulders and ushers me out of the warehouse, leaving my only acknowledged kin to their fate, as we head towards ours.

"We can bring Clary and Honoria with us," he murmurs.

I shake my head, glancing up at the sky to gauge the position of the sun. "They won't come. And we already struck the bargain. If we try to renege, Witch *will* kill us."

"Odd family."

"My son is my family now." We clear Witch's territory and emerge onto cobblestone streets, both of us on alert and watching for pursuit.

I'm uneasy. "There's been no effective pursuit since we left Meadowland's tower."

Are we under protection, or have we gotten lucky and managed to shake those on our heels? I never trust good luck, mostly because it's a myth.

"If want necklace, Fae Lord will keep pursuers away," Gethen says, his thoughts on the same line as mine.

It's the most likely conclusion. Depending on how badly Meadowland wants this necklace without having to fight Witch for it, killing a few thugs to clear a path for us is a small price for him to pay.

I relax a little once we enter the invisible demarcation of Meadowland's territory. We're on his business, no one will mess with us here, and if he doesn't have lookouts posted I'll eat my own corset.

The lookouts I assume are present materialize, a man and a woman of that mixed species look that Meadowland prefers in his mid-level servants, each of them hard eyed but courteous. They escort Gethen and I into the tower and up the flights of stairs until we reach the same receiving room where one wall is crumbled open to give a view of the City and the sky above.

Meadowland turns as we enter. He's in the same red and burgundy attire as if his day hasn't yet ended.

"My son," Gethen growls. "My cousin."

Stepping in front of Gethen, I bow, hoping it will remind him of his manners. "Lord Meadowland."

When I straighten, the Fae Lord is gazing at me, ignoring Gethen. "You were successful," he says. "Where is it?"

Gethen's hand grips my shoulder, his talons digging into

my skin. "You will deal with me. She's mine, and under my protection. You will speak with me, and you will *look* at me, not her."

I stiffen because he snarled the last few words, pushing me behind him. This isn't the time for him to go all alpha protector Orc warrior on me.

"Did I misinterpret?" Meadowland asks. "Has she sworn an oath of allegiance to you? Have you wed?"

I'm too annoyed. There's a form to these interactions, and Gethen is stomping all over them.

"She carried and bore my son," Gethen says. "No other formal oath is required."

There's a beat of silence. "If she doesn't dispute your claim, then I will not." Meadowland's voice is cooler now. "Very well."

"Before she gives you the necklace, you'll bring us our kin."

"Gethen—" I begin, and he cuts me off, his voice hard.

"Be quiet, Tleia."

I blink, staring at his back, and deliberately step around him. He doesn't try to shove me behind him again, instead grabs me and pulls me so my back is against his chest and his arms are wrapped around mine like a cage.

He lowers his mouth to my ear. "Behave," he whispers, "or put you over my lap minute we're alone. But maybe I won't wait, Lei'a."

My abdomen tenses, and for a moment my mind skips off somewhere it really shouldn't be right now.

"This is completely unnecessary," I say, not impugning my dignity with a struggle. "What is wrong with you?"

I glance at Meadowland, prepared to grovel, only to see a brief glint of amusement in his eyes.

"You've made an interesting choice, Mistress Shyncheia," is all he says. He nods at the guard standing behind us, then the door opens and closes. "Your son and cousin will be brought. Well, your son, in any case. The other Orc declined my hospitality."

I want to curse. "Is he alive?"

"If he is not, neither I nor any of mine killed him. I gave no such order."

I can almost hear Gethen grinding his teeth, but abruptly the Orc at my back relaxes. He's probably come to the same conclusion I have. If Hathur escaped, he's alive. Which means he's watching, and will meet up with us—or attempt a rescue depending on how this meeting goes.

Meadowland is being surprisingly indulgent to bring us our son before he demands the necklace. The indulgence tells me this isn't done yet.

"What do you want?" My voice is flat.

He lifts a brow, then straightens from where he's leaning on his desk as the door opens, and I hear a familiar shriek of fury. Gethen releases me before I can drive my heel into his shin, and I run around him towards my son, who runs into my legs and wraps his arms around me.

"Mommy! Mommy, I had cake. And I play with swords. But I didn't cut myself, Pa." Ethan sidles around me and goes to Gethen, who lifts him into his arms. "I want a sword, *Otema.*"

Gethen smiles at him, and the layer of harshness on his expression evaporates.

My son is clean, uninjured, wearing clothes too fine for my current lot in life, and apparently has had a grand old time. A bite of jealousy takes me, because I can't recall a time in my life where I was allowed to have innocent fun. I take a moment to swallow the lump in my throat, and knowing Ethan is secure in Gethen's arms, I turn to Meadowland to conclude our business.

Drawing the necklace off my neck, I hand it to him. It's a thing of exquisite Aeddannar craftsmanship; gold and ruby gemstones, an intricate pendant on a simple chain.

But Meadowland doesn't take it. Gethen murmurs something in his own language to Ethan and the boy settles down his excited chatter, Gethen coming back to stand in his bodyguard position at my right and slightly behind. I suppose since he has what he wants, his son, he's content to let me do the bargaining again. Men.

"You asked me what I want," Meadowland says. "It was a good question." He slants Gethen a slightly sarcastic gaze as if to ask, "Are you going to let her speak now?" then looks back at me. "You travel to the Sorting."

I nod. I haven't moved my arm, it's still held out, slightly bent at the elbow, the gold and ruby necklace dangling from my fingers.

"We are." My heart sinks a little. I don't want to make

assumptions, but he's interested in my destination and he's also not taking the necklace.

The last thing I want is—

"You will take this necklace and deliver it there to a woman who may be present. She has evaded my other couriers thus far. She will not be expecting *you,* however."

—to be used as Lord Meadowland's courier. Especially of a Fae betrothal necklace which is inherently magical, and obviously expensive. If the person who is to receive it doesn't want to be found, that will complicate the situation.

"May be present," I echo. "How certain are you this woman will be there?"

"Certain enough to entrust this errand to you at this time. Will you do this small thing for me? Perhaps your cousin, the one who escaped, may accompany you."

This is a less than subtle reference to the unasked for debt we owe Meadowland for allowing Hathur to escape unscathed. Damn it.

"If we can't find her? If she doesn't accept delivery?"

Meadowland says nothing. Silence from an Aeddannar can mean any number of unpleasant things, but in this circumstance he's simply allowing me to come to my own conclusions.

And to remind myself of the debt, and what happens when the currently friendly Meadowland decides friendliness is no longer in his interest. I don't have any choice if I want to get out of the City alive with my son and Gethen.

I slip the necklace back over my head. "I assume you have

something of a name and a description for me?" I try to keep the anger from my voice. When will I be done with men who have the power to control me?

"I do," he says, lidding his eyes. "Come. I will escort you out of my territory as we speak."

## TWENTY-ONE

Meadowland is generous—or practical, I can't decide which. The escort includes a stop to retrieve already packed bags of supplies, including a buggy big enough for a Human and small child, and a sturdy pony to pull it. Ponies are not inexpensive.

"Mommy! Is that horsie?"

"Yes." I tighten my arms around him, ignoring the pang of regret that the only animals he's ever known are rats.

Gethen presses his hand against the small of my back, his presence at my side constant since we returned to the crumbling tower. He's stiff, but mercifully says nothing except a cool, "Our gratitude."

He's distracted when Ethan flings himself out of my arms making roaring noises, trying to get to the horse—I can't decide if he's issuing a challenge or if he thinks that's the appropriate way to greet another mammal.

I hand the boy to his father, who's big enough to contain a savage, struggling Orcling, and silently take inventory, trying to decide how to respond to this largesse as the men converse. Travel rations, basic camping goods, and supplies for a small child. With the stuffed Orc back in my possession, and the jewels still hidden, I could have afforded to outfit us—but I wouldn't have time or opportunity with trackers on our heels.

I turn to Meadowland.

He flicks his fingers. "The supplies are not a favor. You didn't allow me to apologize for the part I played in the harm done you that night. This is the least I can do." Of course it's in his interest to see us outfitted so we deliver his necklace, but we'll both pretend that's not the reason.

"You will be out of the City by nightfall?" Meadowland asks.

I hesitate. "If our exit is uneventful," I say slowly.

Seacliff. We've heard nothing from him, and that worries me almost more than anything else.

"Leave the matter of Lord Pike to me." From the look in his ruby eyes, this is no more a request than his prompt we get the hells out of Seanna. "I'm better equipped to handle him, and you have a young son to think of."

"Tleia," Gethen says.

I give in. Though I can hold a grudge longer than Gethen, I'm not one to pursue revenge for its own sake, especially when I have a clear path to safety. No, if Lord Meadowland will take care of Seacliff, I'm satisfied. All I want is to know we aren't being chased out of town by Pike thugs.

I bow, and as we turn to leave, Meadowland says, "If you return, Tleia, I will take that as a sign you mean to offer me your service."

"He's exiled us," I say quietly once we've cleared Coho territory. Ethan is in a basket on my back, part of the supplies Meadowland provided. There's no reason to linger. "Do you think Herbert owes him other debts?"

"He's trying to protect you."

"We can't come back."

"Do you want to?"

That's a complicated question, and one I don't have a long-term answer to. But for now, probably forever, the answer is no.

Gethen remains tense but not quite worried, watching for his cousin as well as threats. It isn't until we're two blocks from the City gates that Hathur catches up to us.

We don't stop for greetings, though the men clasp arms briefly.

Hathur reveals that he was never in Meadowland's tender care. "Poisoned darts. Woke up in alley hours later. Guessed where they took the boy but by the time I got to the tower, you and female already gone."

I should be angry, but a Fae Lord lying in order to increase his advantage is nothing new, and also not even close to the worst thing Meadowland's ever done in his life.

"Realized Coho had boy, so kept eye on him. Kept Ethan at his side, but didn't seem like the boy was in danger." Hathur frowns, switching to Uthilsuven. "I didn't know where to look for you but I knew if you lived, you'd return. If you were captured, I'd find and rescue you."

Those with money to hire a carriage—which means those who plan to leave the City and aren't run out of the City—can make the trip from Seanna to the Sorting in seven to ten days with plenty of time to rest the horses.

On foot is between three and five weeks. The buggy cart is sturdy and the pony in good health, but we won't be traveling fast—so two to four weeks for us since the men will stop and hunt to augment our supplies. In four weeks the Sorting fairgrounds will be bursting with traders and artisans, and a village of tents for those who come to either offer themselves or to purchase contracts.

And of course the estimated travel time assumes we aren't attacked by bandits or monsters on the way there.

For the first day we conserve our energy and move as quickly as we can, stopping only when someone needs a tree. I walk to lighten the load on the horse and since I'm not used to this kind of exercise, though we had yard time in the prison, by the time we make camp I'm exhausted.

Hathur takes Ethan and begins to instruct the boy in some small, tedious task I suppose the men think is age-appropriate for an Orcling. I'm too practical to feel useless, but also too practical to deny that's what I am right now.

"A few days of this and I'll be in better shape," I say as a sort of apology.

"Sit, Lei'a," Gethen says, taking my arm and lowering me against a tree.

"So you're talking to me now?"

He's been ignoring me the entire day. I don't require constant attention and maid service, but he hasn't looked at me, hasn't spoken more than a couple of necessary words. One or two times I tried to approach him, touch him, he flinched away.

Gethen pauses, looming over me. The flickering fire casts a subtle light, enough to make him appear sinister. This man will never hurt me unless I ask him to. Looking in his eyes, I begin to wonder if he'll wait for me to ask.

"I know that look on a man's face," I say. "What did I not do?"

"You don't know that look on mine," is the edged reply.

I don't argue.

He crouches in front of me, his gaze intent on my face. "Want return to Seanna?"

"You've lost your mind."

Gethen doesn't smile. "Just checking. Will massage your legs when tent is set up. Rest."

He runs his fingers through my hair, clucks at me like I'm a sleepy toddler who needs soothing and rises to help his cousin set up camp while I focus on getting the blood in my legs to stop feeling like an army of marching ants.

Ethan runs to me, climbs in my lap, and I figure even if I'm useless, this is the one task only I can take on. "Mommy, I want booby."

So I take out my breast and nurse my son. "Isn't it time you gave up the breast?" I ask him.

He detaches with a pop—just long enough to sneer at me

—then latches back on, warm and contented and entirely too big in my lap.

"It's harder to wean boys," Hathur says. "I can't imagine why. The tent is ready."

I crawl into it, still holding Ethan, and settle him on his pallet and blanket before I pull off my boots and settle onto mine with a sigh.

My skin is crawling. I want to bathe, but there's no water nearby so I'll endure. This only proves I had a solid reason for my hesitance in leaving civilization all these years. I'm sure the Orcs don't mind, but I loathe the smell of my own stink.

I'm half asleep when Gethen finally crawls in, my eyes adjusted enough to the dark that I can see him settle near the tent flap, folding his legs as if he intends to sit there and watch us all night.

Maybe it's the dark, maybe it's his silence or the unblinking way he stares, but it heightens my tension. If he doesn't release this need inside him. . .the need will claw its way out anyway. I don't know if Gethen could forgive himself if he left me bloody and bruised—even if I told him I was his to do with as he wished.

"Are you well?" I ask, speaking softly so we don't wake Ethan. "You seem tense." If I think back, he's been like this since we left Witch the first time. Is he still processing the dream we relived? "You've been avoiding me all day."

The look in his eyes clears a little, and he shakes himself. "Will be tense until home. Lei'a, if attacked, take Ethan and hide. Don't try to fight."

"Darling. Why in the world would I try to fight?"

"Have your little charms. Make you brave."

My lips curve in a cat-like smile. "Yes, I do. But they're for emergencies, not basic defense."

He assesses me. "Will you learn, if I try to teach again?"

"I will." I grimace, sigh. "It's a practical skill, but you've attempted to teach me with little success."

"Just need better incentive."

"Survival is the best incentive, and that hasn't worked up until now."

"Because could always talk self out of trouble with big dark eyes and plump lips and sweet voice." His voice deepens into something with a guttural edge. "Can just look at man and his will is yours."

"Not quite, but thank you for the compliment."

I sit up, wriggling out of the covers, and crawl to him, keeping my eyes on his. He doesn't move when I straddle his lap, twining my arms around his neck.

But my plan isn't to seduce. Not yet. I nuzzle his cheek with mine. "Tell me what's wrong, Gethy. I know you. Something's making you unhappy."

Hands clamp around my hips. "Not unhappy. Don't worry about me."

I press my lips on his neck, pulling his hair out of the way, tasting his skin. "Don't you like when I worry about you?"

His voice softens. "Yes." He kisses the skin between my eyebrows. "But don't like your worry-fear."

"Only the dead have no fear." I bite his neck gently.

Gethen makes a rumbling noise deep in his chest, sliding his hand into my hair. "I'm over twice your age, female."

He reminds me of this every couple of years, as if he's complaining I won't let him pull the "older wiser" card on me.

"In Orc years we're the same age." I lift my head and kiss him, sliding my hands over his shoulders and down his chest, enjoying the flex of muscle under my touch. "Let me help you forget that you're worried about my worry."

But he catches my wrist, halting me. "Not now."

I pull back a little, looking at his face. "Are you worried about Ethan? I assure you, he's seen much—"

Gethen scowls at me. "I'm not worried about Ethan, though yes, your screams would wake him."

I try to kiss him again, but he tightens his hand in my hair, his eyes agate. "No, Tleia. What I want needs time and privacy."

"What do you want?" I smile when he remains silent. "You don't have to tell me, though I wonder if you've always had this need or if it's. . .developed during our time apart. Who taught you to desire a woman's pain, Gethen? Who did you fuck?"

"Fucked no one." He wraps a hand around my throat, squeezing. "I'm not settled right now, and don't want to hurt you."

"You can hurt me. Take my pain, it's my gift to you."

My eyes drift shut as I rub my chest against his, feel Gethen's hardness cradled between my legs.

"I don't want your pain." His voice is gentle, but firm. "Will not be like that between us."

"Then show me what it will be like, Gethy." But I know he's lying to himself.

A talon trails down my cheek. "Don't wake boy."

He grasps the edge of my shirt and pulls it up over my head. I've already divested myself of the corset, so my breasts are free, heavy and already aching. He slides an arm around my waist and I arch my back as his free hand clamps around one breast, then squeezes, the talons pricking into my skin.

And pricking.

Moisture dampens my eyes, an automatic reaction to the steadily increasing pain. He lets go of my breast and grabs my nipple, then twists.

I bite my bottom lip, hard, to keep from crying out, and a second later his mouth replaces his fingers, and he's suckling, then biting down, bending me backward so he can bite and nibble.

"I thought you didn't want my pain," I breathe.

"This not pain," he murmurs. "This small thing is nothing."

At least now I have the start of a scale to judge his definition of pain by.

The moment he draws blood, I know it, because he stiffens against me, the arm around my waist tightening, the thick cock I'm undulating against hardening more.

"Hush, female," he admonishes, "or I stop. Boy needs sleep."

I move my hips, the friction of his erection against my clit torture. "I can be quiet." My words are a soft whine. "I can be quiet. I need your cock. I need you to fuck me."

I begin to struggle, not to get away but to get his pants off, at least enough that I can free him and impale myself. If he doesn't want to cooperate, fine, I'll do the work.

But he tosses me onto my back with a snarl, crouching over me with fisted hands on either side of my head. "Not right time, Tleia."

"You deny me?" It's. . .inconceivable. But then he'd kept himself from fucking me for years. I loathe his self-control.

I'll break it again one of these days.

"Be good girl for many days, then will reward you."

Oh. He's one of *those*. Really, I should have known. I stare up at his face. "That's the game we're playing? Denial?"

"Not game. Incentive." He lowers his head and captures my bottom lip, his teeth sinking in. Again, drawing blood, but this time I can taste it, the copper sharpness flooding my mouth.

"Your definition of a good girl?" My voice is strangled.

Teeth graze my neck. "Obey directions, do not complain, do not seduce Hathur."

"How dare you. Hathur can't *afford* me." And it's been decades since I sold myself for pennies or scraps of bread. I think about his other rules. "You're the expert in traveling. I'll obey your instructions. I can't promise about the complaining, though, because it's been several days since I've bathed and—"

He shuts me up with a kiss.

## TWENTY-TWO

I MOAN, SLIPPING MY HAND BETWEEN OUR BODIES, BUT HE grabs my wrist and slams it above my head. "Gethen. Why are you punishing me?"

"Not punishment. Incentive. Proof." The last word is like talons raking across concrete.

"*Proof of what?*" I'm going to strangle him.

He lowers his mouth to my ear, breathes out. "Will make you eat words before eat cock."

I shudder. "What words?"

"'Will not submit to you.'"

My mind flashes back to a few days ago. *"Never again. I won't submit to you."*

He's learned how to hold a grudge.

"That. . .I was upset. I didn't mean it. Don't you want to be inside me?" I smooth my voice, smile at him and cup my breast—he's still imprisoning one wrist. "You can come on my breasts, cover me in your seed so I smell like you. So everyone knows I'm yours. After you make me come."

He stares at me a few heartbeats, his silence thoughtful. "If don't make come, you will be in miserable mood in morning. Will make everyone else miserable."

"It's delightful how well you know me. And now, like then, there's no escape from my misery. You'll have to endure. Give me what I want."

"No. Can't have cock. But will fuck you with tongue till come all over my face. Then you go to sleep."

Gethen releases me and yanks my pants down my legs. I spare a moment to wince at my robust feminine fragrance, but the Orc doesn't blink.

He slides his arms under my thighs, hands grasping my breasts as he lowers his mouth to my clit.

I gasp as his tongue licks up my slit in one long, slow swipe. Gethen mutters a curse and slaps a hand over my mouth.

It's hard to remain silent against the pleasure of his tongue teasing my clit, flicking back-and-forth and dipping inside my core.

He squeezes my bottom as my hips undulate against his tongue, then a single thick finger slides inside me, moving in and out, joined by second as I ride his tongue. More blood floods my mouth as I bite my lip to keep quiet.

"Don't scream," he growls. The fingers inside me move faster and faster.

I arch my back, my bottom coming up from the ground,

and grab his hair, holding on as the pleasure increases. It's taking all my control not to cry out, to remain silent.

"Don't scream."

My mouth opens in a soundless gasp as I come. Gethen rises to his knees, fingers still in my pussy, and continues fucking me, forcing my body to ride the wave and crest over and over. He muffles my cry with his hand again, pressing down until he's almost cutting off my breath.

I meet the sensual cruelty in his gaze, but affection lurks behind the glimpse of darkness.

His fingers slip out of my trembling body and Gethen drapes himself over me, claiming my lips in another kiss. He's careful that his weight isn't crushing as he kisses me, the way he's always careful with his talons, my own taste on my tongue.

"There," he breathes. "Feel better?"

His cock is hard, it must be painful. "Let me taste you."

Gethen kisses the tip of my nose. "No."

"I'm beginning to think you have a masochistic withholding kink. Are you enjoying yourself?"

He flashes a grin, helps me dress and when I settle into his arms, my back to his chest, my eyes drift shut.

———

The men are worried, which makes traveling with them particularly unpleasant.

They devolve into drill sergeants, and I tolerate it for the second day of our travel, all the way up until they set up camp near a wide stream. I struggle to rise, a *heavy* sleeping Ethan cradled in my arms, and hand him to Gethen.

"I'm going to wash," I say.

My Orc almost immediately shakes his head. "Not tonight. Wait until few more days away from City."

"The stream is twenty feet away and the camp site is safe here."

Whether or not to use the common campsites dotted along the main road had been a discussion. If we're being followed, it only makes it that much easier for our enemies.

On the other hand, there's a risk in entering deeper into the forests. The monsters in the vastness know better than to come close to the roads, especially at this time of year. There are patrols organized by the territory's Governor, and those with enough money to travel in style usually also have their own private security, not to mention the trading caravans which are also well secured.

"Give me boy, cousin," I hear Hathur say as I walk away. "Go with female."

I'm half undressed by the time Gethen joins me. Three years in prison edged away some of the fastidiousness I'd developed after ten years as a pampered wife, but still, my skin has been crawling all day from the accumulated dirt of the road. Plus we didn't change clothing yesterday.

I walk knee deep into the stream and bend over, touching my toes to force my muscles to stretch. I groan. So sore. Every part of me is sore.

Behind me, there's a strangled breath.

I look over my shoulder. "Oh, so sorry about that." Poor

Gethen must be getting an eyeful. I straighten, stretch my arms above my head and arch my back. "Hand me the soap."

He splashes toward me a moment later and I pluck the bar from his hands and crouch, beginning to lather my skin. I want to wash my hair, but even with a small fire it will take forever to dry. Can I really go the next several weeks without clean hair?

No. I'll endure the damp.

I ask Gethen to bring me one of our cups, and he does, silently helping me rinse soap off my skin and out of my hair. When I stand, I squeeze as much excess water out as I can and begin to weave it into a loose braid.

"Are you done playing with me?" he says.

I pause, my fingers still in my hair. "*Play* with you? I'm bathing. Oh, right, you're a man, so you think the simple act of a woman bathing is meant as a—"

He yanks me against him, my back pressed against his chest, one of his hands sliding flat on my belly, the other holding me at my throat. I lower my arms, the strength of his erection pressing against me.

"No time to give you cock," he says in my ear. "Stop testing me."

I rub my ass against his groin. "Gethen. All I need is five minutes to have you spilling down my throat."

He whirls me around and pushes me to my knees. The night air is cool against my skin, but his body radiates heat.

"Now," he snarls. "Five minutes. If don't do good job, will add more punishment to tally."

The man who doesn't want my pain. I give him a mental eye roll.

"Please. You insult me." I've already released him from his trousers, wrapping a hand around the thick base of his cock. His breath wheezes from between clenched teeth. "But I can find something else you can punish me for."

Gethen grabs the back of my head with one hand, squeezes my jaw so I open wide, and slams his cock inside my mouth.

I choke, the head against the back of my throat, and recall that he's at his most savage when I'm on my knees in front of him. Placing my hands on his thighs, I let him use me, lifting my gaze to his and relaxing my shoulders so he can experience my complete submission as he thrusts in and out of my mouth.

My jaw aches, and he releases the back of my head to pinch my nostrils closed, forcing me to open my mouth wider.

"Only one place left to fill, Tleia," he says. "I'll have that too. Soon. I'll make it hurt for you."

Moaning, I put my hand between my thighs and rub my clit furiously. His nostrils flare, probably from the scent of my arousal and I moan again, tears streaming down my cheeks as I choke and sputter, gasping for air when he pinches my nostrils closed again.

He grinds against my face and comes with a roar, come pouring down my throat, his cock jerking from the force of his orgasm.

Pulling out, he wraps a hand around my neck and yanks

me to my feet. Turning me so my back is against his chest again, he knocks my hand away from my clit and replaces it with his fingers, working the swollen nub until I cry out, shaking against him.

My knees buckle.

I feel him put himself back in his trousers, then Gethen lifts me in his arms and turns, walking back into the camp.

"I thought you said no bath," Hathur drawls, "and no cock. Way to hold firm with your female. You'll have her trained to be as meek as a baby bird in no time. Do you need some pointers, cousin?"

"Get your own," Gethen mutters, and lowers to duck inside the small tent.

"Put boy to sleep in my tent," he laughs. "You're welcome."

———

I wake, prompted by maternal instinct honed from years of imagining everything that can go wrong with Ethan while I sleep. It's an hour or two before dawn. I poke my head out of the tent and I can just make out the outline of. . .

I frown. My son and his father stand at attention, facing trees, their backs to me.

"What are you doing?" Do I want to know? Probably not.

"Too big now for nappies," Gethen rumbles without turning around.

"Marking territory, Mommy!" Ethan shouts, and whirls. . .a baby stream of piss pointed in my direction.

Marking territory.

I shift my gaze to Gethen, who lowers his hand to Ethan's head and gently urges the boy to turn back around. Gethen advises, "Do not spray mother-girl. Mother-girl cranky before coffee."

I stare a few seconds longer. . .then leave them to it and go back to sleep. I'm tired.

Not my Orcling. Not my circus.

———

Four days into the journey, the men call a day long halt. There's a good sized stream, and Ethan is restless. It's getting more and more difficult to keep him from leaping out of the back of the moving buggy. Gethen and Hathur consider that action a decent training exercise—something about learning how to fall and roll correctly from a moving object—but I'm less than enthusiastic about the prospect of sprained or broken ankles.

Of course, I take the opportunity to wade upstream and promptly strip down to bathe.

"You can look, Hathur," I call out mockingly when I note he's positioned himself with his back to me. "There isn't a male here who hasn't seen breasts before. They're a fine pair, if I say so myself."

"I will yank out your entrails," Gethen says, "and make sausage to feed my son, if you succumb to her teasing."

He swears up and down it's been a thousand years or more since Orcs, on their home planet, consumed sentient mammals. I've always thought he's lying.

"Indeed, my entrails would make him grow big and strong," Hathur says.

"I only eat Mommy booby," Ethan says.

In the interest of peace, I turn my back to them and enjoy my leisurely bath. When I'm done, I dress then approach, squeezing water out of my hair.

Halting, I smile as I see my son crouched on the bank of the gurgling stream, looking fat cheeked and cheerful. Gethen is sprawled on his side, a makeshift fishing pole in his hand and a twig between his teeth. I roll my eyes. As I move forward, Ethan plucks something up from the ground.

I halt.

Ethan examines the fat, wriggling bug in his hand. He's not watching me, so I cringe. Oh well. I suppose this is more boy stuff.

. . .and crunches down.

I lurch forward, shrieking.

Gethen jerks and surges to his feet, roaring. "What? What, Tleia?"

"I'm going to *murder* you," I hiss. "My *son* is eating a bug. *Who taught him that?!*"

"Crunchy, Pa! Crunchy sweet!"

Hathur collapses onto his back, roaring with laughter.

Shrieking, I hold out my hands as Ethan picks up another bug and glances at me, his brows raised in an expression so like Gethen's that it should be funny.

Except that he's *eating* a *bug*. "Share with Mommy?" he says uncertainly.

"Good protein, Tleia," Gethen says in that fake meek tone

he uses when he knows I'm about to make his life *miserable.* "First prey teach Orcling to hunt."

*"My son is eating a bug."*

Gethen has the nerve to look confused as he slowly lowers himself back to the ground. "Tasty." He pauses and speaks more slowly. "I catch you one if you like. Ethan, share!"

"No, Ethan, don't share!" What is wrong with Gethen? "Ethan, don't eat the bugs." I didn't go through my life just to get back to the point where my offspring has to eat insects.

"They won't hurt him, cousin," Hathur says, voice pitched into a soothing tone.

Ethan's bottom lip begins to tremble. "But Mommy, they tasty. Pa said I could eat them."

"Your Pa is a walking dead—"

"Lei'a." Gethen's voice is sharp.

I take a deep breath, let it out. Gethen is watching me carefully.

"Staple of Orc diet, Lei'a," he says after a long, silent moment. Hathur stares at me too. "All Orcs eat when traveling. Good snack."

I turn and walk away.

As usual, I'm experiencing the unintended consequences of my actions.

## TWENTY-THREE

WE'RE ON THE OUTSKIRTS OF THE FAIRGROUNDS WHERE makeshift tents, stalls, and booths crafted from scavenged scrap wood, sheet metal and canvas form haphazard rows. I inhale the scent of roasting meat, skewers and stews over open fires, and my stomach rumbles.

"I want eat, Mommy," Ethan says, proving we're on the same page. "Not booby. Meat. I a big boy now."

"That's right, tiny cousin," Hathur says, "no more breast until you're a married male. Leave the tits to *Otema*."

I glare at Hathur, though I admit it's silly to get irate over the word tits. Ethan is *my* son after all.

Gethen murmurs something to Ethan, probably a promise for all the raw, wriggling, or fried insects he wants.

For the last three days we've shared the widening road and common campsites with other travelers. I watched the carriages and caravans, searching for insignia that might indicate the identity of their occupants. The handful of times I recognized colors or a crest from a family or business association in Seanna, I tensed.

We spent a day longer than necessary camped out since there is no purpose lingering on Sorting grounds. We're here to restock supplies, find Orc kin to travel with, and leave.

I worry the downtime allowed pursuers to catch up to us, but there's no evidence yet of a tail. It's my paranoia assuming Seacliff won't have just let me go.

"I want a bath," I say.

"Mother wants a bath," Ethan echoes. His Uthilsuven is still basic and painstaking, but he can speak simple formal sentences now.

"Shocking," Hathur murmurs. "The female wants to bathe."

"Am poor male," Gethen says. "Bath tent expensive. River free."

We're not married and he's already penny pinching. This is why a woman must *always* have her own money—spend her husband's, yes, but still have her own.

"I want a *hot* bath. My hair is unacceptable."

The Orcs, including my son, braided their hair down as we traveled. Gethy offered to braid mine as well, but the thought of dirt and debris embedded in braids—no, thank you. I need to get clean first.

"When reach steading may have hot bath twice a day. Only cost time to draw and heat water."

We'll have to talk about that. If his homestead doesn't have plumbing, he'll be digging and installing lines all season.

Gethen's focus bores into the back of my neck, the way it's been for the last three days now.

I turn to face the Orc and fix him with my gaze. "I am going to locate the bath tent, and I am going to have a scrub followed by a long soak. Then I'm going to deliver Lord Meadowland's necklace to the simpleton who failed to remain out of his reach. What you choose to do with your time while I'm otherwise occupied is up to you. Take your son with you," I add.

"I'd let the female have her hot bath," Hathur says. "I'm still thinking she's only pretending to be inept with knives. We can look for our kin while she's occupied."

Hathur and Gethen are hoping there will be an Orc caravan traveling in our direction we can join for the added protection.

"Why pay for water when free," Gethen mutters in Gaithean. "I scrub, pay me."

Hathur gives him a pitying look, and says in rapid Uthilsuven I almost can't follow, "No, cousin, you wait until after she marries you to reveal you're a miserly cheapskate who begrudges your wife a few coppers for a hot bath—the way females pretend to be cooperative and good-natured rather than harpies who'll slit your throat before they've had their morning tea."

Gethen glares at him.

"I want to see the swords, Mommy," Ethan says, trying to wriggle out of Gethen's arms. Gethen growls at him, and the boy settles down, hissing through his baby tusks.

But I'm already walking away. "Tell your father."

"Tleia!" Gethen calls after me. "No upgrades! Bath only! I braid hair free!"

I suppose I *could* tell Gethen about the stash of jewels among my supplies, and I slow as guilt pricks at my conscience. I stop, sigh, and loosen the pack on my back, fishing around inside for one of the smaller winking gemstones. I toss it to Gethen.

He glares at me, his fist closing around the shard of rock. "What this?"

"Find a pawn broker," I say, "and stop whining. You boys have fun."

"Knew was holding out on us," I hear Hathur say. "Should find what else she stuffed down bodice. Or I check, if you too afraid."

"Mommy scary when stinky," Ethan agrees.

I sniff. If Gethen really is cash poor, well, he's just going to have to do something about that, isn't he? He has a family to support, and I'm accustomed to living in a certain style. I'll downgrade a bit, I'm not unreasonable. . .but only a bit.

I merge into a motley crowd milling about the sea of tent stalls. A brisk trade in pre-war scrap metal mingles with those who barter for immortal made blades, fabrics, and other goods. There are few children, but those present gaze about as wide-eyed as Ethan.

Before I locate the bathhouse, I begin searching for Meadowland's fool, the weight of that promise literally hanging around my neck. The gemstone and its metal setting have been steadily heating against my skin over the last day since I took it out of my bag and donned it, as if it's telling me in which direction to find its mistress.

I want the thing gone.

"The *ahdramissi* will lead you to its mistress," Meadowland said before we left Seanna. "But in case there is doubt, she goes by the name of Mysterri." The smile he gave me was slight, and droll. "I'm told she tells fortunes."

"What does she look like?"

His expression went neutral. "She is the daughter of an ancient lineage sundered by the crash, and she almost started a war between two Lords who were once closer than brothers. You will know her when you see her."

Her tent stands out. It's small, the entrance draped in strands of beads and seashells that sway gently in the breeze. Drapes are pulled back to reveal the glow of candles within, the diffuse light barely illuminating the interior. It's day, so the candles are a conceit.

I step inside and find it empty except for a small table, two chairs, a stack of aged painted cards and a bowl filled with stones. No, not stones. Runes.

"Hello?"

A bit of darkness detaches suddenly from the corner of the tent and I freeze, then relax as a tall woman with sharp, elegant features steps forward.

I stare.

I stare, and pity stirs, because she's clearly cursed. Long, pin straight dark hair falls past her waist, framing summer gold skin.

Her beauty would almost be repulsive if it weren't for the

slight unevenness of her nose, and that the thin shape of her top lip is not quite symmetrical with the full bottom.

Her eyes are an indeterminate color between green and gold and grey, but despite their ordinary shade, the mind behind them weighs me. She may look to be in her mid-twenties, but if she survived the crash, she's at least as old as Uther Bachdracht.

"I'm accepting petitioners," the woman murmurs and gestures to the table, strands of crystals clinking around her wrists. She wears leather and velvet like the clothing is a costume.

"I'm not here for a telling," I say.

Her eyes brighten for a moment, then dim. She folds her hands into her draped sleeves. "Why are you here?"

She asks like she already knows.

I glance at the pointed ears that peek through her ribboned hair and suppress a sigh. Possibly I should've brought the Orcs with me, because Aeddannari are quick to kill the bearer of bad news. Meadowland hadn't told me she was Fae.

But then, silly me, he might have assumed I was intelligent enough to understand that fact. The Fae marry outside of their species, but it's rare, and it's always a matter of politics or power or inheritance, never love. Certainly never beauty.

No, the beautiful ones with no power they make into toys, or tools, or simply breed.

"Lord Meadowland sent me," I say, "with a gift."

She doesn't move, but I feel both her retreat and the sharpening of threat in the air.

Slowly, I draw the necklace from underneath my shirt and over my head, holding it out. "The *ahdramissi* is yours."

She stares at it, expression unchanging. "I do not want it." But her tone makes this sound more a statement of fact than bald refusal.

The necklace dangles from my fingers. "Take it. If you didn't want your Lord to find you, you should have hidden better."

"None of us can escape our fate unless we choose death," she says, "and I'm not ready to die. Nilarian isn't—yet—a fate worse than annihilation."

She reaches out, so stiff with reluctance I spare her another moment of pity. But this isn't my problem and I want done with it. She takes the necklace and I immediately step back, twisting my hands behind my back.

"May I offer some advice?"

She lifts her gaze from the necklace and looks at me, cool amusement in her eyes. "Certainly. I'm curious what advice a mortal child has to offer."

I hesitate. "He is what he is but he was kind to me. I grew up under his rule, and we never heard of him harming a woman without cause. You can flee, but I don't know if he has other agents present, and rebellion may only anger him. Find something to bargain with, mistress. You're his wife."

The woman chuckles. "I see you have some understanding of what the *ahdramissi* means. He will pay the price for having me."

She gives me another odd smile, the green glint in her eyes growing. "If I see your cousin in the City, I'll offer your greetings, shall I?"

If I were a stupider woman, I would be curious. Fortunately for me, I am not. Time to go.

I bow and back out of the tent, the weight of any further debt owed Meadowland now gone. Gethen lingers nearby with Ethan. I approach and slide myself under my Orc's arm.

"Did the handoff go well?" he asks.

I nod against his chest. "She accepted delivery. We're free of any debt."

"You won't join the line?"

He means will I offer myself at the Sorting to force his hand. I look up. "It's not necessary."

His gaze is steady. "Are you certain, Tleia? You want me to prove myself."

I look at him, weighing my response. "You haven't avenged Herbert's death."

"No."

I smile. "I don't need you to prove you love me. I don't need you to prove you'll sacrifice your honor for me either. You already have, and I'm not a child."

Gethen is the one person who knows many of the unsavory things I've done in my life. He insists I must behave better in the future, but he's never treated me with contempt despite my actions often being the antithesis of his honor system.

"I'm going to the baths now," I say. "Why don't you take Ethan to—"

"Weapon tent," the boy demands. "*Otema* say we see swords."

"Please don't let him cut himself," I say.

Gethen hesitates, the nods. "Don't wander. When finished, stay at bathing tent, and will come for you."

"Where is Hathur?"

"Supplies."

"Do you need more money?"

Gethen's expression sours. "Can provide for female and child."

"You *just* complained about the cost of a bath." I arch a brow. "You already know I'm going to be expensive to keep. Are you certain you still want me?"

"Take your pin money and—"

"It's a bit more than pin money, darling."

If he wants to burn through his funds because of his male ego, that doesn't bother me at all. I'll do exactly as he requests, and save my money. For now. We'll see the state of his homestead once we arrive.

## TWENTY-FOUR

On my way to the bath tent, I purchase a new set of clothing from a stall manned by an Orc female. It's better made and more suited to the travel conditions than what I'd scrounged together in Seanna, but not quite as well-made as the three sets of clothing Lord Meadowland had provided—he really must have felt guilty.

"Travel North?" she asks

"Yes. To the Bachdracht clan holdings. Any news of raiders or monsters on the roads?"

She sucks on her teeth, eyeing me. I try to look innocent, or at least not like trouble.

"Eh. Always are, but the closer you get to Bachdracht holdings, the better defended the roads are. Ya got kin up there?"

"My son's father is taking me there to live. He's cousin to the Bachdrachts, or so he tells me."

She nods, bends over and rummages in a trunk, then pulls out a set of bone and bead tribal jewelry, placing it on the stack of clothing I purchased.

"A gift. The design is from the Bachdracht female's circle. They distribute through us. They're good circle. A little too fond of their drink and their knives, and they keep their males on a short chain, but good circle."

"Thank you."

I slip the clothing into my bag after fondling the necklace a bit, smiling to myself. Once I'm clean, I'll don it with. . .an odd emotion. I almost think what I'm feeling is pride.

I find the tent, pay for an oil scrape, a long soak, and enough fragrant herbal soap to scrub my long hair. I'm tempted to linger and chat a bit, gather more gossip about the roads and who's shown up at the Sorting, but I don't trust my Orcs being left to their own devices for too long and I don't want to linger here longer than necessary.

Once I'm thoroughly cleaned and scraped and I've rubbed cocoa butter into my skin, I dress, tip the boy who washed and braided my hair into four thick rows close to my scalp— an Orcish style he called Allmother braids in his language— and exit the tent.

I wonder what Gethen will think of my leathers, jewelry, and braids. I'm weaving through the crowd when the senses I developed as a girl on the streets of Seanna City go off.

I'm being followed, and not with any stealth. A man, lanky and tall with the broad shoulders and elongated arms of the Icarians, but wingless, his skin gray cast rather than a shade of pewter. Mixed species then, which means he could possess any number of skills and power, or none, being as mundane as an average mortal footpad.

He, or his master, could be someone who thinks I'm here for the Sorting and is watching me.

Or my suspicion that our flight from Seanna has gone suspiciously uncontested is about to be proved true.

Oh, well. I'd estimated a fifty percent chance I'd wind up being bait today—another reason I'd wanted away from my Orcs. As long as I appear to be protected, my pursuers won't crawl out of the slime and show themselves. If they're going to attack, I'd rather they do it here than on the road, or worse, follow us all the way to the homestead.

As I skirt through the crowd, it becomes clear I'm being herded, especially when I catch glimpse of three more thugs too focused on me. The Icarian is the hunter, and he's using the common foot pads to help capture me. There's another Icarian, a Fae mixed species, and an Orc halfling. Too many for Gethen to handle on his own without endangering Ethan.

I need to find Hathur.

Supply tents. Supply tents. I find him in the fourth I check, this one selling a variety of camping gear. He glances over as I step through the raised flap, lifting a brow.

"Where are my cousins?"

"I need you to tell Gethen I'm entering the Sorting," I answer in Uthilsuven.

Hathur's friendly expression fades. "Why? You told him it wasn't necessary."

"Circumstances have changed. There are complications.

I do have a yearning to stand on the cliffs near Gethen's home and look out over the sea, catch some fish in the lake he's been telling me about, but he has to prove himself worthy first. I shan't be pursued easily, nor taken without a fight."

I hold Hathur's gaze, hoping he's not as country dumb as he sometimes pretends—to annoy me, I suspect.

He sighs, tugging on one of his braids, and casually looks over my shoulder, scanning the crowd. *"Right,"* he says after a minute. "I guess I'm on babysitting duty while your male comes to fetch you, stubborn female."

"I think that's the ideal plan. And that we can resolve this once and for all before we're on the road. We don't want any complications dogging our heels."

"Will you make it to the stadium?"

I give him a small, grim smile, though there's some genuine amusement in it because his words are funny. "I'm not much of a warrior, but I've never met anyone who could catch me when I don't want to be caught."

"Good luck, female."

I hesitate, step into his body to disguise my movements, and reach between my breasts for one of the little pouches I'd extricated from my bag earlier. I might have to drop the bag at some point, and the last thing I want to do is lose the gemstones.

"Hold on to these for me." I'll keep the charms with me, though I doubt I'll have to use them unless the thugs use magic. Two Orcs with axes and the Sorting security should do well enough.

He palms the bag, muttering, "Knew there was more money, female."

I run my fingertips along his jaw with another smile, then turn and take off through the crowd, forcing my pursuers to abandon even the pretense of stealth, and follow at full speed.

———

## GETHEN

"This is a risk," I mutter in Uthilsuven, eyeing my son as he sorts through bins of toys.

He's set aside a small sword, a fishing pole, and a doll that looks like his mother, and I've told him he must choose only two. He'll try to talk me into three and if he negotiates well, *without* resorting to Lei'a's manipulative tactics, I'll allow it.

"I don't like it, but Uthsha will guide."

"It's better to eliminate all your pursuers now than lead them to the homestead," Hathur says. "You knew she was going to try to act as bait. I think she thinks we're dumb country brutes, Gethen."

A diplomatic response is best. "She has a warrior's heart, if she lacks the muscle. And the discipline." And, in some ways, the ability to judge her quarry. She should know I know her well enough to understand she is trying to get rid of us so she can draw her pursuers out.

"You have your hands full with her," Hathur says with a chuckle, "but it's too late to rue your choice now."

"It was too late a decade ago, when I met her." When I'd felt as if I'd met my opposing half.

"Will she take you to husband?"

"That's female's circle business." But I have hopes.

Tleia isn't a female to confide. She makes plans, she executes them as she pulls the strings of her puppets and arranges her pawns on a board as she sees fit, whether the pawns or puppets object. She rarely apologizes. Her ruthlessness gives me sleepless nights, and Hathur is right. She'll cause havoc.

At least once she's done playing house. I'm not fool enough to think she'll enjoy being a farmer's wife for much longer than it takes the novelty of it to wear off.

Right now the goal is to draw out her pursuers, which is why I allow her to dangle herself as bait.

Better to let her think I'm stupid; that way she won't exert herself to hide her schemes from me.

That's probably the better way to handle a wife.

"Ethan," I call. "Choose two and come."

As expected, he begins negotiations with big—dry—eyes and a trembling bottom lip. I avert my gaze while I gather my will. He looks too much like his mother, and I have worked to keep from her how much she controls me. I suspect she knows, regardless.

But I won't be ruled by an almost four-year-old infant.

"Look me in the eye and state your case," I say. "Do not try to use my love as a weapon."

"Mommy say when we have a house I can have all the toys I want. And a pet, but not a rat," he adds.

Two impulses strike me. One, to indulge mother and son, and two, to rein both in. I understand why Lei'a wants to give her child everything he hasn't had until now. But also I've seen the sons of mothers who spoil them. Unpleasant, and often, short-lived.

"Your mother loves you," I say, "so she says much."

"Mommy say when people love you they give you things."

Mommy is manipulative and used to solving most of her problems by weaponizing her allure, and is raising Ethan in her own tactics. I don't tell my son this; I will discuss it with his mother, however.

"He is going to be hells on the female's circle before they declare him fit to take a mate," Hathur mutters.

I cross my arms over my chest. "I love you too, son, but I am not Mommy, I am Pa. Now; why should you have three toys when I have already said only two? You have two minutes."

During the four week trip I've taught my son simple sentences in our language, and introduced him to the concept of discipline. He has his mother wrapped around his finger and though she can be brusque and is desperately trying to wean him, she rarely tells him no. Ethan and I have locked tusks on more than one occasion, but every boy must learn the chain of command and the consequences of breaking it.

Because Ethan has experienced those consequences, he quickly adjusts his tactics. "Pa, the fishing pole is to catch food and the sword is a tool." He looks up at me, eyes still wide, but mouth now firm. "The doll is only one toy." He holds up his pointer finger to emphasize.

I try to find fault in his logic, and cannot.

Hathur pays the vendor, laughing his head off, and I lift my son and his three toys into my arms.

"Eughair of homestead Gretdrath has agreed to protect him," Hathur murmurs as we begin walking through the crowd. "He brought his sisters and six more warriors with them to protect their goods, all well armed and trained. Three of them first gen soldiers."

Eughair Gretdrath lives west of Bachdracht holdings by only six days. We have not feuded with them, and there have been inter-marriages. I hand Ethan to Hathur.

"Hathur is taking you to our marriage-kin," I tell the boy, holding his gaze and giving him my serious face. "You will obey Eughair's orders and remain hidden in their caravan. You will wait with them until I or cousin Hathur come to fetch you."

"Where's Mommy?" Ethan demands.

"We go to retrieve your mother now. We may be several hours, up to a day. Repeat to me the rules."

He repeats to me—in Gaithean—the instructions I gave and I nod and speak to Hathur. "I'll follow Tleia. Join me when my son is settled."

"He knows to take Ethan to our kin if we don't return," Hathur says quietly. "I sent a messenger to Uther. Your mother will be informed, and she'll come down from the mountains."

I nod. There's risk, but I base my strategy on Seacliff

having given orders that Tleia is to be lured away from her protectors and then captured. If her pursuers engage Hathur and I, there's every likelihood they won't survive.

When Hathur finds me again, it's to tell me Ethan is safely stashed and that my mate is, as we guessed and allowed, being hunted.

## TWENTY-FIVE

**TLEIA**

If I make it to the stadium line where guards protect supplicants and personnel, I'll be safe. There's no authority on the market side of the fair, it's up to every person to defend self and property. But the Sorting belongs to the ruling immortals, and anyone who makes trouble is punished.

I burst through the crowds, slowing only once I've passed a chalk line. I jog to the nearest guard in the gray and black livery of the Sorting, a male Aeddannar with shoulder length brown hair and a calm blue gaze that looks past me and assesses the situation.

I hold my hands up. "I'm a supplicant for the Sorting. I'm being pursued."

Those two lines give him the authority to protect or attack. His gaze turns flinty as a winged woman in an armored breastplate, leggings and arm guards swoops down. Her dark hair is braided and wrapped around her head, her gray heart-shaped face almost sweet.

"Stay behind Alijah," the Icarian says in a voice too gritty for her face.

I obey, watching my pursuers emerge from the crowd and cross the chalk line.

There's the Icarian mixed-species, two Humans, and an Aeddannar. "I feel the sudden urge to make a bad joke."

The female guard glances at me.

"I have no sense of humor," I add. "Which is why the urge is unusual."

"The girly belongs to us," one of the Humans says. He has a craggy face and sun brown skin, his accent placing him from the outlands. "She ain't eligible to join the Sorting since she's already owned."

"Have the Aeddannar next to you repeat those words," I retort.

"What is your purpose?" Alijah asks.

The Fae smiles genially. He's focused on Alijah, probably as the most potent threat. There's none of the usual signs of travel about him, his pale hair too neat even for Fae—they aren't immune to dirt and weariness—his clothes too clean. If he arrived before us in enough time to settle in, then Seacliff knew all along the best chance of catching me was to wait until I was out of Meadowland's protection.

"We were ordered to pursue the Human for our employer, who is owed a debt."

Slippery. The first half of the sentence is absolutely true, it's the second-half that's more ambiguous. He hopes the guards will accept as truth the implication that I'm the one owing the debt to the employer.

The Icarian guard snorts. "Does this Human owe your employer a debt?"

"As I understand it."

"I owe his employer no such debt," I say. One, because I can't be for certain who his employer is, and two—

"Lord Seacliff," the Fae interjects smoothly.

"I haven't placed myself in debt to Seacliff," I say.

Now I'm skirting the absolute truth as well. Legally, a widow or widower inherits the debts of their deceased spouse. But I didn't incur them. Also, technically, I have no direct or implied knowledge of any debt Herbert owes Seacliff. I know Seacliff believes there's a debt, but with neither my eyes nor my ears have I confirmed this as fact.

Not that it matters, since I don't have a drop of Fae blood in me and I can lie through my teeth if I want. But most of the Aeddannari are skilled at detecting deception from other species; not magic, but training.

Alijah shifts slightly, and there's a blade in his hand. "If the Human female owes your Lord a debt then they may take that up with her new master. I see no reason to eject her from the Sorting grounds, and thus she is under our protection. You may remain, and you may join the Sorting to offer a contract, but you may not attack her, and you may not take her without her express permission."

"I give no such permission," I drawl, "in case there was any doubt."

"We got that," the Icarian guard says, voice as dry as mine. "Go to the front of the line. Tell them your entry has been contested and overruled, and Kore and Alijah said to process you inside while we take out the trash."

"It's been too quiet this session anyway," Alijah murmurs to her. She snorts.

I back up one step, then the second, and then Gethen's roar blankets the general din. I turn in his direction as he tears out of the crowd, and for one fierce moment our gazes clash.

Kore sighs. "Who is this?"

"The man whose contract I will accept," I say. "If anyone owns me, he does, and I grant permission for him to act on my behalf." Then I smile at him, slow and sensual. "Come for me."

He snarls, tusks gleaming, eyes bright with rage and growing battle lust. He nods and I turn and run, my last sight of him charging towards my attackers, chanting in Uthilsuven.

———

**GETHEN**

Three Humans charge me. I swing, catching one across the torso and rip him open, bloody spray across my face as I twist to thrust a powerful kick into the middle of the second. He stumbles back, doubling over.

"Do you require rescue, cousin?" Hathur calls out.

"Their blood is mine," I snap. "Keep eyes on Tleia."

The third Human grabs my arm and swings, but I slam my fist into his jaw, which makes a satisfying crack.

"We'll leave you to it, then," the female Icarian says. She and the Fae partner step back, giving me the field.

The Human I'd left gasping for breath returns. I roar, swinging my ax as I slide my free hand to my side and snatch a small throwing dagger.

It hits him in the eye seconds later and he's down, leaving the immortal and the half-blood.

I charge the Fae, swinging my ax in a deadly arc. He leaps away, a sword appearing in his hand. The use of brute strength puts me at disadvantage when it comes to speed and grace. The half-Icarian creeps forward, cautious.

Baring my teeth, I growl, "Two almost fair odds. Bring more."

Whirling, I counter the Fae, the Icarian lunging into my reach—he's slow, and his job was likely to help herd Tleia, or to handle her once caught.

My ax slams into his head when he all but trips over the Fae, who snarls at him, proving they are no unit or they would not fight so poorly around each other.

The Icarian's skull splinters and the Fae leaps back, circling me.

Then he dances close, scoring slices with his pretty blade, landing a kick on my jaw moments later.

I stagger back and bend like Tleia does when she panics, letting my braids drape over my face as I groan. He darts close and I grab his pointed ear then slam him face first into the ground, bringing my heel down on his neck with a crunch.

"Behind you!" Hathur shouts. "They have reserves!"

He sounds too cheerful. But then, I'm hardly winded. A puny roar sounds behind me and I wince in second-hand embarrassment. A half-Orc, ax raised, charges. I meet his blow with mine, metal clanging, each seeking an opening.

Feigning a stumble, I lure him close, dubious the same trick will work twice.

He rushes in, eager for the kill. Uther would not stop shouting for days if I fell for such a tactic.

I drop my ax and seize his tusks, using his own momentum to flip him over onto his back, hammer several punches at his face then grab his face and twist, snapping his neck.

"Follow Tleia!"

I rise, whipping around to glance at Hathur. He's running toward the stadium entrance and I follow, heart thudding.

Icarians swoop down and hover as ground guards surround us, weapons drawn.

I drop my ax and raise my hands. "I'd like to register as a claimant," I say politely.

The Icarian female who'd spoken to Lei'a lands. "There's paperwork."

I don't sneer at her—Icarians do nothing without documenting it, then documenting their documentation. In triplicate. "Yes, mistress. There always is."

The Fae guard marches me to the appropriate station and

I get in line, which is much shorter than it is for those who wish to offer themselves.

The Human orderly eyes me, but slides a thin, ancient tablet in my direction and begins to explain terms and conditions.

No one seems to care blood and brain matter covers me.

Certainly Tleia will insist I bathe as soon as we are done, however.

———

## TLEIA

As I run to the stadium entrance, the two people posted beckon and usher me inside.

"There's always is a handful of contested entries each sess," one of them says cheerfully. "Keeps the guards on their toes, don't ya know."

The other one points. "That way for food line. An orderly will come inside to process you."

"There's an Orc coming for me whose contract I want to accept."

"We saw. You have fun with that, mistress. No fighting inside the stadium." He drones a series of other rules.

I nod my thanks and walk in the direction they indicate. I've forgotten one of the perks of the Sorting is that while the entrants wait the three days the event allows for people to sign up and enter the stadium, the entrants are fed, watered, and provided with a place to sleep at a fire.

I listen to the bored orderly who catches up to me repeat a list of rules, my heart rate slowing as the immediate threat is gone.

Unfortunately, that means I have time to worry. About Ethan—though I assume he's with Hathur—about Gethen. Though clearly he can handle himself.

I chuckle as I accept a plate. "Don't mind me," I tell the man who hands me the food. "It's been a long few weeks."

He nods and I move along, eat, take my place by the fire, then there's nothing else to do but worry, and wait.

Half an hour later the gong sounds, and the immortals enter the stadium.

## TWENTY-SIX

COMMON SENSE TELLS ME TO REMAIN STILL AND LET GETHEN find me, but I must be more upset than I thought because I immediately begin searching faces for him.

There are Aeddannari, Icarians, other Uthilsen Orcs. A handful of Humans who've either bribed their way into being granted the opportunity to offer contracts, or who act as proxies for other immortals.

I'm waylaid once or twice by other Orcs, considering the identifying necklace I wear around my neck. I rip it off and drop it onto the ground, heart in my throat because I don't see his face.

Finally I stop searching, nausea beginning to swirl in the pit of my stomach because it's possible the worst has happened.

I just. . .assumed he would be fine. He's a warrior; I've

watched him fight, and he has incentive to win. It never occurred to me he could be defeated.

Panic unfurls as I begin to bend and rest my hands on my knees, when there's a rough voice behind me.

"Tleia!"

I straighten and whirl, then beeline towards him, flinging myself at the Orc who holds his arms open, lifting me as I bury my face in his neck and wrap my legs around his waist.

He's covered in blood, but I've never minded blood except for the scent. I don't like the scent. But right now I don't care, my hands in his hair tugging at the tangled locks and thin braids because I need to punish him for worrying me.

"Are you hurt?" I manage to ask. "Are you hurt?"

He chuckles in my ear. "Barely even fair fight. Not hurt, Lei'a."

Gethen's arms tighten, then slowly loose and I slide down his body until I'm on my feet again, looking up at him.

The smile on his face fades. "Can't leave unless accept contract."

I shake my head impatiently. "I don't care about that. I'll sign your stupid contract. I'm already yours."

He lifts me again into his arms, turns and strides out of the stadium.

The paperwork.

I wonder about a people who feel the need to document everything. Some things are best left in one's head, where the only witness against you is your mouth if you're foolish enough to open it. Our son waits for us so we agree to the standard contract but amend to be altered at a later date. Gethen barely reads it, and I know he can read.

Once that is done, we meet up with Hathur outside the stadium boundaries.

"So you got your man," a feminine voice calls out.

I look up at the whoosh of air as the Icarian guard, Kore, lands. She arches a brow at me. "Did you read the contract?"

"Our contract," I tell her, "was written in blood many years ago." I smile. "I read it."

"No do overs." She lifts off the ground then, laughing, and we leave.

We skirt the fairgrounds and as we pass by tents, I notice the spot where Mysterri's had been. She's gone.

On the outskirts of the grounds, we meet up with my new neighbors.

"Mommy!" Ethan shouts.

The men had assured me he was well protected, and looking at the dozen plus bristling Orcs who surround a caravan of wagons, I relax.

Then turn to my son, who is being swung down from a wagon and put on his feet so he can run towards me.

"Mommy, Pa, where were you," he demands in a voice pitched high in borderline distress.

I drop to my knees and open my arms, gathering him close. I blink away tears because I know that for him, once again I disappeared unexpectedly. Here with strangers, even if they do look like his paternal kin, he must have been afraid.

"Mommy and Pa and Cousin had to run some errands," I say. "Were you a smart boy? Did you make friends?"

"Were you obedient?" Gethen asks.

We clearly have different survival philosophies.

"I got one toy, Mommy."

"Oh, surely we can do better than that." I stand, lifting him in my arms and turn to Gethen who gives me an odd, sidelong look, then transfers that look to Ethan, who burrows his face against my chest. Is Gethen penny pinching again? "I have money."

Hathur coughs.

"We don't want to encounter any other friends, Tleia," Gethen says. "Maybe next time?"

He has a point.

"When we get home, we'll make inquires," I tell my son, "and we will buy you many toys."

Gethen says nothing. His silence is loud, but I decide to ignore him. If he has something to say, he knows how to use his multi-lingual vocabulary.

———

Ethan and Gethen enjoy traveling, especially with a caravan of Orcs. I'm enjoying it less, not because of the company, though that's also somewhat of a trial.

The Orc women keep asking personal questions as if nosiness is an accepted species trait, but I'm reluctant to outright lie. Orcs, the women especially, ignore polite deflection.

"They're curious," Gethen tells me.

I sigh, because he's probably right.

Gethen cradles me in his arms at the evening fire. Camp is set up for the night and sentries assigned. Sitting between his legs, I lean my back against his chest, his embrace a comforting prison. Ethan is playing dice with Hathur and two other Orcs—learning all manner of colorful language— his small face somber as he crouches. He truly thinks he's grown. He's only almost four.

Gethen nuzzles the side of my face and places his lips next to my ear.

"Stop plotting against our neighbors," he says.

"I'm not plotting."

"Lei'a. I know you. Only this sweet when think you might have to arrange for someone's death."

"Allegedly. You've never actually proved I was involved in—"

"Always thought it adorable you think I don't know when you lie. Which, in spirit of honesty, is eighty percent of the time. Other twenty percent I'm not paying attention."

"Darling, what you don't know for certain can never be held against me. Or you." There are certain things I won't never confirm, best friend and son's father or not. Not really for my sake, but for his.

"You don't have to protect me anymore, Lei'a." He bites my earlobe, blowing a stream of warm breath into the canal and I shudder, letting my eyes drift closed.

"Ethan," Gethen rumbles. "Your mother is cold. Bring her a blanket."

"It's summer, Gethy."

"I don't want you to catch a chill," he croons.

He's up to something. I watch my son, who rises obediently and walks to our tent, disappearing inside.

"I see you finally mastered the time-honored tradition of using your small child as an errand runner."

"Every soldier starts at the bottom and works their way up."

Someone near us snorts. I agree.

Ethan emerges with a blanket and hands it off to Gethen, who pats his head and sends him back to Hathur, then drapes the blanket around me like a cloak, tucking the edges behind my back. His arms, most specifically his hands, remain concealed beneath.

Like I thought.

Gethen begins a conversation with the neighbor sitting a polite distance from us. At the same time, my Orc slides a hand under the waistband of my pants and cups my mound. He pauses.

I understand the assignment.

"Child's play," I murmur.

"A challenge," he returns just as quietly as his fingers touch my clit and begin to rub.

I lean my head against his shoulder and close my eyes, pretending to drift off. "What's the forfeit when you lose?"

"Are you certain I will?"

"The forfeit, Gethen."

"If I lose, I'll let you tie me up and ride my mouth."

Someone next to us coughs. Perhaps it's the smoke from the fire.

"And if you lose—" Gethen continues against my ear.

"Don't think there're any losers in this game," Someone mutters.

We ignore them.

"Then you'll invite Defne and Ratha and Ilotha for tea when we arrive home," Gethen says.

"Never mind," Someone says. "There clearly is one loser."

I freeze. "Why can't you be normal and ask for a perverted sexual favor?"

"I agree," Someone adds.

"Are you joining the bet?" I ask them. "Throw down your stakes, or hush."

They hold up their hands, and mime zipping their mouth closed.

"Prepare to learn how to bake bread," Gethen growls, and begins to finger me with all due seriousness.

His movements are subtle enough that no one who didn't overhear the bet would know what he's up to—if I maintain my composure.

He's determined, but I have a vested interest in winning.

I bite into my bottom lip, savoring the small pain. "What are you trying to prove?" My voice is too deep, too breathy, too broken. I begin to shift in his arms, my legs restless, and I tighten my muscles.

"Only that I'm well trained," he says, a teasing note in his gravelly voice. "But not well behaved."

I have to chuckle, though it's more of a gasp. Gethen is

about as poorly behaved as a salmon is blue. "The lessons you learned from the luscious widow Salkoya?"

He bites my earlobe again, then trails his lips down my neck. Careful because of the tusks, and the teeth aren't entirely dull either. "She's waiting to meet you."

"I'm sure you told her all about me," I growl. It's to cover a high-pitched whine that tries to escape my throat the more his fingers work me.

"Oh, fu. . ." I cut the Gaithean expletive off before it escapes my mouth, but if he's a stickler for technicalities, then I've lost the bet.

A moment later I come against his fingers, blood flooding my mouth as I gnaw on my lip to keep from crying out.

"Think it's a draw," Someone murmurs. "Might try that game with the wife when I get home. She always says I need to be more adventurous."

## TWENTY-SEVEN

I'VE BEEN CARRYING ETHAN FOR THE LAST TWENTY MINUTES because he decided the only way he can nap is if I hold him. I'd hopped out of the covered wagon Gethen, Hathur, Ethan and I share because I'm thoroughly sick of the rocking motion. Literally sick. My thighs and calves don't burn as much anymore, and my endurance has improved in the last weeks of travel.

But carrying an almost forty-pound child proves that I'm not in as good condition as I was stupidly hoping.

"Don't you want to walk?" I ask Ethan for the twentieth time.

He shakes his head. At least he's not asking to nurse. Gethen and I are waging a battle, using bribery to lure Ethan away from his comfort chewing. He's half Orc and could go for another year or two, but I'm tired of it.

I want my breasts back.

Gethen trots towards me from the front of the caravan. Ethan and I walk in the protected middle.

"I'll take him," he says, holding out his arms.

I try to shove Ethan towards his father, but the little arms around my neck tighten and he shrieks in protest. "Want Mommy!"

"I have crickets," Gethen says in a cajoling tone.

I grind my teeth, but at this point I'm desperate enough to hand him over that I don't protest. It's not as if I have to watch them happily munching on the insects. I can look the other way, and frequently do—this reminds me to make Gethen wash his mouth out before he kisses me so I don't accidentally get a little insect leg. One of the Orc women tried to convince me to eat one of the salted bugs, and I almost slapped her.

As the pitch of Gethen's voice goes increasingly higher as he abandons dignity to negotiate with a child, my impatience begins to take me somewhere dark where I consider denying my son supper to teach him the consequences of trying to bully me with his tears.

I'm about to start issuing threats when the caravan slows. There's a rumble of the usual evening conversation as a campsite is chosen, scouts deployed to secure our perimeter, and tasks for the evening are agreed on.

Oddly enough, as a nursing mother I'm not expected to do much besides sit out of the way and tend to my son, but I'd rather do chores.

"Enough of this," I snap, and shove Ethan at Gethen. "Just take him."

Ethan shrieks again but I don't care.

I turn on my heels—determined to find something to do that's productive enough Gethen won't drag me back to coddle his little hellhound—when a sudden cry goes out.

I whirl, dash back towards Gethen who tosses Ethan at me and whips out his ax.

I run to our covered wagon and push Ethan inside, crawling in after him and snatching up a rope I'd secured to the wagon and tying it around Ethan's waist. He's jumped out of the moving wagon before when I drifted off into a nap, enough times that I decided tying him down was warranted. If I have to leave the covered wagon to help the warriors, I need to know my child won't try to throw himself into the fray.

"We're under attack," I tell him, staring into his eyes and crouching down so we're level. "Remember prison yard fight rules?"

He nods, resting his back against the wagon. "Stay out of the way, stay quiet, don't try to help Mommy."

"Good boy." I grab his stuffed Orcling and hand it to him. "This is fight yard rules, Ethan. Stay here. I'm going to go help Pa."

His expression is too flat for an almost four-year-old, but there's no time to mourn that lost aspect of his innocence. I scramble out of the wagon, pause to assess the situation, and grab the bag of charms underneath my shirt.

It's organized chaos. Monsters emerge from the shadows of the evening forest as shrieks and howls fill the air.

The Orcs form a loose perimeter, defending our

campsite. Gethen roars, swinging his massive ax at a chameleon like creature who swoops down from above, it's snake like tail lashing.

"Watch the skies!" he yells.

A trio of monsters descend on Gethen, other clusters attacking. I've been told the magic and radiation twisted creatures in this forest are smart, I just hadn't believed it.

But I prepared anyway.

A grizzly bear twice the normal size with quills running down its back swipes vicious claws at Gethen. It roars, an odd coughing squeal at the end.

I run towards Gethen, the first charm I extract warming in the palm of my hand. I feel the etched symbol with the pad of my thumb and whisper the activation word, wait until I have an opening, and throw it.

"Gethen, spike charm spike charm!" I scream.

He disengages from an elk with bloody antlers and tentacles where its nostrils should have been, leaping away just as my charm strikes the ground in front of the monsters attacking him, and activates.

Spikes erupt from the ground under their feet. The charm has a six-foot radius and Gethen barely cleared it.

I head toward a female warrior battling a skinless squirrel with a long, venomous stinger on its tail. It strikes, fast and agile but she's as quick, hissing at it while it chitters at her.

"Eat my ax, you overgrown naked mole rat!" she shouts as it strikes.

She's enjoying herself, and that won't do because she's needed elsewhere.

"Stop playing," I snap, "we've got bigger hairless squirrels to fry."

My only charm that's not single use is the one that activates into a long knife, and I withdraw that now and start to head towards her when Gethen shouts.

"Tleia, drop!"

I drop to the ground, rolling blindly, my instinct to evade an unknown threat taking over my muscles. It's been decades since I've been in a fight in the streets, but trauma never forgets.

Fire rakes down my arm as a wolf with giant fangs—the most normal looking of the creatures who's attacking us—is trying to tear out my throat. I scream, having lifted my arms to cover my face, pulled my knees up and kicked out, no stranger to being thrown on my back and attacked by something more dangerous than me.

But Gethen is there, his ax biting into the wolf's side. It releases my arm and leaps over me towards Gethen, who meets its attack with contempt.

The speed at which he kills the wolf shocks me, but my arm is on fire, blood dripping down in the steady rivulet. He's at my side a minute later, helping me up and ushering me towards the wagon.

"What were you thinking?" he snarls. "You were told not to fight!"

I'm shaking, with pain and fear and adrenaline. "I don't want anyone to die if I can help."

"You can help by staying alive and protecting our son," he says, pushing me into the wagon. Gethen hesitates, his eyes on my arm, then he swears.

I shake my head. "You know I can handle a flesh wound, go."

He takes me at my word and disappears.

I set myself to pulling out a stash of medical supplies, distantly realizing the adrenaline running through my body is keeping me from feeling most of the pain, but also keeping me from feeling most of anything at all. I listen to the sounds of the fight outside of the wagon, tensing whenever one comes too close.

"Mommy, can I move now?" Ethan asks.

I glance at him as I begin to rinse out the wound while holding my arm over the basin. There's nothing to indicate there was poison in the wolf's mouth, but there were plenty of germs. Gaithea may not have labs anymore, but we haven't lost all of our scientific knowledge.

"Do you want to watch me stitch up the wound?" I ask, my voice shaking but calm.

His eyes alight with curiosity, but his bottom lip trembles. "Does it hurt?"

"A little, but that's fine. Pain tells you something is wrong. Come watch, and one day I'll let you try too."

It's the only thing I can think of to lance the potential trauma of the situation, to turn it into a lesson. I dredge up the strength to at least smile at him as he crawls closer and settles next to me.

The slashes are deep enough to warrant stitches, and I

down half a bottle of strong brandy before gritting my teeth and beginning to poke the needle through my skin.

This is also something I haven't had to do for several decades, at least until I went to prison.

The sounds of the battle lesson, and a shout goes up giving instructions to chase down the monsters who fled, leaving no enemy at our backs.

More scouts are dispatched, and I hear scattered discussions regarding wounds and whether to maintain the evening's campsite or move along. From what I glean, an attack like this isn't uncommon, and if there are no deaths then it's not considered an emergency.

I untie Ethan after I'm done binding my arm and let him climb into my lap, carefully holding my arm off to the side so he doesn't accidentally bump it. Bound, it's a dull throbbing pain and I finish off the alcohol for good measure.

I'm trying to distract him from his usual comfort mechanism when Gethen crawls back into the wagon, a deep wooden bowl of food in his hand.

He settles down in front of us, crossing his legs, and gives Ethan a solemn look. "Did you help Mother tend her wound?"

"I holded her stuff," he says. "Next I can do the needle too."

Gethen nods. "We will teach you to sew soon. Here, are you hungry? Let Mother eat first."

I demur, having no appetite, and watch my son eat.

The bowl has several rolled balls of animal fat mixed with dried fruit, dried meat, and various herbs and seasonings.

There's also flatbread, a handful of foraged nuts, and some hard travel cheese. I used up the water we had in the wagon to wash my wound, so Gethen leaves then returns shortly later with two more flagons.

I wouldn't mind another few shots of whiskey, but my edges are already dulled, and this night calls for sobriety in case there's another attack. Which reminds me.

I look at Gethen and hesitate. "One of the charms is for a ward."

He nods. "May we use it? In two days, will be in clan controlled lands and the creatures won't breach our borders. If we're going to be attacked again, it may be tonight."

I fish out in the ward, leaving Ethan to his meal, and walk the perimeter of the camp with Gethen to activate the charm and set the magical barrier.

"Go back to the wagon," he tells me when we're done.

I face him. He's been terse, almost cold since he brought us food. This isn't Gethen's normal after battle demeanor. Normally, he's giddy.

"What's wrong?"

He gives me a long look, then turns, saying over his shoulder, "I'm going to gather wood. Go back to the wagon, Tleia."

Wood?

I don't think so.

I catch up with him in three steps, grabbing his forearm.

In a second he switches our grip, so his hand is wrapped around my uninjured arm and the other, the back of my neck. It happens so fast, I don't have time to startle, but the press of his fingers is not gentle.

He squeezes, slowly, then lets go, looking down at me.

"Let me gather wood, Tleia," he says quietly, turns and walks into the forest.

This time, I don't follow.

But that doesn't last long.

## TWENTY-EIGHT

I HUNT DOWN HATHUR AND PUT HIM IN CHARGE OF ETHAN, then gather blankets and go after Gethen.

If he really doesn't want to talk to me, I'll leave him alone, but I can count on one hand the number of times during the years we've known each other that that was the case. Talking is the cornerstone of our relationship. Talking, daydreaming, reading, arguing. No matter what it is, there are always words between us.

The last few weeks have been off because most of our words were geared towards survival, and of course we have a child now. We've been separated for three years, and we've had to get back into a rhythm. But Gethen has never stonewalled me, and I'm not about to let him start now.

"The problem," I say several minutes later, stopping enough distance away that he can't pull that fast grab trick of his again, "is that we've always talked to each other when we were upset. Why are you shutting me out?"

I drop the blankets to the ground in a pile.

He turns to me, eyes narrowed, his expression that of a man suppressing foul curses. "I need some time alone, Tleia."

"If that were true, then I'd give you time alone." I walk towards him. "But it's not time alone you need. It's your hands around my throat."

I watch unironically as his fingers flex, then still.

"What are you mad at me about? Don't lie. You're a terrible liar."

A sardonic smile curves one corner of his mouth, then fades. "I've gotten better."

"Darling, not that much better."

I close another few feet between us, and halt. We're still inside the ward's perimeter, within earshot of the campsite but there's enough visual privacy, and if we speak in quiet voices, no one will hear us either.

"Talk to me. We've paid too dear a price to get to this point."

"Fine."

He steps towards me, and I instinctively stiffen. I'm not afraid he'll hurt me, but every man is capable of aggression and Gethen's riding the wave of that fight. His cheeks are still darkened with color, his dark eyes bright.

Another step.

I don't think he'll hurt me. But I think he wants to put those hands around my neck and take my breath.

I recognize the look in his eyes.

Fucking in place of violence.

"We had an agreement, Tleia." His voice is restrained.

"What agreement?"

"If there was an attack, you would take Ethan and go to the wagon and stay. You wouldn't try to fight."

"Oh. That agreement."

"Does your word mean nothing to you?" True anger in his voice now.

I hesitate. I don't want to lie to him—I should, for the sake of peace—and I also know the truth is more complicated than me breaking a promise.

"I know I said I would stay out of the fighting," I say. "That was my intent. But—"

"There are no buts when you make a promise. How many times do I have to tell you this?"

I frown, tilting my head back because there's no space between us now. "If you say so, Uther. But I have the charms, and I knew I could help without getting myself killed."

"Almost got your throat ripped out!" he roars, restraint gone.

"None of the other women retreated to the wagons."

As soon as I say that I know it's a weak argument. All of the other women are weapons trained, and I am not. Not really.

"I'm sorry," I say finally. "The charms are keyed to me, no one else can use them. What do you expect me to do?"

"Expect you to follow orders. The charms will keep. Your life won't if you get yourself killed. What if a monster had slipped behind us and gotten to Ethan?"

"I thought about that. But a monster could've slipped past you and attacked both of us."

"That," he says through gritted teeth, "would have been the appropriate time to use a charm."

"Not in an enclosed space, Gethen! I'd get both of us killed. Gethy, you can't wrap me in cotton wool—"

He grabs my shoulders and shakes me. "And if that's what I want to do?" He's shouting now. "If what I need is to wrap you in cotton wool for a few hellsdamn years? Don't you think I'm tired of seeing you hurt?"

Gethen kisses me, more an expression of frustration than desire. I know it's coming, and I brace.

My wound should hurt more than it does when I lift my arms to tangle my hands in his hair, holding his ravaging lips against mine. I should be in more pain; I should be more alert as the not distant sounds of the camp fade from my focus. I should be more everything, but right now all I want is Gethen. It's been too long, and we've waited, and waited, and in the aftermath of the battle when once again I could have lost him, all I need is to feel his mouth on me, his hands on me, his body inside me.

I try to tug him down to the pile of blankets I dropped.

He resists at first, pulling away with a curse. "Now is not the time."

"We're alive, the camp is warded and Ethan is safe. I need you." I'm shaking now, tears pricking my eyes and instead of regathering my aplomb, I let the tears leak down. "Why do you make me beg you? Is it revenge?"

"No, Lei'a." He gathers me up in his arms again, holding

me tight, but careful of my wound. "No revenge." Gethen
closes his eyes for a moment, then opens them. "I want to fall
on you like a beast. But you deserve a man to touch you
gently for once."

Head tilted back slightly, I study his expression. "Are you
afraid you'll hurt me? You already know how much. . ." abuse
would be the wrong word to say right now ". . .rough
handling I can take."

His mouth firms. "Not from me." He turns away from me.
"Please, go back to the wagon."

"You know I don't mind." My voice is soft. "You know I'll
take you any way I can have you. You don't have to hold back
with me."

His laughter is bitter, but there's genuine amusement in
it. "You're Human, Tleia. I'll always hold back with you. On a
normal day, this is no problem. But the last few weeks have
been—"

"Why don't you let me worry about what I can and
cannot take? Do you think I chased you out here after weeks
of abstinence, moments after battle, and didn't know what I
would be getting if I poked a monster?"

His shoulders stiffen. I almost have him.

I close the distance between us, running my hands up his
muscled back, settling on his neck and beginning to massage
the tension out of him.

"You already know I'm not a woman who wants to make
love. I'm a woman who wants to fuck."

He turns so fast I jump, but his hands are gripping my

waist, holding me still. "And I'm a man who wants to fuck. Do you understand? That's all I want right now."

I roll my eyes to make my point. "It's almost as if you think you're talking to a young, blushing virgin. I was a professional sex worker, Gethen. Believe me, I understand."

In a way, it's kind of adorable that he treats me like some sort of debutante when really he wants to treat me the exact opposite.

It hits me then. "You're afraid you'll be like all the others. And you don't want to be."

He rears back as if I struck him.

I laugh.

His nostrils flare, and he actually snarls at me.

"No, no, I'm not laughing at you. Not really. It's only. . .Gethen. You couldn't be like them if you tried. I *love* you. That makes all the difference in the world."

The more I think about it, the funnier it is, and I've needed a good laugh, so I indulge myself.

He lets that go on for about thirty seconds before he's lifting me into his arms, striding towards the blanket and lowering me down.

"I warned you," he growls. "I should spank you for laughing at me."

I slide my arms around his neck, wincing a little at the pain from my wound. "You're so cute, Gethy. No wonder why I spoil Ethan. He's just like you. So cute and adorable and sweet and cuddly."

Gethen is staring down at me, his eyes steadily darkening.

"None of those adjectives will be in your head when I'm done fucking the breath out of you."

"Oh? You're still all talk."

He presses his body into mine, his weight almost too heavy. He could crush me, crack my bones, truly suffocate me, and I feel the tremble through his body, the tension as he still keeps himself from doing just that.

Gethen lowers his head, brushing his lips against mine. I open my mouth, accepting him, and his tongue slides inside.

In a second the pace of the kiss changes. I run my hands up and down his chest, down his shoulders and muscled arms as his mouth conquers mine. A hand sliding into my hair, he tilts my head this way or that, controlling the angle so he can take what he wants, and the kiss goes on so long I have to pull away to breathe.

He whispers something harsh against my skin as he lowers his head to the curve of my neck.

"Give up," I say.

The last of his restraints shatter, and he's stripping the clothing from my body, slowing only when he's handling my shirt to make sure he doesn't cause any more pain. He yanks down his leather trousers to free his cock then his hands are on my ankles, spreading my legs wide, pushing them up and draping them over his shoulders.

"Will probably regret this, but it's too late, Tleia." He locks his eyes with mine, lines his cock up to my entrance, and shoves inside.

"Gethen!" I arch my back, my nails digging into his

shoulders. "Wait, wait." My body isn't quite ready, my opening still tight.

"No wait. Warned you."

He shifts, pulls out, then pushes back in. I shut my mouth because he's right, he did warn me and I underestimated the warning, which is my fault.

His girth—I knew from having him in my mouth that when the time came the initial entry would be difficult. I was roaring drunk the night Ethan was conceived; clearly I forgot the important details.

My body scrambles to stretch and open for him; it's painful. "Gethy, please." I don't know what I'm begging him for, but from the flare in his eyes, I know he likes it.

Pain edges pleasure as he slams into me over and over again, his heavy sacs slapping against my bottom with each thrust.

"Hands and knees," he says hoarsely, pulling out long enough for me to obey him.

Strong fingers wrap around my hips in a punishing grip as he pushes inside me again with a guttural groan.

I collapse to the ground, taking the weight off my arms and lay pliant beneath him as he ruts.

He yanks my head back, his fingers now in my hair, and he says, "Quiet, female. They'll think I'm killing you."

"You are killing me."

I can feel him in my stomach, feel the strength of the warrior above me, taking my body with a brutality I truly hadn't thought Gethen capable of.

He shifts his hips, maneuvers me so the angle is different,

and suddenly I *am* screaming. His cock hits my internal spot in a relentless rhythm. If I wasn't willing, if I didn't love him, if my body wasn't already on the brink of orgasm, this would be torture.

I crash into the orgasm, my entire body shattering with the force of the release.

"You truly are a brute," I rasp. "You fuck like you're single-handedly assaulting a fortress. No sophistication at all."

Gethen laughs. The more sophisticated a man, I've always said, the less able he is to make a woman come. I've never needed much foreplay when I at least marginally liked the man in my bed. With Gethen, I need none.

I whine as he pulls out because it's like having a battering ram that was going full speed between my thighs try to unwedge itself. I'm pulsing in the aftermath, and I'll probably feel him inside me for the next twenty-four hours.

"I'll make it up to you," he murmurs, stroking my hair, my back, my bottom.

When his mouth settles between my thighs, his tongue beginning a long, languorous lick, I shudder again.

He more than makes it up to me.

## TWENTY-NINE

"WAKE UP, BABY," I SAY, GENTLY SHAKING ETHAN'S SHOULDER. He's curled in the wagon, fast asleep, but I'd promised I'd wake him as soon as we were home.

It takes time to finally process that we *do* have a home; I hadn't let myself believe.

Until now.

He sits up, blinking away sleep, and raises his arms. Lifting him, I turn to Gethen, who's exiting the house after doing a quick interior search.

The cottage is sparsely furnished but cozy, lit by candles that flicker in the sea breeze drifting through open windows.

"The beach is a mile from here," Gethen says for the tenth time, hovering in the doorway.

"We'll have to teach Ethan to swim," I reply—also for the tenth time.

We're being careful, neither of us wanting to mar this

first moment. As I enter the house, setting Ethan on his feet, Gethen lets me explore in silence.

The fireplace in the main room looks as if it's only for warmth since there's a small kitchen through an open doorway. The wooden floors are swept clean, but bare.

I wander into the kitchen, inspect the pantry and a small mudroom with fishnets, harpoons for whale hunting I presume, baskets, tools and foul-weather gear hung from pegs on the walls.

The kitchen contains a dry sink, open cupboards stacked with pots and dishes, an oak table with benches. Glancing out the window, I see a pitcher pump which I assume is our source of fresh water.

"Not much," Gethen says once I've inspected the bedrooms. "Sent word ahead and the others offered what could. Have budget for you to select furniture and things."

"Save your money. I'll buy the furnishings." Mostly so he has no say in how I decorate.

Gethen crosses his arms over his chest, giving me a look. "Not so poor, Lei'a."

"It won't feel like my home if I don't contribute."

He nods after a moment. "Don't spend all your money."

"I have no intention of doing so." Especially since I've spent the trip interrogating Hathur about the businesses in the community and pinpointed a glaringly obvious missing service.

I'm going to open a brothel.

It will be quite respectable, with clean, well-trained professionals and a selection of locally crafted beers—wines imported from the City—and a small menu. Perhaps evening entertainment, though I'm dubious what talent the community can provide.

But Gethen doesn't need to know all of that right now, especially since I expect he'll object, rather strenuously.

That's going to be an interesting discussion.

"You see bathroom?" Gethen demands.

He begins rambling on about pipes, drains, valves and pumps and how it all connects to the homestead's well, starting in Gaithean and sliding into Uthilsuven. I listen enough to make sure that means we have running water and a flushing toilet, then I let my mind drift.

He leads me out back next, though we both keep an ear out for Ethan, who's dragged a chair up to the kitchen counter and is happily extracting the meager contents of the cupboards. I expect he'll drag the pots and plates outside into the dirt soon enough, which doesn't bother me at all. It will keep him occupied.

But as I cast my gaze around, I realize there's no way currently to keep him contained. "We need a fence. A tall one, with a strong, complicated lock."

Gethen glances at me, and we share a look of understanding. He grimaces. "Maybe a leash," he mutters.

"These are garden beds?" I ask, eyeing the neat rows of freshly turned over ground. "It looks like someone's been here."

"Hathur sent word ahead to ready the cottage. Female's circle clean, male's circle tend to beds." He pauses. "When decide what plants you want, they donate seed. Newlywed gift."

There's something odd about the way he says the Gaithean word for newlywed. I glance at him. "What, you don't want to marry me?"

Fascinated, I watch his cheeks darken in a blush. He crosses his arms over his chest again, avoiding my gaze and says nothing. I don't know what that's all about, but I suppose he'll tell me when he's ready. I don't particularly care if he marries me or not.

"Is my name on the deed to this house?"

Gethen rolls his eyes. "Only Icarians worry about paper. House mine. Tleia mine. So house yours. All know it."

"I think I'd like a piece of paper, properly filed with the local authorities, if it's all the same to you."

Gethen approaches then swings me up into his arms and twirls me around, nuzzling my neck. "Suspicious female. Don't trust me at all?"

"Of course I trust you." I pat his chest. "But business is business, my love."

I need that piece of paper as collateral to open my brothel.

But again, there's no need for him to know all of that yet.

"Like house, Tleia?" he asks, looking at me through his lashes, adorably uncertain for a man his age and size.

This isn't the time to tease so I smile, cupping his face in my palm. "I adore the house. Once I'm done with it, it will be perfect. We can build on if we need extra room."

His expression brightens. "Are you pregnant?"

"No, Gethen, I am not. I was thinking more like a library or a parlor. Not a nursery."

"Oh."

I eye him, resigned to his train of thought. Of course he wants more children. He didn't have to birth the one that already came feet first into the world.

"You know," I say, "you haven't gotten me a push present."

He frowns. "What is this?"

"Allow me to explain."

———

**GETHEN**

There will be no sleep for me tonight. Because I am awake listening to Tleia breathe, my son next to her, I see the flash of movement outside my bedroom window.

I rise from bed, taking care not to disturb the small ones, and leave the house.

An Orc stands twenty feet outside the front door, facing in the direction of the ocean. His shoulders are broad, heavily muscled, and scars stripe his back that are hundreds of years older than I. He's wearing his hair below his shoulder blades now, the top half a mess of thin braids, the bottom half left free.

He turns, and I stare into the rough hewn face of the man I call uncle, but who I think of as father.

"Commander," I say.

He stares at me, expressionless, then a smile cracks his

face. "You must've done something terrible indeed," he jokes. He speaks our original tongue with a fluidity I try to match. "Commander?"

His arms are crossed over his chest but he opens them now. Like I am Ethan, my son, I walk to my uncle and let him envelop me, inhaling his familiar scent.

"It's good to see you, boy. You brought home your female and son? They are well?"

I swallow and pull away, casting my gaze down. "They are, with little thanks to me."

"I'm certain that's not true." I don't look up. He sighs. "Come, tell me. Kathien will watch the house to ease your mind. We won't go far."

It's almost morning before I am done telling my uncle everything I excluded from the few letters I sent home over the years.

"I will not judge you," Uther says finally. "It's stupid to question the decisions of the soldier in the field in the heat of battle, when you're commanding from a comfortable distance away."

We're facing each other, sitting crosslegged in the sand, the ocean waves only inches away.

"Speak bluntly, Uncle. It's not like you to hem and haw like a merchant."

His brows lower as he stares at me. "I am not hemming and hawing," is the testy reply. "I'm telling you that I understand you made the best decisions you thought you could at the time."

"To allow Tleia to be raped and tortured for years while I

held an oath to my employer above the principle of protecting the one who was mine?"

He shakes his head. "She was another man's wife. You were right in that. You had no rights to do anything save what you were given the authority by her husband to do. Even if she told you what she wanted, she did not have the authority to absolve you of your oath."

"But I did have the authority to absolve me of my oath."

"And you have learned." He leans forward, clasping my shoulder. "These aren't lessons that can be taught around a bonfire, son. They must be lived. In the end, everything has worked out?"

I laugh bitterly. "She has nightmares. I don't think she realizes it. Panic attacks. She won't let our son wander more than a few feet away from us before she starts to lose her mind."

"None of that sounds egregious, son. You've never seen a soldier after a long, thankless battle. It takes years to heal from those scars, and sometimes the scar tissue still hurts. Can you handle that? That the cost of being with her is that sometimes when you look at her, you'll see your mistakes? That you'll see hers?"

"I can handle it."

He rises. "Then I suggest you get home in time to make breakfast for your female." He gives me a sidelong look, the corner of his mouth twisting up. "Will she take you to husband?"

I stand too, using the excuse of dusting sand off me to avoid the question. "I haven't discussed that with her."

Uther begins to chuckle. "She doesn't know our custom surrounding marriage proposals, does she?"

"I haven't discussed that with her."

"Well, leave it to the female's circle if you're too modest to bring it up." His expression softens, going distant. "I'll tell you about how Defne married me over a beer this week."

I smile. "Did she draw blood?"

"I wear my scar with pride. Ah, I almost forgot. Ratha and Ilotha are coming to greet Tleia this morning."

"Tueven's balls."

"So maybe on second thought, you don't want to be at the house when they come around."

## THIRTY

## TLEIA

"YOU LIKE SLEEP," AN UNFAMILIAR FEMININE VOICE SAYS. IT'S A rich, slightly raspy contralto with a faint Uthilsuven accent. "Know you're awake, City girl. But happy to play game with you."

I open my eyes and yawn, stretching my arms above my head and arching my back, the bed sheet sliding down to reveal my naked chest.

I smile up at the Orc woman. She's about typical for the female of the species. Dark green skin with yellow undertones, tall, well-toned shoulders and arms bared by a leather vest which also displays her chiseled abdomen— obviously she's never had a baby. The leather vest also barely covers her generous breasts, and I thought I was well-endowed. Her hair is long and dark and braided, tipped with beads, and she has a wide mouth with slightly smaller tusks than a typical male's, and inscrutable dark eyes. She has that quasi-immortal youthfulness which means she could be anywhere from one hundred to several hundred years old.

But since I think I know who she is, I know she's a first gen which puts her around four centuries of life plus. There's no telling how old she was when the dreadnought crashed.

"Good morning," I greet. "Now get the fuck out of my bedroom."

There's a chuckle from the threshold of the bedroom door. "Oh, we're going to like her. We're going to like her very much once we teach her civilized manners."

"Been a few years since we've had new Human," the Orc staring down at me says. "Defne was a little smarter."

"Pragmatic. Defne believes in picking her battles." The second Orc woman steps next to the one who still hasn't budged from my bedside, and looks down at me too.

Orc Two is leaner, a bit shorter, her skin a shade of medium green with gray undertones. Her hair is braided around her crown, and she wears a loose sleeveless tunic and pants instead of the older one's Warrior-Am-I leathers. "Do you believe in picking your battles, Tleia?"

Because both their gazes are fixed on me and I recognize the glint in their eyes, I decide to play with them a little. I push the sheet off my body and slowly spread my legs open, lowering my hand until my fingers rest lightly on my clit.

"It's morning, and I usually indulge myself before I rise," I say. "If you will not get the fuck out, well then, I guess you'll just have to watch me fuck."

The second Orc female frowns, then grabs the first's hand and jerks her out of the bedroom. "Hurry up," the second snarls.

My laughter chases them down the hallway.

I take my time because I might as well finish what I began.

When I enter my kitchen, Orc woman One is sprawled in a chair at the table, Orc woman Two hovering over her. Two aims a slight glare at my face as I saunter in.

"Relax," I say, "I have no designs on your wife. Ratha and Ilotha, I presume?" I dip into a curtsy that's perfectly done, and only slightly mocking.

Ratha lifts an eyebrow. "How know who we are?"

"Gethen has described you well enough over the years." My guess is they're here to drag me off to the female's circle, the community women who rule everything with a pussy.

No one rules me. I've already decided to abandon my usual tactics of seduction and ingratiating myself with potential enemies—I don't want to spend my life like that.

So we will start out as we mean to go on.

Ratha studies me. "And you are female he refused to leave."

"Stuck in that damn City too many years," Ilotha mutters. "Should come home a decade ago."

I frown. "Where are they?"

"Male and boy?" Ratha shrugs. "Told them to leave. This is female's circle business."

I fix her with an unfriendly stare. "I would appreciate if in the future you don't eject my man and my son out of our home."

Ratha begins to laugh. "Always thought Gethen would choose bunny rabbit. Soft, fluffy, big sweet eyes. Pet and coo over. But he brings home krutzve'e."

I finally take a seat at the table. "In his defense, he thought I was a fluffy bunny for quite a while." I cross my legs and my robe slithers open, revealing a line of thigh.

Ilotha scowls, moving closer to her wife.

I smile at her, slow and taunting. "If you had knocked, or better yet, if you had not come into my room uninvited while I was sleeping, perhaps even now your wife wouldn't be presented with such a temptation as I."

Ratha frowns. "Think highly of yourself."

"I'm realistic." But I decide to stop teasing Ilotha and straighten, adjusting my robe. I glance at the basket sitting on the table. There are wrapped loaves of bread, produce, a jug of milk and some other things. "Staples?"

Ratha nods. "Weren't certain when would arrive, so circle put together things to tide you over until can shop."

"What do I owe you?"

She bares her teeth. I drop the matter of debt.

"There *is* shopping here, correct?"

Ilotha runs her tongue over her teeth, eyeing me. "Not what you're used to, City girl."

I sigh. "Well, I was expecting to have to do something about that anyway. Did my son eat before you kicked him out without my permission?"

"Did, but if hungry, his father will take care of him."

"You don't ask if Gethen ate," Ilotha says.

"I don't mother grown men, darling."

Ratha stands abruptly. "Enough pleasantries. Let's talk business."

"By all means. Business."

"You signed a Sorting contract, and it's binding. But we have our own traditions. First—"

"Let her dress first," Ilotha says.

Ratha rolls her eyes, but I laugh and return to my bedroom.

———

". . .has role in community. All must work." Ratha squints at me. "Been warned about your lack of enthusiasm with weaponry."

I sip the tea I made after perusing the basket of supplies. Because I'm not a barbarian, I offered tea to the women as well as putting together a plate of sliced fruit and cheese. All very civilized.

"Not all of us can be warriors," I say.

"Then what you want to do?" Ratha demands.

I purse my lips. "I intend to contribute to the economy. I have connections in Seanna City—" I'll have to go through intermediaries, of course "—and funding to start a small business or two."

"Huh. What have in mind?"

"Nothing specific at this point." A lie, but I'll need to practice some diplomacy. "I need to tour the town square, meet the local homesteaders and everyone in the community. There's no rush. The key to starting a successful business is to find an untapped need." And sex is usually the most lucrative untapped need.

"Verhen is selling the tavern," Ilotha says. "It could use some updating. He's let it go to seed, which is a shame because if there's no evening bonfire there's not much else to do but fuck or fight."

That interests me. A tavern? I can do something with that. "Is the building sound?"

Ilotha shrugs. "It's old, but we live in the middle of a forest." She grins. "And there are youth and apprentices willing to charge a pittance for labor so they can practice their trade."

"Properly supervised, of course. Do we have a restaurant?"

The expression on Ratha's face is priceless, but Ilotha leans forward, eager. "We do not. Some of the locals who cook well sell dinners, but you have to ask around to see who has what and when. There's a bread wench who comes to market daily."

I tap the tabletop with my fingernail. "Sounds like there's some potential there." I smile at her. "Why don't you give me a tour of the community and tell me more about it, darling?"

This time it's Ratha who growls.

Oh, they are going to be so much fun. I hadn't expected to find a source of amusement so soon.

"Maybe should focus on setting up and keeping your house," Ratha says. "Our males are trained well enough, but they prefer the outdoor labor." She looks around in a slow, exaggerated motion. "See no servants here. This is farm. Not manor house."

Not yet, anyway.

"She don't look like much of a housekeeper, my one," Ilotha says.

I chuckle. "Oh, darling, I don't do manual labor. I barely even wash my own hair. There must be a youth or a placid young househusband willing to clean for coin."

"Not a female?" Ratha says.

"I prefer males."

"They're coming to clean your house, not lick your pussy."

"There's no reason not to enjoy a tolerable view," I purr. "And, please, don't put out any horrible rumors that I disdain females. I welcome anyone with skill."

Ilotha's brows lift. "Does Gethen know you're. . .like this? Mated Orcs are monogamous. He *did* tell you that?"

I laugh. And laugh. And laugh. I'm still laughing when my Orc hesitantly knocks on the kitchen door and sticks his head in.

"Ratha?" He says her name meekly, gaze lowered. "Defne ask for Tleia."

I stop laughing. "Where is my son?"

He blinks at me. "Sal'a has him."

"Salkoya?" I stand. "*You gave your mistress my son?*" I don't care that she fucked him years ago, I care that she might care that he's currently fucking me. Jealous women are demons.

"Calm down, City girl," Ilotha says. "She won't hurt the boy. We don't suffer child abusers to live."

"I don't know you. I don't know any of you." I feel panic begin to rise and don't know if I can stifle it without help. "Gethen! Bring him back."

His arms are around me a minute later as he sweeps me against his chest, murmuring in my ear. "It's all right, Lei'a. It's all right. Will go get him now. Forgive me." He hustles me out of the kitchen door.

Ratha and Ilotha follow, silent.

———

Salkoya is a perfectly boring widow who speaks to Gethen more like a favorite cousin than a former lover, and she's about as dangerous as Ethan's stuffed Orc. I note that after she introduces herself to me, she keeps a respectful distance from him, beckoning for Ethan to come greet his mother.

I clutch my wriggling son to me. He allows this for all of thirty seconds before he's pushing away to join the other children again. I rest on my knees, watching him, relearning how to breathe. The fear hadn't really been about her, especially now. It will take some time to trust these strangers with my son.

"It'll get better," a new voice says. I place the cadence —outlands.

A Human woman approaches, a slender girl at her side. They look like the old southern tribes, where my people are from the colder north. Dark eyes big and round where mine have more of a slope, long dark hair with a slight wave where mine is straight. Skin of birth rather than sun bronzed brown. The adult is taller than me, with the curvy figure of a well-fed housewife too, except her sleeveless shirt and fitted pants reveal the muscle of a girl who's always worked under the layer of feminine fat.

"I've been here two years, and I still don't like it when my daughter wanders too far," she continues. Her gaze is assessing. Not cold, but reserved with a contained, hard-bitten wariness that reminds me of the streets I grew up on.

I glance at the girl, who wanders off to join the other children, my gaze snagging on the—I blink. An *ahdramissi?* Why does a Human outland girl wear a Fae betrothal necklace? It's not a simple design, either.

The woman glances at Gethen, her expression flat but not unfriendly. "You're still here? Go talk to Uther. Ya got male's business to discuss." She glances once at my son, her eyes narrowing. "A bit overdue, too."

"I'll go get a pitcher of lemonade," Salkoya says and walks into the house. "We can sit outside and talk while the children play."

I watch, bemused, as Gethen slinks off at the command of this Human. "I'm a little disturbed at how easily other women order about my man, and how easily he obeys." Slowly, I rise. "I'm the female who holds his leash."

Three women face me, two Orcs, and the Human. Then the Human sighs. "Right. You're a live one, ain't ya? I'm Defne. The welcoming committee for female Humans who come through the Sorting. Let's talk."

"We'll discuss that leash," Ratha says, "and requirements to be one who holds it."

"Little late for that," Defne says. "He already knocked 'er up. I expect their circle will 'ave somethin' to say about that."

"This is why we don't let our males leave the community much," Ilotha says. "They start forgetting their home training."

"Is my son's existence a problem?" I ask. If this outland wench looks at Ethan askance one more time, I'll consider learning how to use a knife in a serious fashion.

"He'll make a fine father, Tleia," Salkoya says, emerging with a pitcher in one hand and a platter in another, cups tucked under her arm. I take the platter and put it on the table she indicates. "I tried to train him up as best I could— he was good with my girls and earned himself a fair name in bed. But, well, no telling what bad habits he picked up in the City. You send him my way if he needs a scolding."

"It's not the order in which we do these things," Ratha says, answering my original question as we settle around the table. "Babies before marriage. But you will make honest man of him. In time."

It sounds like a threat. "He hasn't asked me to marry him."

"Yeah," Defne says, picking up a cookie and shoving it in her mouth. "About that."

## THIRTY-ONE

*THREE MONTHS LATER*

GETHEN'S FINGERS ARE TWINED WITH MINE. IT'S BEEN OUR habit for the last few weeks to put Ethan to bed right after the sun goes down, then set up a nest of blankets outside and fall asleep talking and staring up at the stars.

Not that there isn't plenty of sex. His appetite is bottomless, and even I'm hard pressed to keep up with him some days.

But we do talk. Some things the mind forgets, but I've never forgotten how much I loved to talking to Gethen, how hidden and hurried our physical interactions had to be even though we never did more than hug.

If Herbert had found out. . .

I set aside those thoughts. Herbert's dead, and even though I can torture myself in endless loops about what might have gone wrong, I'm getting better at accepting that maybe I am suited to a normal life.

Boredom is an issue, though. Also, it's not as if I ever intended to settle down as a homesteader.

Gethen squeezes my hand. "Thoughts? Too quiet. I'm always scared when you're too quiet."

I smile then roll on my side and prop myself on my elbow, sliding a hand on his chest.

He turns his head to look at me, brows raised. "Lusty female. I need at least an hour before—"

He speaks as if I'm the one initiating these marathon sessions. "I'm not asking for round three." I pause. "We've been settling in well, I think. Ethan. . .I've never seen him so happy."

His skin is dark from all the sun, his eyes and cheeks bright with health. He's grown several inches taller and lost some of the baby fat in his face. He still wants to cuddle at my breast at night, but he doesn't ask to chew on me anymore.

Gethen draws a talon gently across my lips, his eyes soft. "Everything I want is here."

I give him a warm, sensual smile to reward his pretty words. "I want to open a business. What do you think?"

"What kind of business?"

"I've talked to Hathur a bit—"

He frowns at me. "Talk to Hathur first?"

"You've been busy."

Gethen sits up, eyes narrowed. "I'm never too busy for you. Why speak to Hathur? *What* business, Tleia?"

Sometimes I hate that he knows me so well.

"The community is small, and you've done a good job bringing in businesses to address basic needs as well as amenities. There's one glaring underserved opportunity I noted, however."

"What business, Tleia." His voice deepens, going smooth and cool.

"Well—as you know—I have a certain set of dearly paid for skills. It would be a shame to—"

"No." He rises to his feet.

I crane my neck to look up at him, leaning back on the palms of my hands. "You don't even know what I was going to say."

He pins me with a glare, crossing his arms over his chest. "Know you very well, Lei'a. No."

"Brothel. Small and tasteful, of course. A select number of diverse professionals and enthusiastic amateurs seeking a wilderness adventure, whom I will train well, and a handful of. . .local enthusiastic amateurs for clients where cost is a consideration—"

"No. Will not discuss this, Tleia."

He whirls and stomps away, giving me his back. Sometimes I wonder if he crosses his arms over his chest and slides his hands under his armpits like that because he's trying to prevent himself from strangling me. After all, there's not really anyone to stop him now.

If I could just get him to do that during sex. . .but he still shies away from fully letting go. He's still afraid of himself.

"Hear me out," I say. "It's a legitimate need in the

community. I've spoken with Hathur and Ratha enough to know that while sexual relationships outside of marriage here aren't frowned on, they're approached with extreme caution."

Gaithea doesn't have pharmaceutical birth control anymore—none of the immortals are interested in population control—and Orcs are family oriented. They believe in strong marriages and don't like when couples wed because of an accidental pregnancy. But professional sex workers are meticulous about the use of contraceptives. Not only to prevent pregnancy, but the spread of disease among Human clients.

"There's a need for sex workers, Gethen. We have the opportunity to set the standard for how the community handles such a business. With class and discretion."

I chatter on about my ideas, mostly to cover his ominous silence and give him time to calm. Sourcing locally made craft beers, ordering wines from all over the continent. Putting on regular evening entertainment, and opening the brothel to the families in the community several times a month for musical entertainment. I know I'll need buy in from the female's circle, but I'm thinking that once the women realize they can be serviced as well, their attitudes will change. A high quality, no strings attached fuck?

Put me on the waiting list. If I was single, that is.

"We won't accept married or partnered individuals as clients," I add, "unless they have consent from their partner. My establishment will not cater to cheaters. There will, of course, be a minimum age requirement."

Though, really, I'm of a mind that if young people are going to fuck—and they will—they should have the option to purchase their first experience from someone who knows what they're doing.

"We can even offer lessons. You know, teach these males how to find a clit so the older single women of the community don't have to shoulder the entire burden."

Gethen turns, fixes his gaze on me. "Are you unhappy with me, Tleia?"

"This isn't about you. This is about me wanting to use my skills to contribute to the community and make money. I need a life outside of this homestead, Gethen. You know me. Did you really expect I would—"

"No. But I thought we agreed we'd leave all of that filth behind us."

I give him an even look, despite the sting in his words. "Sex work is not filth."

He walks towards me, very slowly, his hands now at his sides. "You barely escaped that madness with your mind intact. You can't handle it. It's too much like our old life. You'll never let go of the memories. It will hurt you."

"Are you sure it's my hurt you're worried about, Gethy? Or yours?"

He stiffens. "What I'm not sure of is if one man between your thighs is enough for you. Maybe it took you so long to leave because—" he stops.

I can't speak, and I don't know how long passes before I manage to say something civil. "I don't have any other skills."

"Then learn new skills." He raises his voice, then forces it back down. "You are a mother, a homesteader. Approach the female's circle to be involved in adjudicating issues in the community. Why are you bored already? There's plenty for you to do—unless you're so addicted to the filth that you can't let it go."

"I don't want to do any of that. I'll participate, it's good business, but that's not what I want the entirety of my life to be. All of my decades of training, going to waste? I don't think so."

A flash of cruelty crosses his face. "Is this about me refusing to hurt you in bed? If I can't do it, you'll find someone who will? Several someones?" He crouches in front of me and seizes my chin, his fingers biting into my face. "Are you so shattered that you can only find pleasure in pain and degradation, Tleia?"

I can't look at him anymore. I stare at the ground, not fighting his grip, struggling to find the part of me that will fight back, but it keeps slipping away. I can't fight Gethen. He was always my last harbor, the one person who could still look at me and see something, anything, of value.

"You know I would never take another man to my bed. If you don't know it, nothing I can say will convince you."

"The answer is no. You are my son's mother. You will be a worthy member of this community, and not a City madam."

I take a deep breath. "You can't forbid me to do anything I want to do. You are not my husband."

He flinches, then hisses at me. "But I *am* your master, Tleia. We have a contract, remember?"

I don't move. He gets ahold of himself, releasing me, and runs his hands over his face, then stands again.

"I'll make sure no one patronizes your business, Tleia."

"You'd blacklist me?"

"Blacklist? Yes. And who will sell you a building?"

"The tavern keeper is looking to retire."

He shakes his head. "If I say no, he will not sell."

I give him a bitter smile and do exactly what he expects. "What man has *ever* told me no to anything I wanted when I exerted myself, darling?"

His eyes burn. "See? Not even in business yet and already speak of dark things. Dishonoring me, and yourself."

"I have no honor, Gethen. You already knew that. Just as you already know I have nothing else to offer—anyone." I stand, turning away from him. "The contract is a year and a day. Get rid of me then."

"Tleia—"

I can't take any more. I walk away.

## THIRTY-TWO

## GETHEN

I swore I would never hurt Tleia, but I see pain in her eyes before I turn and storm away instead of following her into the house. I leave before I say anything else I regret.

We have not argued like this since the first two years we were thrust together.

She is who she is. My uncle speaks at length of the futility in trying to change loved ones. It brings resentment, pain, slow decay where once there was love and happiness.

I've known who she is over ten years. I struggle, I rail. At times I hated her for being the one who captured my heart and wrapped the leash around my throat, when she is the exact opposite of everything I want.

But she is what I need.

She is perfect.

And I spent too many years unable to do more than steal discreet embraces, or offer comfort as she cried. Worse still —for me—the nights she returned smiling and sated. I will never take for granted what we now have.

The problem is not Tleia, the problem is me. A festering stew of loathing, anger, pain and anguish I never lanced.

I am a warrior, a Bachdracht of my community through my father's line and yet I have not offered penance for my failures. I suffered, Tleia suffered, Ethan suffered. But suffering is not penance.

And she was right. She is not the one who needs to offer it.

I go to my uncle as soon as the sun rises, and he must see something on my face when I approach because he drops his hoe. Defne takes one look at my face, and quietly excuses herself.

"Son?" Uther says.

I fall to my knees in front of him. "Father. I hurt Tleia."

A hand settles on my head. "What did you do?"

I tell him. Tell him the bitter, twisted words I hurled at her. The accusation she has no honor. How I raised my voice and bruised her jaw, watched her flinch and withdraw into herself to fight the lash of my words but I *did not stop* until *she* walked away.

I made her feel small. Unworthy.

I rest my forehead against his knees and weep. "Is this what I've become? Has that cursed City ruined me?"

My uncle sighs. "Young males," he says under his breath.

"I am over ninety years old."

"A grand old age. Come, boy, what do you want?"

I look up. "Penance."

His expression stills. There's a weight, a gravity to the word I use.

"Penance isn't undertaken lightly," he says finally. "It's broken males stronger than you. Are you certain?"

"Tueven is my witness, I will offer blood and flesh for my failures. I will visit the same pain on myself that my failures visited on my female and child." I swallow. "Every time I begin to say something that will hurt her, I will remember that penance. And I will stop. She's been through enough, and I—" I shove the words through my mouth like forcing stone through a grater "—I must excise this."

After a long enough silence—in which I do not retract my request—Uther finally nods.

"I'll gather the male's circle. Go to the forest and wait for us."

I stand, then hesitate, glancing in the direction Defne went.

"Will your wife tell Tleia not to worry? I don't want her to think I'm not coming home because of our argument."

Uther's expression softens. "You are good boy, Gethen. A good male. Defne will keep Tleia company." He pauses, and sort of winces at the corner of his eyes. "Probably Ratha and Ilotha too. They might. . .have some things to say if Tleia tells them your words."

Uthsha save me. That is no less than what I deserve.

———

I'm already kneeling in the circle as the males gather, stripped down to loincloths, scars, and the clan jewelry that marks a warrior's prowess, their footsteps an ominous drumbeat.

Towering firs sway in the early autumn wind, bringing the scent of the ocean and mingling with pungent damp earth and my own sweat. Acrid smoke assaults my nostrils as I wait in grim silence, head bowed and hands on my thighs in the posture of a penitent. I built the fire and waited the entire day, no food and no water. Fasting will be the gentlest form of suffering I will welcome tonight.

Uther gazes into the fire, face stern, his eyes distant. "I tell the tale as my father told me, and his father told him. In the beginning of the days of the Orcs of Uthilsen, our gods and goddesses still walked among us. We were little better than savages, brutes who had to be taught to stand upright and build fire to cook our food. But our gods were true immortals and could wield magic much like the Fae still do."

I listen, mesmerized by the cadence of his voice, my gaze lost in the flickering fire as images seem to leap from the flames. My brothers surround me, silent, attentive.

"At that time Uthsha, now our warrior goddess, was a maiden of the forest and after Tueven, sorcerer of storms and raging rivers, proved his worth, she took him as husband. The true immortals know love as we do, and between them they had five children.

"But Tueven was known for his hasty, explosive temper, and he was easily baited into mischief. One day the deceitful Lord of the Dark Horde tricked hotheaded Tueven into a fearsome battle, luring him into the Dark Horde's shadowy depths.

"Mighty Tueven fought for three days and nights, but finally succumbed to the fell dark magic, and was imprisoned.

"Rotting in the underworld dungeons, his fury and strength turned against him, eating him from the inside out."

Uther lifts his gaze and stares at me. I don't look away, letting him see my own rot. A year in prison is nothing, not against Tleia's three.

"When Uthsha realized her husband was missing, she picked up his ax and traveled into the pit of the Dark to save her beloved even though she was heavy with their sixth child. Through her wisdom and connection to living things, she defeated monsters and reached the bowels of the planet where Tueven languished.

"With magic and claw, fang and fury, she freed the Storm God from his shackles. But as they climbed back towards the light, the Dark Lord's servants fell upon them for one last attack. Brave Uthsha and Tueven fought them off, but they paid the price of Tueven's freedom, and Uthsha miscarried the babe.

"Tueven's heart turned heavy with shame. He hid his face from his wife and retreated from the world, consumed by guilt. For who but he had brought this fate upon their unborn child?

"The great god-king of the Orcs saw this and spoke: 'Though the fault is yours, do not flee from what you have wrought. Make amends through sacrifice and honest penance, then continue on the path of honor.'

"So it was Tueven went to the sacred circle marked in ancient stones and laid himself bare. He offered his own blood and flesh in payment for his reckless actions that brought harm to his family. The oaths he spoke resonated through the realm, and when it was done, Uthsha forgave him, though she had not blamed him in the first place, for the females among us learn wisdom much earlier than the males. Wisdom, and compassion.

"Thus was born the tradition that when an Orc warrior's carelessness brings sorrow to his wife or clan, he must humble himself with public penance to cleanse his spirit. Only then can honor be restored.

"Our fathers bid us remember this tale. Let it guide you to take responsibility and make right what you have wronged through foolishness. Our ways are built on honor and we forsake life before we forsake honor."

Uther stands. "Speak your shame, Gethen Bachdracht."

Withdrawing the single blade I am allowed, I slash it across my chest.

"I did not protect my female from great harm." I will not speak of the particular tortures she endured; that is for her to tell if she wishes. "I put my oath to my employer over the greater duty of guarding the one who holds my leash."

Another slash.

"I got her with child before she took me to husband, putting her in harm's way."

Slash.

"She gave birth to our son in prison, alone and in pain, with no female's circle to comfort her and no husband to serve her. My son knew no home but a City prison and played with no companions but rats and roaches." Another slash, slower, deeper. "I spoke words that brought my son's mother shame and grief."

Blood drips in steady rivulets down my chest and into the ground. As I speak, my brothers close in a circle around me.

"Your shame is witnessed," Uther says, "now we will remind you the cost of dishonor."

I endure the blows. No one takes my blade, because I will not wield it. The beating is methodical, and brutal. Bones do not break, but they come close.

At the end, a hand digs into my hair and yanks my head back. The male holding me pauses.

Uther gives me a considering look. "Half a shave," he says.

I stiffen. "A full."

His eyes harden. "I have spoken."

He nods at the warrior, and half of my hair and the braids that mark me as a clan warrior are cut off. Someone brings out a razor and takes the cut down to the scalp, scraping away even stubble.

When it's done, I pick up the hair and toss it into the fire.

"Dedicate yourself anew to the path of the warrior, the path of honor," Uther says.

"I am Gethen Bachdracht, a warrior of this clan. I kneel before the spirits of my ancestors and swear this oath by blood and bone:

"I will walk the path of the honorable warrior with

renewed vigilance and wisdom. My blade will only be drawn in protection of mate, clan, and the sacred rites of our people.

"No longer will I be swayed from my purpose by oaths that are lesser. I will speak no ill words to my mate and think no ill thoughts of her. I will protect her, even from herself."

The plea Lei'a had made so many times. Because she knew, even as I did, that she is always her worst enemy. Why else would she need me, if not to be her shield against the dark things in her soul?

"My blood sanctifies this oath and only death will break it."

When they bring out a bucket of salted water and pour it over my wounds, I cry out for the first time, then grit my teeth.

"Salt water purifies," Uther says. "As it washes away blood, it cleanses anger, guilt, and shame. But water is also life, and a new beginning. Help him stand."

Hands under my arms, because my legs are numb from hours of kneeling. My brothers hold me upright.

"This is also a lesson," Uther says, "that when we are weak, our brothers will shore us up until we find firm footing. Embrace your kin, and may Uthsha and Tueven accept your penance, and bless your household."

———

When I walk through the door of our home, for a moment I fear I've already broken my oath. But the hollow look clears out of Tleia's eyes after she sweeps me with a thorough gaze.

She pushes back from the kitchen table.

"What the hells?" she snarls in Uthilsuven at Hathur and Kathien, who are in charge of ensuring I didn't collapse flat on my face on the walk home.

"He'll be fine," Hathur says. "Though he should eat."

"There's dinner?" Kathien asks, walking around the both of us and beginning to nose through my kitchen.

"Did you cook?" Ratha asks him, tone scathing. "If you didn't cook, then there's no dinner. Why don't you do something about that?"

He mutters something under his breath, but Ratha lifts a brow. She outranks him, and even if she didn't, Ratha is scary.

As Ethan would say.

"*Otema!*" My son enters the kitchen, his head tousled as if he was sleeping. "Are you hurt?"

At four, he is too young to join the male's circle. He'll remain with the females for another four or five years, then they will give him over to us to begin his training until he's a young adult and must learn how to please a woman and maintain a household. Then the females will take over from there.

"Pa is fine," Tleia says, picking him up and putting him in a chair. "He was out playing with the other children."

Hathur snorts.

Lei'a turns back to us, the flames of the hells in her eyes.

"Does someone want to explain to me why Gethen is sliced up like—like. . ." She stops speaking and turns away.

I go to her, sliding my arms around her shoulders and pulling her back against my chest. I nuzzle the side of her head with my nose. "I really am all right. But aren't you mad at me?"

I feel her take a deep breath, exhale. "I don't want to have this discussion in front of witnesses."

"The clan already witnessed," Hathur says. "He made penance. The wounds were doused in salt water, so they're clean enough, but one or two might need stitching."

My Lei'a may look and talk and walk like a high courtesan, but she's from the streets of Seanna. She can stitch wounds without blinking.

I take her to the bedroom while Hathur entertains Ethan, and Ratha stands over Kathien as he makes a late supper.

"What is penance?" she asks, walking to the bedroom window and looking out, her back still to me.

The bedroom was empty of anything but the bed frame, mattress, and a wardrobe when we first arrived. She's added thick blankets in an emerald green, and pillows in an armchair, two woven tapestries on the walls that depict the myths of her people. She is slowly leaving her distinct mark on the house.

"I'm sorry," I say. "I said things to you that were cruel."

"But still true."

"No, they are not true. And one day, you stop forcing yourself to think of yourself in the worst possible way because you're afraid that—" I stop talking. Those words won't help her. "I love you, Tleia. I told you before that I love the dark sides of you. I was angry, and jealous."

She turns to me. "I still want to open the brothel. But I won't do it until you want to open it with me. Which means we're probably going to have some version of the same argument at least once a week until you give in."

I laugh, more with relief than with amusement. She isn't going to leave me. Either physically, or emotionally. I walk forward and pull her into my arms again.

Then I wince.

She pulls away, frowning, and surveys my body. "Penance means you knife yourself up and then what. . .the male's circle beats you within an inch of your life? And Gethen, what did you do to your hair." She purses her lips, tilting her head a little. "Do you know, I almost like it. It makes you look. . .dangerous."

What did I look before? "I am an Orc warrior. I already looked dangerous."

"You dress like a banking clerk. Very respectable. Law-abiding. Probably a virgin."

"I do not." I pause. "You know I would never leave. No matter how angry I was. And I won't ever speak to you that way again."

She looks up at me, and then away. "I'm. . .focused on my own needs, as usual. I always have been selfish. I know you want to cut all ties with Seanna, and I—I don't know what to do with my life. It was all I knew."

"I like the idea of the restaurant and entertainment. Can we start there? You may be happy without the other aspects."

She's silent, then she nods. "Compromise. We can try it your way."

I hesitate, then decide to compromise too. "The training you mentioned. Perhaps that might be a good thing, for the young adults. To learn simple things, like a proper kiss, before they try to inflict their wet, slobbering tongue on some poor lover."

Tleia grins.

"But not you. You will not train."

She widens her eyes and nods. She looks just like Ethan when he thinks I don't know he's lying to me. I sigh.

## THIRTY-THREE

"YOU NEED TO MAKE A DECISION," DEFNE TELLS ME.

"I have a week left." One week until the contract from the Sorting ends—and I haven't married Gethen yet.

"What's the hold up?" As usual, she's blunt.

I shrug. "I'm giving him time to change his mind." But also I don't want to marry him as an indentured woman. I want our only bonds when we marry to be the ones we choose.

Defne stares at me. Her three-year-old son plays in the corner with a basket of toys Ethan has almost grown out of —or abandoned rather. Ethan has the attention span of a guppy.

"He chose his wedding jewelry," she says.

I grimace. "He did. Pointedly."

The female's circle told me months ago the Orc marriage tradition—which involves the woman kidnapping the groom, dragging him off by his hair and marrying him at knife point as a battle ensues over his virtue—is mostly symbolic now. They stopped allowing the women to take unwilling grooms because it somehow impacted the birthrate, but tradition forbids he propose or even prompt me to ask him.

But there *is* a set of wedding jewelry strategically displayed on top of the chest of drawers in our bedroom.

I sigh.

"If he breaks tradition and marries you first, he'll be in trouble with the male's circle," Defne warns. "They let 'im off with a slap on the hand with Ethan, but if he breaks tradition a second time, Uther won't be so kind."

"Noted."

The relationship has been interesting.

Transitioning from being hidden best friends to now a couple living together with a child wasn't as seamless as I thought it would be.

Our upbringings, and much of our values, still clash. But every time we lock horns, we're able to fall back on a familiar crutch; talking. Reminding each other of how long we wanted this. How much we paid for this. How much our son is worth this.

I know it's not going to be easy, but even on the bad days Gethen hasn't wavered.

There are times he has to walk away when he's angry, but he's never abused me, and he kept his promise to never speak harsh words in anger again.

I set aside the swath of fabric samples I ordered from the

last trading caravan. The owner of the Tavern isn't ready to sell yet—I'll give him my full attention soon—and in the meantime I've done a small but growing business as a seamstress. In a desperate quest for a hobby that wouldn't bore me to tears and Gethen would approve of, I discovered sewing. Very well, a desperate quest for clothing with a little more style than one can get in the mountain forests of the Pasifik Northwest.

"I'll do it the evening the contract expires," I say into Defne's waiting silence.

She fixes me with a look. "Ya want me to tell Ratha?"

"If you tell Ratha then I wont be able to change my mind."

"Exactly."

I laugh. "Tell her. Tell her I'm finally ready to make an honest man of him. Uthsha bless poor Gethen."

She stands. "If you think that male is at all hesitant when it comes to marrying you, ya haven't been paying attention."

That's what she thinks.

———

**GETHEN**

It's the monthly evening session of the male's circle, when we discuss weighty business and adjudicate the issues among the males in the community.

Mostly it's an excuse to get away from our females— wives, lovers, mothers, sisters—without having to explain ourselves. The one night each month they watch us walk out the front door and head into the forest and they keep their silence.

They do not know what we do during the monthly circle. We do not know what they do during theirs. Everyone prefers it like this.

Tonight we lounge on the beach in front of a roaring bonfire, roasting fish and drinking ale. The gentle roar of the waves lapping against the shore is soothing, or would be if it didn't remind me of a constant push and pull in my relationship with Tleia.

Kathien passes a rolled smoke around the circle. I inhale, pass it along. "The stars are quiet tonight," I say. "Peaceful."

Peaceful is not what Lei'a has been lately. Nor I, considering her contract expires at sunrise. Legally, she will no longer be mine. Ethan is my acknowledged son, and even Lei'a I would fight so I did not lose him. But she's said nothing of her intentions, and in this I am not allowed to *ask*. It's driven me to drink.

What is she going to do when the contract expires? More pointedly, what am I going to do if what she wants to do is not what I want her to do?

I cringe.

Uther snorts, glancing at me. "Ready to give in yet?"

"I am a warrior." I try not to sound sulky.

"Ready to give in yet?"

I swear. "She is so *difficult*. Do you know what scheme she devised this week to get my cooperation with her brothel?"

"Let the female have her brothel," Tilleth mutters. There's a chorus of assent.

I glare at them all.

"It might not be so bad," Uther says.

"You too, Uncle? Has she seduced all of you?"

"Brother, go easy on the word seduced," someone says. "I have a wife."

"There is no other word. That is the word for what she has done to convince you all that—"

Uther stands, and we all go silent.

I jerk my head up as a moment later wild, high-pitched undulating begins to spill from the cliffs above. It sounds like a pack of screeching mountain lions.

Or harpies.

I imagine this is how harpies sound.

What it is, however, is a very specific war cry. My heart begins to beat faster, a grin tugging at the corner of my mouth.

"It's the females," Kathien says. "They're attacking."

Uther crosses his arms over his chest, frowning. "Hold your ground, brothers. We are warriors. We defend our circle from all oncomers."

"Even the female's circle?"

"All oncomers."

"It's Lei'a," I say happily, then frown. "Unless it's one of your lovers."

Hathur snorts and stands, getting out his ax. "It's not for us. Congratulations, cousin. Are you ready?"

I can no longer suppress my grin. I must look like a fool. My brothers won't hold it against me, at least not the married males.

The females appear over the cliff moments later and stream down, a war party of heavily armed Orcs, Humans, and mixed species. I search for Tleia, and she emerges and takes to the front, half dried blood running down her bare chest and back.

I still, and blink away the moisture in my eyes as I see her. She's fierce, beautiful.

She's been blooded into the clan, finally.

"Should I rise?" I ask Uther. "Or stay on my knees? What did you do? I'm not certain the best way to meet her." I shut my mouth, realizing I'm fussing like an adolescent about to receive his first kiss, and ignore the amusement in Uther's gaze.

I decide to stand, and meet my fate head on.

Tleia stops in front of me, her dark eyes impassive, her lush mouth smiling. Then she half turns to a stone faced Ratha, and gestures. "Here, give me the knife."

I watch in growing horror as Tleia grips a slender silver blade, holding it like it's a tool.

"It's not a lip pot brush," I tell her. I'm almost sputtering—before I shut my mouth as my brain catches up with me. The other females glare my way, incensed at the insult.

I had not *meant* it as an insult. I just don't want Lei'a to cut herself.

Behind me my brothers are spreading out, growls filling the air as some beat at their arms and chest, others brandishing weapons, others silently crouched and awaiting the attack.

"I've come to claim this male as my husband," Tleia says,

her voice cool. She speaks Uthilsuven flawlessly. Flawlessly. I feel a punch of irritation. If she can speak this well, then why does she pretend—nevermind. I keep forgetting. This is Tleia. The female who entertains herself at night by keeping unnecessary secrets.

"You can't have him," Hathur growls. "Only a worthy female will claim a warrior of the Bachdracht line."

"Sisters," Tleia says, "I presume this is our cue. Retrieve my husband."

Tleia leaps forward, blood in her gaze as the other females attack.

"Don't cut yourself," I tell her, and go down on one knee and offer my wrists. "You've already bled enough today and it will upset Ethan." I grin. "How was the blooding?"

She makes a face. "I'm unamused by the fact I'm required to allow the wounds to scar."

"Scars are beautiful."

"Says the Orc." She eyes me. "Aren't you supposed to run around and act as if you're an unwilling groom rather than a man who's been moping for weeks on end in order to get his way?"

I throw one of her favorite phrases back in her face. "Have you lost your mind? I want this over with before you change your mind." The moping worked, so I will not take offense to her statement. Uther Bachdracht is my uncle. I understand tactics.

She gives me a long, slow smile. "But we must make a good show. I won't have the female's circle saying your proposal was shoddy." She lowers her voice in a deep growl. "Run, Gethen Bachdracht."

———

## TLEIA

His run is more of a leisurely lope down the beach, the swing of his arms entirely too happy. He's pleased with himself, and I have a notion to make him regret that at some point in the future, but I set aside thoughts of petty revenge and focus on catching him. I'm fast, but his legs are longer so he has to slow.

Behind us the battle morphs into laughter and good-natured groans as well as the sounds of mocking jibes. Suddenly Gethen stops and whirls, baring his teeth at me and holding his arms out at his side as if in challenge. Humor glints in his eyes as he crouches into a defensive position.

I slow, sauntering to him as I wag the knife in front of his face. He winces. Ratha has been trying to teach me more, and I have been trying to learn, but I'm not any good at it.

Still, I know my job. I plant my feet in the sand, jab the blade towards him, and bare my teeth in return. "Surrender to me. If you come willingly, I'll treat you gently."

He snorts. "I've had bruises after a night in bed with you when you supposedly were treating me gently."

"I was just attempting to demonstrate my own needs."

His expression somber. "I will never cause you pain,

Lei'a." His voice is soft, firm, the look in his eyes resolute. "Even if you want it."

"And if I say I won't marry you unless you agree to what I want?"

Gethen straightens slowly, fixing his gaze on my face. "Then we will not marry. But no other will have you, Tleia. You will not leave my home, my bed, and will not take my son."

"You'll live in shame as an unwed male?"

"Greater shame is causing you pain."

No relationship is perfect, I've learned that by now.

Gethen must see the acceptance on my face because he lowers himself down to one knee, and inclines his head in submission. I press the flat of the blade against his throat because I don't trust myself with a sharp edge, and bury my free hand in his hair.

I "escort" my betrothed back to the waiting circles where Uther watches us, one arm loosely around his wife's shoulders.

"You've caught your prey," Ilotha says. "Fine hunting."

Hathur snorts. "The prey wasn't running very hard."

"I didn't need to run," Gethen says. "I've always been hers."

If there was any part of my heart left that didn't belong to Gethen, he would own it now. I drop the knife in the sand, probably too close to my toes, and launch towards him, wrapping him in my arms. He returns the embrace, burying his face in my hair.

"Love you more than anything, Lei'a," he says, his voice

harsh with held back tears. I know, because I've heard that voice before. "I love you more than anything. Make me your husband."

We speak our oaths, and I'm not certain I remember what we say. I'm not certain it matters because standing there with the moon high in the night sky and the waves lapping against the beach—someone fetched Ethan and Uther holds our son in his arms—all I see are the stars in Gethen's eyes and then his face goes blurry. But not because I am weeping. There's probably sand in my eyes.

When we are formally bound as husband and wife in front of the community as witnesses, I know everything has been worth it.

All the struggle, the starvation, pain. The rape and abuse. . .yes, yes that has to be worth it too. Because if anything changed, even one moment, would I still have Gethen now? Would I still have Ethan?

This is what I will tell myself every day, to get through the days when regrets and nightmares are a thick enough blanket I want to choke on them.

I'll get through the days by looking into my husband's eyes and seeing that he knows me, and loves me still.

*Thank you for reading and please Smash a Star!*

**Want the bonus epilogue? Click to download.**

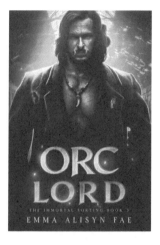

Book 3 is ORC LORD, featuring Sajena (Honoria's sister) and Lord Cythro of OakHorde street.

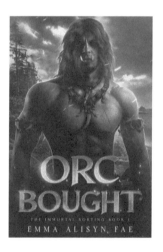

Did you miss Book 1? Read Uther and Defne's story.

Book 4 will pick up on Mysterri and Lord Meadowland's story.

**Interested in the Fae? Start here.**

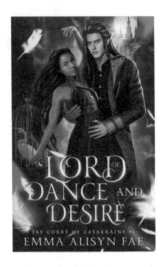

Made in United States
Troutdale, OR
12/12/2023